1

Amy Tierney grew up in Dublin and now lives in Wicklow where she is married with three children and two dogs.

30 days hath September is Amy's debut novel and the first of the "Calendar Days series".

To Becca,
Hope you enjoy
the read,
thanks for the
support.

Amy Tierney

Amy Tierney .

April '17 .

30 days hath September

Finn
Tierney

Email: Amie.Tierney@hotmail.com

Edited by Eamon O'Cleirigh

Clearview Fiction Editing

ISBN -13: **978-1516979134**

For Colm, Amelia, Conor and Finn

X

1st September 2013

SUNDAY

Cathy woke with her tongue stuck to the roof of her mouth, a cold wet hangover pounding at her temples.

"Thank God it's Sunday," she said, groaning as she rolled over to check the time. 11.45am the clock blinked. *Damn*, she would have to get up soon to collect the kids. They were starting back at school the next day and she still had pencil cases and new lunchboxes to buy. She knew this task could take all day if she wasn't careful. Depending on the availability of school accessories in the first shop they went to, she could end up having to spend the whole day in Dundrum Shopping Centre.

Once she managed to struggle out of bed, she headed for the shower, where she let the hot-water jets wash the night off her face and massage her shoulders, working her thick blonde hair into a shampoo lather. For Cathy, her morning shower was like the universe's way of giving her a fresh start; a blank canvas, to create on it whatever she chose. Some days she crafted beautiful masterpieces, akin to Michelangelo's work in the Sistine chapel. Sometimes she created crap, splashes of colour pulled together in no specific rhyme or reason, but mostly, she formed a nice simple pencil drawing detailing the easy, carefree attitude to life she'd begun to lead.

7

For a while, after she'd kicked Gary to touch, her canvases were black and grey, with a few spots of childish colour. It had been so hard dealing with her husband's betrayal, his cheating, forceful manner, and all the lying. The list went on and on like a bad song, scratching at her memory. While the first few weeks had passed in a daze of negative emotions, she'd eventually realised she could do one of two things: continue to paint a dull lifeless canvas for the rest of her days, or get out, cop on, and start living her life again. There was no option but to choose the latter. She had two children who were just as hurt and confused about the sudden change in their cosy family life. It broke her heart trying to comfort them while she also cursed Gary to hell for what he had done. It was clear to see that Jack and Millie were hurt enough without having to watch their mother wallow in a black hole.

One morning, after dropping the children to school, Cathy drove to the Black Castle beach, pent up and needing to find peace. With it being mid-November and still early, the small pebble bay lay deserted. As she breathed in the salty air, the ocean's energy caught her heart, its magnetic surge pulling her closer to the crashing waves. She dug her feet into the pebbles, took the deepest breath, and let it out in a long agonising scream. Not just once, but again, and again, screaming while hot tears rolled down her face, her hands clenched by her side, roaring into the wind, willing it to take her pain away, continuing until her eyes stung and her throat turned raw. Then she screamed a bit more, just for good measure.

Standing at the edge of the grey sea, she vowed to the seagulls circling above that she was done with the dark. These would be the last tears she would shed over that bastard. She banished her demons to the wind, forgiving her child within for all the rotten things she had thought about herself; for trying to understand and excuse why Gary had treated her so badly.

"It's over," she yelled at the seagulls. They duly obliged by swooping down to collect her sorrow and take it away. That chapter of her life was written and she was choosing to close the book. From now on, it was her and her children; Cathy's hopes and Cathy's dreams; her worries and sorrows, strengths and weaknesses. She had positives and negatives, rights and wrongs, for her to do with whatever she wanted. Right there, that morning, she started running, for herself.

*

Having dressed as fast as she could after her shower, she pulled her damp hair into a loose knot on top of her head. Once she'd applied mascara, she slid pale lip-gloss across her full lips, pouting into the bedroom mirror, telling herself she would have to do. When she grabbed her jacket off the chair, she realised it still smelled from last night.

Being a Sunday afternoon, the traffic was light, and she enjoyed the sunny drive into Dublin to collect the children from the pub where Gary worked as a bar manager. Usually she didn't like the children being in a pub, but this was a family-run establishment and at this time on a Sunday would be full of parents with their kids enjoying a bit of pub grub for lunch.

After finding a space in the back car park, she made her way into the lounge, bubbling at the prospect of seeing her children. Gary, she could do without, but she missed Millie & Jack so much when they were with their dad. Even though Millie's constant yapping, and the inevitable arguments between the twins, drove her crazy, she suffered a terrible loneliness without them. After all, she had looked after them every day since they were born, nearly 6 years ago, and it came as no surprise that she still found it hard to deal with their absence, both when they went to school and to stay with their dad.

Making her way through the lounge, she spotted the twins sitting together on one side of a corner booth, Gary opposite them, looking confused. The children were eating lunch, which she was grateful to see. From the look of it, Gary had ordered a roast-beef dinner, and as she neared the table, the delicious aroma hit her. Scooting in beside the children, she gathered them into a bear hug and kissed the tops of their heads. Millie and Jack bounced beside her on the seat.

"Mammy! You're here," said Millie. "We are just having our lunch and telling Daddy about how it's okay for people to have two houses and two homes. Not everyone in our class has two houses, but some do, and that's okay. Right?"

Cathy glanced at Gary. Where had this come from? "Yep, it sure is," she said and gave Jack a quick wink. "Your lunch looks delicious, so be good and eat it all up before we go." Without thinking, she went into mammy mode by cutting their chicken nuggets a little smaller on each plate, making it easier for them to eat. She looked across at Gary.

"Hi, Cathy. How's things?"

She didn't want to get into any sort of conversation with Gary, but realised she had two sets of eyes watching her, so she made an effort to be civil.

"Great, not bad at all. That carvery looks nice." She nodded at his half-eaten dinner, then embarrassed herself with a loud grumble from her still-empty stomach, cursing her treacherous body. She agreed, at his suggestion, that she have some lunch before leaving. Usually, she would do anything to avoid spending even an extra second in her ex-husband's company, but today she was hungover, due her period, and in need of stodgy food to fill her up. Gary went to the bar to order her food,,and returned with a jug of ice-cold water and a clean glass.

"Here, you look like you could use some of this."

He filled the glass and slid it across the table to her, always the professional barman, always ready to satisfy his customers' needs. Thing was, he'd never stopped at satisfying their drinking needs, taking it upon himself to look after their sexual requirements too.

A lounge boy came over with the food. As she looked up to pay him, she noticed a guy staring at her from behind the bar. The man focused on her with an intense, smouldering look. She squirmed before tearing her eyes away. Who is this hot guy checking her out in such an obvious way? She glanced at Gary, then looked back over to the bar and took in all that she could.

Tall, dark, and handsome. What a cliché. But that's what he was, his dark brown hair curling over the collar of his pristine-white shirt. Even at a distance, she made out the chocolate colour of his eyes, framed by long black lashes. He looked fit, too; strong, and oh-so-yummy.

He leaned forward as he spoke to a customer, but continued to look back to where Cathy sat. She tore her eyes away when he grinned at her, embarrassed to have been caught staring. Now, squirming in her seat, heat flushed into her face, and a knot tightened in the pit of her stomach.

"Who's the tall guy behind the bar?" she asked Gary, casual as could be.

"Sam?" He looked over. "He's been here a while."

"I don't recognise him." How could she have missed him before? "I thought I knew all the staff here?"

Gary smirked. "Oh, he's not staff, he's the boss."

"What?" She looked over to the bar to see if they were talking about the same person. "He couldn't be the boss. He's too young." And hot.

Gary filled her in on the mystery man.

"He's Sam O'Keeffe, son of Michael O'Keeffe. Part of the O'Keeffe Empire and all who sails in her. They own this place and a few more around town. Pubs and Clubs. That's their tipple and it's done them well over the years."

"But how come I've never seen him before? Has he just been released from prison or something?" Maybe he'd been put away for crimes against passion. Jesus, where was this coming from? She flushed again at the thought.

She sensed that Gary wasn't happy with her new interest in Sam O'Keeffe, but he answered her anyway.

"He just came back from abroad. Ibiza, I think, and the Balearic Islands. As far as I know, he's been there for a few years. Now he's taken on the area-manager's job for the pub chain. This and two clubs on Leeson Street are part of his patch."

Cathy finished eating, checking that the children had enough and were happy with the colouring book Gary had brought. She looked back over to the bar, catching a glimpse of Sam as he disappeared into the back room. I shouldn't be checking him out.

He's my ex-husband's boss. The ex-husband I'm sitting here with, having lunch with for the first time since we split. The ex-husband who I'm having the longest conversation with in a year, and it's about another man. A sexy man. A man whose eyes, even from here, melted into her. A man whose body looked like he could hold up to a marathon session in the bedroom. And a man who really was out of her league.

If Gary was right about Sam's family and pedigree, Cathy imagined he had women falling at his feet, throwing themselves at him, and generally had the pick of the bunch. No, she wasn't interested in heartbreak, but it was still nice to appreciate the dessert menu, even if you are on a diet. Sam O'Keeffe was dessert for sure. The chocolate kind.

Dragging her thoughts out of the gutter, she told Gary that she'd enrolled the twins in a local after-school drama and dance class. It would help build Jack's confidence and social skills, and Millie would be right at home having a stage to perform on.

"Sounds good," he said. "When does it start?"

She hated having to ask him for money, but when it was for the kids, it made it easier.

"That's the thing, it starts next week. I'm a bit short for the term fees, and was wondering if you could help out at all?"

"Of course, no problem." He said this as if money was never an issue for him, which it didn't seem to be. Gary earned a good wage, and always looked after them when they had been a family. Since the split, he still paid the mortgage and deposited a set amount into Cathy's account each month for the kids. It wasn't a fortune, and sometimes things were tight, but she managed. During the summer months, she took in ironing from a local B&B, and this gave her a few extra Euro to enjoy a bit of breathing space. She rarely had much left at the end of any week for the usual niceties, but she did her best to make sure the children didn't go without.

"It's just with the kids going back to school this week, it's a bit tight. You know, two of everything, and that includes term fees for any extra activities."

It annoyed her that she needed to justify to herself how she used the money Gary gave her. She didn't flit it away on nights out with the girls, or pampering weekends away when Gary had the kids. If he had noticed that she was taking better care of herself, he hadn't said anything. No, the money was spent on essentials like food, clothes, bills, except for the odd bottle of wine which she opened on a Friday and made last 'til Sunday. In fact, last night's drinks were a result of her friends Byron and Annabel dragging her out, plying her with cocktails to celebrate her surviving the past year, and coming out the other side of the wringer in one piece.

"It's not a problem, Cathy," Gary said, pulling her back to the moment. "How much do you need?"

She told him how much half the fees would be.

"I'll have it for you by the end of the week." He looked at this watch, then glanced up at the clock over the bar. "My shift will be starting soon."

"Right. Thing is, Gary, I'll need it by Wednesday at the latest. They start their first class after school and I need to have it paid by then. I appreciate the help-out. It takes the pressure off." She didn't miss that he failed to offer her any extra money, even though he knew she was struggling.

She leaned on the table so he would hear her over the general pub noise. "The drama and dance school will be great for them. They need to start mixing with other kids outside school. You know how dependent they are on each other. They even have the same friends in their class."

After the breakup, the children had clung to each other for comfort and familiarity in their changing world. Amazing as children are, they adjusted to their new family situation a lot quicker than Cathy had, but she still worried. They were so close, she dreaded the day when extravert Millie woke up interested in boys, with Jack, being the quieter of the two, getting left behind.

That was a few years away yet, but she didn't want them getting into any habits now that might hinder either of them in the future. They loved each other. They would always be each other's twin, but they were also individuals and they needed to be treated as such.

When the lounge boy returned to clear the table, Cathy gathered Millie and Jack up to leave.

"I'll walk you out to the car," Gary offered. He went over to the bar and returned with the twins' overnight bag. Cathy noticed Sam leave the office and make his way over to where they stood.

"Hi, Gary. Sorry to intrude. Are you on today?" Sam glanced at Cathy and the children.

"Yes, yes," Gary said, annoyance obvious in his response. "I'm just finishing up here. I'll be around to help in a minute."

Sam didn't make any move to leave so Gary took a deep breath and gestured between them with both hands. "Sorry, yeah, Sam, this is Cathy. Cathy, Sam O'Keeffe."

Sam reached out and shook Cathy's hand with a firm grip. Not sure if Gary could see the spark that flew, she shook Sam's hand once then withdrew.

"Hi, guys," he said to Millie and Jack.

Cathy rubbed her hand on her thigh, noting how he was already familiar with her children.

"Thanks for the crisps yesterday, Sam," Millie said, grinning up at him. "They were yummy."

Sam smiled back. "Anytime, little lady." He leaned to his left. "How's your knee today, Jack? Is it better?"

Jack gave Sam a thumbs up as Cathy threw a sharp glare at Gary. She bent to inspect Jack's knees.

"I fell yesterday, Mammy," Jack said, a serious expression on his tiny upturned face, "and my knee was bleeding the red stuff. Sam got me a blue plaster from the kitchen and it fixed my broken leg."

"Good stuff, little man." Sam ruffled Jack's hair, winking at him. Millie giggled with delight at her new friend.

Cathy took it all in. How much time did the children spent here with their dad? It was obvious that they were used to Sam. She vowed to tackle Gary on the issue another time.

"We better get going," she said, eager to get away from this man who was sending shivers down her spine, and away from this other man who she wanted to kill with her bare hands for being so irresponsible with her children.

"Nice to meet you, Cathy," Sam said as she stepped away from the table.

Not wanting to be rude, Cathy paused, but then turned, catching her breath as her cheeks flushed. How is this guy having such an effect on me? She tightened her stomach muscles. "Nice to meet you, too, Sam. Enjoy the rest of your day." She didn't give him a chance to respond, walking with the twins out of the pub and into fresh air.

As she headed for the car, the children and Gary in tow, her blood boiled. How many times had Gary brought the kids here? She'd only collected them from here on a couple of occasions. It seemed, thought, they were here more than she knew. Enough that they knew the bar staff. And the bar staff knew them – even the new, hot, sexy, area manager, whose touch Cathy was trying hard to forget.

Strapping the kids into their car seats, she told Gary to call her about his days off next week. They would need to work something out if he was taking them mid-week. With them being back at school, she needed to know if he was able for the early-morning school runs.

*

She drove the twins to Dundrum Shopping Centre, going first to Tesco's for lunchboxes and then Eason's for the pencil cases, striking it lucky in both, delighted that she'd accomplished her objectives without having to trawl through a dozen shops.

Once home, they all got into their fluffy pyjamas, pulled the curtains closed, and snuggled up on the sofa to watch a Disney DVD. Cathy didn't pay much attention to the film she'd already seen about seventeen times. Instead, she thought back to the man she'd met earlier. Sam O'Keeffe. Every time she thought about him, her belly flipped. She couldn't get his face out of her mind. The way he'd looked at her. He was charming. Although, something told her he was also trouble, and with her usual stubborn revolve she decided to steer well clear of him. She couldn't get involved with a heartbreaker again. No, she wouldn't survive it. She took her phone from her pocket and googled his name. Yes, she knew it, trouble. It was all there in black and white. Big trouble.

2nd September

Monday

Eight weeks of summer holidays had given Cathy plenty of precious time with Millie and Jack. Any warm and sunny day, she'd dropped everything, packed a bag, and headed to the beach with the children. Calm hot days were a rarity in Ireland and when the rain disappeared for three days in a row, it felt like they were in the south of France. The last two weeks of August had been wet and unpredictable, though, so she'd tried to entertain them at home, but there was only so much she could do.

Now, their first day back at school was a welcome relief for all of them. By 9.05 that morning, Millie and Jack were safely settled in the Senior-Infant classroom, sharing a small wooden table and sitting on miniature chairs. Excited shouts of welcome had greeted the children as they reconnected with friends, and parents gave brief rundowns of the exotics of their summer break.

Miffed at first for being unable to moan about delayed flights and lost luggage this year, Cathy brightened up after a quick chat with a few of the adults, realising that not everyone had been able to get abroad. More and more people were struggling in the economic downturn. Plenty of other families, like her own, had battled their way through the Irish summer and lived it up on the Costa Del Courtown, or headed out West instead.

*

Cathy changed into three-quarter-length leggings when she got home. A sloppy-white t-shirt and running shoes completed the outfit. Bringing her I-Pod, she drove to the port road in Wicklow Town, parking near the Black Castle beach. She stretched and twisted as she warmed up, then set off running.

After her screaming session with the seagulls last year, she'd often started her run from here, from what she saw as her symbolic spot. Her objective was to run at least twice, if not three times a week. In the beginning she'd nearly killed herself by going too far, too fast. The need to run away from her old life drove her forward, pushing herself into a new one. Then, after a while, she found her rhythm and it no longer caused her physical pain; the cramps in her legs disappeared and the burning in her lungs subsided.

These days she ran because she enjoyed it, free and uninhibited. Perhaps she still used it as a stress release, but whatever the reason for her running, it was working, both in her body and mind. She'd lost a huge amount of baby weight, slimming to a body she was comfortable with. Her legs and calves were toned and sculpted, and her skin had a beautiful sun-kissed, red-cheeked glow from being out in the fresh air. The extra exercise helped with her sleep too, sliding into a coma for the best part of six hours each night, exhausted from being a busy mammy and running 5km on a regular basis.

Gone were the times where she tossed and turned, tormenting herself with the haves and what-ifs. Insomnia had darkened her canvas and brought her to a new low. Now, night times were for sleeping, allowing her body and brain to recharge. Running was the time for thinking, for pounding out any worries or niggles with the ever-solid beat of her feet.

Sam O'Keeffe's face kept popping up during her run, easing her pounding to a soft thread as she imagined him. Indulging in her fantasy, she endeavoured to block out all the crazy stuff she'd read about him on Google, concentrating instead on the feelings she'd experienced when he'd looked at her, right into her soul. She visualised him coming on to her, wanting her, drawing her into his space. The spark that flew with an electrical jolt when their hands touched was not the result of carpet static, that's for sure.

What would he want with me? Twenty-five years of age, almost divorced, with two children in tow. Judging from his Wikipedia page - yes he had a Wikipedia page - this man was one hot, eligible bachelor. The most sought-after man in Ireland.

Sam O'Keeffe. Age 31. Born in Kildare, Ireland. The eldest son of Michael and Ann O'Keeffe of the mega-rich O'Keeffe family. Studied business in UCD and worked for a short time in Sales before living abroad for a number of years. Had recently returned to work as an Area Manager for his family's business. He played guitar in an Indie-rock band, had a black belt in Taekwon-Do, and had earned the reputation of Ireland's Most Eligible Bachelor by being linked to a long list of some of Ireland's hottest socialites. There were plenty of pictures to support this detail. All the photos showed Sam

23

O'Keeffe attending function after function, with a different woman on his arm each time.

Cathy vowed to steer well clear of that potential nightmare. She'd had enough of the heartbreakers and playboys. It was never going to happen between them. They didn't frequent the same groups or social circles. She had the twins and her best friends, Byron and Annabel. Sam had the world, a whole planet of beautiful woman to choose from.

Wiping sweat from her face and neck, she slowed to a jog for the last kilometre. She doubted she would even see him again. Plenty more fish in the sea, darling. "Stop looking at the sharks," she added out loud, for good measure.

*

Sam O'Keeffe was on a mission, pulling in favours to find out more about the absolute beauty that had walked into his pub yesterday afternoon. With two stunning children, Gary and his wife had made an attractive family. However, Sam had dug a little and discovered that all was not rosy in the garden. Gary was separated from Cathy for about a year. Something to do with him being a dick, and her kicking him out. The details were fuzzy. Either way, Gary's stupidity was his dream come true.

Somewhat surprised, Sam had become aroused when he'd seen Cathy sitting in the lounge. Unable to tear his eyes away, he'd smiled back when she'd looked at him, hoping to gauge her reaction.

With a close eye on the CCTV monitor, he'd seen her preparing to leave and knew he had to talk to her. The least thing would be to get closer to her to see if the attraction was mutual, or all in his pants.

A jolt shot up his arm when their hands met and he damn near exploded. Acting like a nervous teenager, he couldn't get any words out of his mouth, so ended up focusing all his attention on the twins. After she'd left, he'd started asking questions.

Cathy was the reason he'd got short swift answers from Gary when quizzed about his ex-wife. She was the reason for Sam's uncomfortable night alone in his bed, and the reason he was up and out before noon on a Monday morning. He needed to know more about this woman. Gary wasn't forthcoming, and the other staff in the pub knew little or nothing about her, apart from her being Gary's ex-wife.

Sam needed to find another source. And that would be Tony, his brother, friend of everyone, foe of none. Tony knew everyone in Dublin. He was like a telephone operator when it came to knowing people's business. Fortunately for Sam, he also worked for the family company as the HR Manager, with access to files for all employees, the type of information Sam needed to put his plan into action.

3rd September

Tuesday

Cathy was sorting whites and darks when her phone pinged. A new text. She took the phone out of her jeans pocket and looked at the unfamiliar number. Okay, let's see who this is.

Hi Cathy, Sam O'Keeffe from the pub. We met the other day. Would like to meet again, if you're interested. You have my number, call or text. Sam

Jesus, where in the universe had that come from? She stood stock still, digesting the message, her stomach and heart doing summersaults. What the hell?

Her natural reaction was to text back a big *NOT INTERESTED, THANKS*. But she didn't. Being out of the *flirting and dirting* scene for so long, she'd no idea what the protocol for text-dating was. If you met someone in a bar, you dealt with the person there and then. Over the phone, a date could be made or avoided a lot easier as it didn't involve eye contact. Implausible excuses could be used that you wouldn't get away with in a bar. If a guy phones asking you out, *yippee* if it's someone you like and were waiting for the call, or the 'Sorry, I can't make it, my granny just died' fat lie, then block all future calls from that number.

In a bar, however, if the guy you've been eyeing all night makes his way over to you and starts to chat, then *yippee*. On the other hand, if the scutt from the corner you've been trying to avoid makes a play, the dead-granny lie can't be employed. You'd have been having way too much fun with your friends all night to be in deep mourning over Nana.

Text-dating, though, that was a new one. Should I answer him straight away? Yay or Nay – get it out of the way. Should I ignore the text, pretend he got the wrong number? Or should I rally the troops and get advice from the two women who have much more experience at this game than me?

She went with number three and rang Byron, her best friend, telling her to grab wine and Pringles and come over after work, giving her the briefest report on why there was a need for a mini-summit. "See if Annabel could come, too." She might know a thing or two about this Sam O'Keeffe fella that could help her decide, one way or the other.

After hanging up, it occurred to her that it might be considered rude not to reply to Sam's message, so to get herself out of a bad-manners' argument with her conscience, she texted, *We'll see.*

Hold on, how does he have my number? Had to be Gary. She fumed at the thought he'd give her number to a complete stranger. Well, not a complete stranger, he was Gary's boss, and they had been introduced. And sparks did fly when they met, and her stomach did do a flip when she received his text.

But still. Thanks for thinking of my safety, Gary. Letting me get hit on by any oddball that comes your way. Men, sometimes you were just better off without them. There was one man, though.

She smiled, re-reading Sam's text. If only he wasn't such a player; a ladies' man, she might have considered a date with him. Sometimes it got lonely, like when the kids were in bed. Even with Gary, there was no friendship or companionship. When she was married to him, he *worked late* so often, and Cathy always relied on the bond of her wedding vows to hold her secure in their relationship. Well, that bond and those vows were shot to threads now, but she still longed for that security again. Maybe she should start putting herself out there, meet more men, even arrange to go on a date with the cute guy from the chemist.

She knew cute-chemist guy had a crush on her, the way he blushed beetroot every time she went in for Calpol. Should she give it a go? At least with beetroot man she knew he fancied her, so half the battle was already won. Only thing was, she'd have to do the asking. Could she do that? Yes she could. She made a mental note to pick up some Calpol tomorrow.

*

Sam grinned when he opened the text. *We'll see.* It wasn't a yes, but it wasn't an outright no. With a bit of luck she'd assume that her ex-husband had given him her number. He didn't want to reveal he'd breached confidential HR files to find Gary's ICE number. It was fortunate the guy had been lazy about updating his personal information since his split from Cathy.

He'd never gone to such extremes over a girl before, and was surprised at his obsession with wanting to know Cathy. Ever since their meeting on Sunday, he had a semi-hard on that wouldn't go away. He wanted to speak to her, laugh with her, kiss her, but most of all, take her.

He snapped out of his fantasising. What would his next move be? He wanted a chance with Cathy, and if that meant grovelling at her feet, so be it. For now, though, he had to wait and see what the *We'll see* text turned out to be.

*

Cathy stretched her arms and rolled her shoulders as she made her way down the stairs, content that the twins were settled into bed. She was looking forward to spending the rest of the night with the girls. Byron and Annabel were her backbone. She paused in the hallway when she heard Annabel laughing at how Byron was cursing her inability to use the corkscrew.

"I know Sam O'Keeffe," Annabel said. "Not well, but we've crossed paths a couple of times since he's been back in the country."

Byron snorted. "He's some boy, thinking Cathy's going to be a notch on his bedpost. He has another thing coming, because she's having none of it."

"Why not?" Annabel asked, her voice close to a shriek. "The guy is sex on legs, yummy from top to toe. If he'd given me a second glance, I would've been in there like Flynn."

Cathy wiped the smile off her face and coughed before entering the room. "Who is she trying to shag now?"

"Your man," Byron said, a mischievous grin reaching almost to her eyes.

Cathy stopped mid-stride. "Who, Gary?" She stared hard at Annabel. "Don't tell me…"

"Eeewwwww!" was the chorused response.

Byron laughed out loud. "I thought we were never to speak that man's name again, unless it was followed by the words, *May He Rest In Peace*."

"It's Sam," Annabel said. "Sam? Remember, hunk almighty? The one who's chasing you, and the one you're trying to run away from. Sam!"

Cathy smiled. "Yes, I get it, Sam O'Keeffe."

Annabel clapped her hands. "Tall, dark, handsome. Has the ability to cause wetness with one look, and could probably give tantric sex a good run for its money."

"Annabel!" Cathy grabbed her refilled wine glass and took a long slug. "Is this the same Sam O'Keeffe, playboy of the world, and man of many beds? The man about town who could have any beautiful young socialite of his choosing, and by the look of the gossip pages, has already taken down at least half of them?"

"Yep," Byron said, still struggling with the corkscrew, "that's the one."

Annabel slapped the countertop. "What? That's bull. Seriously, Cathy, don't believe everything you read in those rags. Most of it is absolute gossip. Pure speculation."

Cathy placed her glass down and took the wine bottle and corkscrew from Byron. "But I saw the photos, Annabel. Lots of them. Sam being papped with a different babe on his arm each time. Now don't try to tell me that at the end of the night, he takes them home, sees them safely to their front door, and kisses their hand goodnight."

"You don't know. Maybe he does."

Cathy and Byron both raised a sculpted eyebrow at Annabel, who shrugged and held her hands up. "Okay, but it's well known that young, free, and single party girls attach themselves to anything that's eligible. They need to get noticed if they're to work it on the social ladder." She waved Cathy's protest off. "When a hottie like Sam O'Keeffe is let back onto the Dublin circuit, chances are there's a queue of women needing to be photographed with him. Come hell or high water, they'd have their night on the arm of Ireland's most attractive newcomer."

"That's rubbish," Byron said, taking the opened wine bottle from Cathy. "He's a player, and there's nothing more to be said about it."

Annabel rolled her eyes. "Just because he's photographed with these girls doesn't mean he's playing them. It's the socialite game. Most of the girls have more respect for themselves than to sleep with everyone they date. Believe me, they have bigger goals than sex."

Cathy didn't know what to say. Byron and Annabel looked at her, waiting for a response. Annabel had just blown her whole argument out of the water. What if he isn't such a bad guy after all?

Annabel touched her arm, her voice soft. "Cathy, I've met Sam a couple of times. He comes across as a nice guy. Ordinary, unassuming, certainly not the guy the gossip rags make him out to be." She straightened up on her stool and looked from Byron to Cathy. "I think you should give him a chance."

"Damn it, me too," Byron said. "At the very least, give him a chance. Look, there hasn't been anyone since Gar, the prick, and it's obvious you have an attraction to this guy. Yeah, give yourself a break. Relax, go have coffee with the man. No pressure." She smiled, her teeth blazing white. "If he is a womaniser, out to break your heart, you'll know about it soon enough. Anyway, he's not going to jump you in Bewleys' café, is he?"

"Byron!" Cathy took another slug from her glass to cover her embarrassment. Bewleys, eh?

Byron continued. "If he doesn't try to get you into bed after a latte and scone, then your preconceived notions about him might be a tiny bit unjustified. I think you should give him a chance."

Cathy eyed them both, hoping they couldn't see the little mouse running around inside her head, scampering this way and that through her scattered thoughts. She picked up her glass, necked the rest of her wine, then grabbed the phone off the table. Gesturing for Byron to fill the glass again, she sent a three-worded text: *How about coffee?*

4th September

Wednesday

Cathy parked at the back of Gary's pub. Sam's pub. Her stomach flipped. Was he here? She checked the time. 10.30 am. Once she got the money Gary had promised her for the kids' drama classes, she could get away. She didn't want to go inside in case she ran into Sam. He hadn't replied to her text and her confidence wasn't the best. She also didn't want him thinking she'd come looking for him. Stalking him. Get that thought out of your head, girl. She stayed in the car and sent Gary a text asking him come out to meet her.

Gary appeared at the lounge entrance and scanned the car park. What's he looking for? It's not like she was hard to find, still driving the same blue Nissan Micra she'd had when they were together, and there were only two other cars in the car park.

"Here you go," he said, offering her a white envelope through the open window. "For God's sake, Cathy, I didn't know you needed it today. You should have said."

Cathy bit back her anger. "I did say. I told you the kids were starting drama after school today and the fees would need to be paid." She wasn't in the mood for Gary's crap. He always managed to get her back up, and this time was no different. She hated how he made her feel like she was begging for money, or that any request was unreasonable.

He looked back at the pub, then leaned down to the window. "Right, right, sorry, I guess I forgot. I, eh, didn't have enough on me and had to borrow from one of the lads."

Cathy took a breath and focused on finishing this so she could leave. "Look, thanks for the money. It should be the last of the unexpected expenses until Christmas." So he was short. Big deal. What about all the times she had to do without for the sake of her children. It wouldn't kill him to watch his wallet for a couple of days until he got paid again.

Gary sifted from foot to foot, keeping his eyes locked on hers. "Sam O'Keeffe was asking questions about you the other day."

"Oh, Yeah? By the way, thanks for thinking of my safety. The next guy who pumps you for my phone number, tell them you can't remember it. I don't appreciate it, Gary."

"What? He rang you?" He nearly stuck his head in the window.

Cathy remained silent. Time to get out of here.

"Did he ring you?"

"No, actually, I was just…oh, forget it." She bit her tongue, unwilling to turn this into an ugly spat outside his workplace. He was clearly jealous of Sam's curiosity. But why had he given Sam her phone number if he was so bent out of shape about it?

She hadn't seen him so wound up in ages, so she changed the subject to avoid an argument.

"What days can you take the children this week?"

He straightened up, as if to shake off whatever had bugged him. "I'm off tomorrow and Sunday. I can collect them from school and bring them in on Friday morning. Then if you drop them off to my flat on Sunday, I'll keep them overnight. Is that okay?"

Cathy let out a silent sigh of relief, thankful that a situation had been avoided. She had to admit that Gary shared much of his time off with the children. The truth was, he spent more time alone with them now than when they were all living in the same house.

"Thursday's a strange day for you to be off," she said.

"Yeah, I got an email this morning saying the rosters had been changed for this week. A pain in the arse, but it's a case of shut up or put up."

Cathy knew that as manager Gary liked having the pick of prime days off, and that this change in his work rota was bound to piss him off. Maybe Sam, the new area manager, had something to do with it. But why? She dismissed the thought, knowing there could be a hundred different reasons for it.

"Right, I have to go." She pressed the button to raise the window. There were things to be done, and Gary's moodiness irritated her.

"I'll see you Sunday when I drop the kids off," he said before striding away with a wave of his hand.

"Narky Bastard," Cathy mumbled, then reached for her phone which had just pinged.

Coffee sounds good. Are you free now? Sam.

Before she had a chance to reply, her phone rang, and Sam's number flashed onto the screen. Jesus! What the…? She took a deep breath, gripped by nerves, then answered, her stomach turning mini-somersaults.

"Hi, Sam, I just got your text," she said, sounding far more casual than the reality. "I'm not sure I can get away right now. Not right this minute."

Even though she'd agreed to meet him for coffee, and knowing it wasn't a proper date, she wanted to at least look presentable when she gave him his chance. At this moment in time her tracksuit pants, fleece jacket, and scruffy running shoes didn't go anywhere near hitting the mark. Her hair was greasy, too, pulled back tight at the nape of her neck, and she'd no makeup on, either. Not even mascara, and a PMT spot niggled at her chin. Her only saving grace was that her teeth were brushed and she was minty fresh. Otherwise, she looked exactly how she appeared every morning when she dropped the kids to school; not glamorous at all.

"It doesn't really suit at the moment." Thank goodness this was a phone call and not a face to face meeting. She needed to rearrange for a more suitable time to have coffee with this man, a time when she didn't look like a bag lady. She jumped a mile when someone knocked on the passenger window.

"Hi," Sam said into her ear via the phone, but waving at her through the window. Cathy noted a stiffness to his shoulders, like he was on a mission of some kind. Had he known she was here all along?

"Hi," Cathy answered, embarrassed to have been caught in her lie, but then a rush of anticipation and longing filled her, turned on by the way Sam O'Keeffe's smouldering gaze burned through her.

Ending their phone call, she gestured for him to get into the car. The knowledge that her cheeks were burning did nothing to improve her already overwrought state.

"Okay, you caught me." She held her hands up in a joking manner. "I'm here sitting outside your pub, but I'm not stalking you. I swear." No! Can't believe I said that. She looked away from Sam, who remained silent. "I came to collect money from Gary for the children's drama class. I was just leaving when you texted, and didn't really want you to see me like this."

She wiped a hand on the front of her fleece, and noticed a slight smile pulling at the corners of his mouth. That's nice. She flushed, thinking of the things she'd like him to do with that mouth, then snapped her head back to reality. Jesus! She glanced at him, doing her best not to linger on his impeccably-fitted dark navy suit. A light blue shirt and stripped tie completed the outfit, making him look like he'd just walked out of the Brown Thomas catalogue. Was there even such a thing? My God, how am I going to play this?

"Are you free for half an hour, Cathy? I'd like to take you for that coffee you mentioned."

His smile nearly stopped her heart, but not her brain. That sprang into action. Well, he's seen the state of me now, and he still wants to take me out. I've no valid excuse to say no, and because he's looking at me with those long-lashed, chocolate-brown eyes, I most certainly am going to say yes. Why live a life left wondering?

"Sure," she said, "why not." She touched the keys in the ignition. "Nowhere fancy, though. I'm not dressed for the Shelburne. My ball gown is in the dry cleaners."

Sam laughed and, to Cathy's surprise, looked relieved.

"Just let me make a quick phone call," he said, "then we can go to Insomnia around the corner." He excused himself and climbed out of the car.

Cathy waited until he'd entered the pub before taking advantage of his absence and letting her hair fall loose to her shoulders. She ran her fingers through it to detangle some of the knots, then glossed her lips and nearly choked herself with the amount of body spray she used. Once satisfied, she hopped out and locked the car.

*

She settled at a small table by the window while Sam waited by the counter to be served. Wow, he is some guy. She used the distance between them to check him out. He wore his custom-made suit like a second skin, and even from this distance, she could tell his body was strong and well looked after, and no doubt with wall-to-wall muscle underneath that shirt.

He was tall, with broad, confident shoulders leading up to a sharp, well-chiselled jaw, and such a handsome face. She squirmed in her seat. What else was underneath that suit? She turned away so he wouldn't see her flushed cheeks as he made his way over to her.

After placing the tray on the table, he offered her a choice of pastries. "Chocolate or Blueberry?"

"Eh, stupid question. Chocolate, please." She grinned and reached for her purse.

Please, Cathy." Sam put a hand out to stop her. "My treat."

A shock run up her arm at his touch and heat flooded through her veins. She looked at him. Had he felt it too? She could tell from the look on his face that he was no more immune to her than she was to him. As he removed his hand, she thought she caught a glint of desire in his eyes. Then he blinked and it was gone.

Stunned by their obvious attraction to each other, she didn't know where to go, or what to say. The one thing she did know was that if someone didn't start taking soon, the ground would open up and swallow her. Maybe both of them.

Sam continued to look at her, his lips parted just enough to reveal his perfect teeth. Cathy blinked and took a deep breath.

"So, I believe..." She hesitated, the list of things she'd researched about him jumbled in her head. "Eh, I believe you play the guitar?"

Sam spooned two sugars into his coffee and stirred. Cathy watched him, hoping this wasn't going to be a big mistake.

"Agh, you Googled me?" he said, a grin lighting up his eyes. His shoulders relaxed and soon they were talking about stuff Cathy had gleaned from the internet, and how he felt about having his private life splashed all over the press.

"Don't believe everything you read, Cathy," he said in response to her mention of photos of him and his bevy of beauties. She had trouble hearing him the way he kept his voice so low.

"I didn't read it, I saw it, with my own eyes." Her face flushed again while trying to defend herself. Why did he feel the need to pick her up on it, and then set the record straight? Touchy.

"Look, Cathy, I've only been back in Ireland a few months." He shifted his pastry aside. "My parents were pushing for me to mix a bit more, to get my face out there. Mostly, I go to charity or Vintner events. The press photographers are always at stuff like that

41

so it's a good way to get your name back in the papers and cause a bit of a media stir, or so my parents think. They're well connected. People in high places and all that."

He paused, took a sip of coffee, then grimaced. "When the daughter of a family friend or some business associate needed a date for a function, I was pushed in their direction. Mostly business. It got the girl's face in the paper and my name bandied about, so win-win for everyone." He looked uncomfortable having to admit that he let himself be used in such a way.

"I'm not mad about the way the whole thing works. It's fake and boring, to be honest. But sometimes, a man's gotta do what a man's gotta do." He said this last piece with an American drawl. "As I said, don't bother reading all the crap that goes with the photos. I don't, it's not worth the hassle. The press mostly get it wrong anyway, but if my name gets out there as a good addition to the O'Keeffe group, then it can't be all that bad, right?"

Cathy found it fascinating. Everything he'd told her was so far removed from her life and the everyday things she had to put up with. A different world, where privacy was sacrificed for the sake of a business deal. The concept was alien to her, and she wasn't sure she liked it. Being photographed when you went out to a club or pub on a night out? How could you ever relax and be yourself with the pressure to look good all of the time?

She looked around, checking for paparazzi lurking in the bushes outside, snapping candid shots of them. My God, she'd die if a picture of her, in her tracksuit and fleece, ended up on the internet, or in a glossy magazine. Now she wished she hadn't picked a window seat. She should have thought this through. Damn, she should have said no to coffee.

"Stop panicking, Cathy," Sam said, his tone so reassuring. "They only come out at night. Anyway, you look beautiful."

Cathy caught Sam's gaze drift over her. Oh, God! She covered her boiling cheeks. "Jesus, what am I like? I'm making such a balls of this."

"I think you're better at this than you think you are," he said, his glinting eyes sending another flush through her to the extent that she had to remind herself to breathe.

"Will you come on a proper date with me?" he blurted out, the smooth-talking Adonis taking a brief step back. "Tomorrow night."

The unexpected vulnerability on his face touched Cathy, so much so she didn't want to hurt him with a direct rejection. She still wasn't sure if she could trust him, or how much of a player he was, but she had to admit that she liked him, and that made it difficult to say no.

"I play guitar, as you know, and there's an open-mic session in Temple Bar tomorrow night. I'd love if you could be there."

Sam's invitation took her by surprise. What to do? This was so hard. She knew she wanted to see him again, but she wanted to be careful.

"Can I bring a friend?" She knew she sounded like a teenager, but there was no way she'd go out with him alone. Not yet.

He shrugged. "Eh, okay. Why not? Does your friend have a name?"

"Byron, my friend's name is Byron, and her fiancé is Tom." It came as a relief that he didn't have a problem with the extra company. She released a breath and studied him. Did he have a problem with her request? Was he hiding it? It was good to be able to include Byron. Any time spent with Sam tomorrow would be so much easier having her there for support.

Sam coughed into his hand. "Why not ask them both to come? I'll be on stage for a while and we can all go grab something to eat afterwards."

She agreed, praying that Byron and Tom would be free the following night. It was too soon for a one-on-one date night, but a couples' date could work. And as luck would have it, Gary had the children tomorrow night. She wouldn't have to beg her sister, Becky, to babysit on a school night. Also, Gary wouldn't need to know about her date with Sam.

She couldn't believe how well things had gone, or that she was actually looking forward to going out. I'm going on a date. With

Sam O'Keefe. She hugged herself, finished off her coffee, and made arrangements with Sam for the following night.

*

Sam was happy with how things had gone. He'd been holding off replying to Cathy's text until he could figure out the best time and place for them to meet.

He had a problem, though. Earlier, he'd been in the pub's office and noticed Gary on the CCTV monitor hovering around the till at the bar. It was strange. There were no customers in the pub. Sam witnessed Gary taking money from the till and put it in an envelope before leaving the pub.

He cursed at the CCTV screen. What the hell is Gary playing at, stealing from the pub? Fury blazed through him as he tracked his manager on the outside CCTV cameras. He watched him leave the pub and walk to a blue car in the back car park. When he zoomed in to see who he was meeting, he almost choked when he realised it was Cathy in the car.

"Fuck it," he'd shouted. "The little bastard has his ex-wife in on his scam." Damn. He acted fast, determined to find out what was going on. Why did it have to be Cathy? He grabbed his phone and sent off a quick text, needing to see if she was involved in any of this.

An unexpected dread gripped him as he made his way through the bar and out the exit, following in Gary's footsteps. He was also angry with himself for thinking Cathy was as pure as the driven snow. Fuck it, he'd fantasized about her for the past three nights, suffering through uncomfortable erections until he'd had to release the tension himself.

He just couldn't believe she was involved in something like this. But then, what did he know about her? Nothing. He'd met her once, and knew nothing else except she'd been married to Gary at some stage and they were now separated. Right now he needed to find out what the hell was going on. But he had to be careful. They couldn't discover that he knew what was going on. No, he needed to keep a level head, and get his facts straight.

He passed Gary in the car park and gave him a curt nod. I'll deal with that sneaky scumbag later. He needed to make sure Cathy didn't leave before he got a chance to talk to her. She was reading the text he'd sent so he decided to phone her to stop her driving away.

He said hello, doing his best to speak as though nothing was wrong, listening while Cathy fumbled through her greeting. She blurted out an excuse as to why she wasn't free to meet him. Sam walked up to her car and knocked on the front-passenger window. She nearly dropped her phone with the fright.

"Hi," he said into his phone. She answered and gestured for him to get into the car, which was a bit of a struggle, folding his large frame into the small space. He waited for her to speak, conveying a sense of outer calm while burning up inside.

"Okay, you caught me," she was saying, holding her hands up. "I'm here sitting outside your pub, but I'm not stalking you, I swear." Sam remained silent while she went on to explain. "I came to collect money from Gary for the children's drama class. I was just leaving when you texted, and didn't really want you to see me like this." She pointed at her clothing and hair.

From the apologetic look on her face, and the fact that she was upfront about Gary giving her the money, he knew she wasn't involved in the theft. He could bet she had no idea where Gary's money came from. She wouldn't have offered her reason for being there if she was trying to cover up something. It was there in her eyes, a genuine innocence, mixed with the guilt and embarrassment at having been caught red-handed trying to blow off his coffee invitation.

He relaxed and made a mental note to take a good, close look at the pub's lodgement books. Relief flooded through him when Cathy agreed to spend some time with him now, and excused himself to make a quick phone call. He rang Tony and asked that the pub's account sheets be emailed to him ASAP.

"Discreetly," Sam said, making sure Tony understood.

"Is everything okay, Sam?"

"Nothing I can't handle for the moment." Sam knew he wasn't doing a good job of hiding the anger in his voice. "I'll keep you posted if anything comes up."

Back in the office, he poured over spreadsheets and lodgement statements. When he took a break, he sat back and reflected on his coffee date with Cathy.

"Jesus, she's so sweet," he said to himself, pushing against his hard on, a common occurrence these past few days since she'd entered his life. It was such a relief to know now that she had no involvement in the mess he was starting to uncover. Someone had been skimming the bar tills for months now.

How had it gone un-noticed for so long? He resolved to bide his time. No point running out and throwing accusations about with no proof. He would uncover what was going on, and when he did, whoever was robbing from his family would regret ever setting foot in the same space as Sam O'Keeffe.

5th September

Thursday

Wrapped tight in a towel after her bubble bath, Cathy scanned the clothes in her wardrobe. What to wear? That was the question. Taking advantage of having a free house, she'd spent the afternoon preparing for her date, using all her fancy lotions and potions, shaving and buffing her body to within an inch of its life. Now all she had to do was choose what to wear.

Deciding on a pair of skinny jeans and knee-high boots, she fished out a black-sequined top that would go perfect. This outfit always made her look and feel good. The jeans hugged her curves, and the small heel on her boots gave an extra few inches to her five foot eight height.

With her curling iron, she created a waterfall of loose waves in her fresh-washed hair. A rush of emotions swirled through her body as her mind flitted back to her impromptu coffee date with Sam yesterday morning. Heat crept into her face as she recalled how gorgeous he was, but also how much at ease he made her feel in his presence. He was easy to talk to, and she had to admit she was looking forward to going out with him tonight.

She used clips to secure some hair she'd teased out over her brow, allowing a few tendrils to hang loose at the front. Wearing it like that showed off her face, on which she had used just a little makeup, preferring to keep it light and fresh. She finished her look by accessorising with heavy gold bangles and costume jewellery. Taking a deep breath, she surveyed herself in the mirror one last time. Butterflies flitted through her and her fingertips tingled as she blew a kiss at her reflection and wished herself luck.

They had arranged to meet in a pub in town, not far from the club Sam would be playing in later. When she arrived she found Byron and Tom already there. She pecked Byron on her cheek, giving her a light squeeze, then hugged Tom. Byron smiled, her beautiful teeth lighting up her face. Cathy was grateful that the best friend she could ever wish for had agreed to come out with her and Sam tonight.

Tom was a friend of Gary's. He'd met Byron at the afters of Cathy and Gary's wedding four years earlier. After a couple of years dating, Byron and Tom had gotten engaged, and were finally going to get married in June coming. Her heart set on a June wedding, they'd waited three years for a free Saturday at their chosen hotel.

Even though Tom was a friend of Gary's, they were cut from different cloth. Tom was a sweetheart, loyal and strong, and head-over-heels in love with Byron. He'd agreed to wait three years to get married because he knew it was what Byron wanted. The man would do anything to make her happy, wanting to give his lady her dream wedding, though he would've been happy to elope the day after their engagement. They'd settled in and started saving, well aware that their wedding wasn't going to be a cheap one.

"You look beautiful, Cathy," Byron said, while Tom went to the bar. "What time did you say Sam would be here?"

Cathy licked her lips and shook the nerves away, then checked her watch. Nearly half seven? Goodness. "He should be here soon." She thanked Tom for the vodka and coke before taking a huge gulp to calm her nerves. They kept an eye on the door, and she kicked Byron under the table when Sam walked in.

With a jolt in her gut and a new-found bravado, she stood up, took a deep breath, and walked over to meet Sam. She placed a soft kiss on his cheek and said hello.

"Hello, yourself."

Cathy almost melted when he smiled down at her. Their eyes connected and electricity shot up her arm when he touched her hand. With legs shaking, acting much braver than she knew she was, she took his hand and led him over to meet her friends.

"Sam, this is my BFF, Byron Kelly, and her wonderful fiancé, Tom Byrne".

Sam reached over and shook hands, thanking them for coming. "It was the only way I could get Cathy to go on a date with me," he said, his tone one of gentle teasing.

Cathy noticed that he looked nervous, too, and was glad it wasn't just her having trouble holding it together.

Sam continued. "I'm not sure what it means when my date needs a bodyguard, but I'm pretty sure she won't need protecting. Not from me, anyway." They all laughed and settled down around the table. "Will I get a round in before we leave here?"

"Pint for me, thanks," Tom said, rubbing his hands together. "I'm on a late shift tomorrow so I'm going to enjoy myself tonight."

Cathy caught Byron shooting a warning look at Tom, to which he responded with a playful wink. Cathy agreed to one more vodka and coke, and Byron was okay sipping her half-full glass of wine.

"I'll give you a hand, Sam," Tom said. He drained his pint and followed Sam to the bar.

"Oh, my God, Cathy, he's gorgeous. Much better looking in real life."

"I know, By, he's so cute." Cathy sipped her drink and checked to see who was within earshot. "And I'm not joking. When he touches me, I'm ready to explode there and then!"

"Diiiirrrtttyy Birdiiiie!" Byron looked over to where Sam waited at the bar. "How could you have ever doubted that guy? He's the whole package, Cathy. Look at the body on him."

"Stop drooling, By. That's just the outside, what about the inside and all the other stuff?"

Byron leaned closer. "Don't worry about what's inside, honey. You should be more interested in what's underneath those clothes." She winked and looked back to the bar.

Cathy kicked her under the table again, doing her best to keep the smile off her face. "Byron Kelly, for God's sake, put your tongue away. You're a good as a married woman."

"Not yet, I'm not. I could be convinced to be a runaway bride, if that man there was doing the asking."

Cathy shook her head and smiled. Byron was the best, which was why her messing didn't bother her in the least. There would never be anyone but Tom for her. Their relationship was a solid as a rock. I bet she'll cool her jets when the lads came back to the table.

After their drinks, they made their way to the club hosting the open-mic session, with Byron and Tom walking ahead. Cathy couldn't believe how self-conscious she felt, fidgeting with her bag and hair, talking too fast. Damn her nerves. Sam relaxed her by placing a gentle, warm hand on the small of her back. They chatted about the night so far and Sam commented on how nice Byron and Tom where.

"They seem like really good friends."

"They are. They helped me a lot, especially Byron, when Gary and I broke up. Actually, she was the one who finally got me to see what he'd been up to. I'm ashamed to admit that I blamed her initially for not telling me sooner. We fell out for a while over it."

"Sorry to hear that," Sam said. "It must have been hard for you."

Cathy nodded, shocked that she was sharing this with him. She took a deep breath and relayed a brief version of what to her was her life tragedy.

"It turns out that Gary had been putting it about all over town. Almost as long as we were married. Byron had her suspicions, and then about two years ago she caught him in the act, but she didn't tell me at first." She paused, hoping she wasn't sounding like a martyr.

"Go on," Sam said. "I'm interested."

"She wanted to tell me. Apparently, everybody knew about it, but no one had the guts to come to me. Then one evening I overheard her talking about it with Annabel." She looked up at him and shrugged. "Let's just say the shit hit the proverbial fan."

Sam's hand pressed a little harder into her back. Then he slid it up around her shoulders and gave her a quick hug.

"It's all good now, with me and Byron, I mean. Gary's still an ass, though." She took a breath, looking up under lashes to gauge Sam's reaction.

"Anyway, I copped on, got myself sorted, and the rest, as they say, is history. That's it, my life is full of clichés." She threw her hands up and gave another shrug.

Sam could well imagine the crap Cathy had gone through. He knew at first-hand what betrayal felt like; giving every part of yourself to someone only to have it flung back with a bag full of rubbish to sort through. Even though he'd been hurt, at least he was on his own, with only himself to worry about. Cathy had her twins to look after.

When it had happened to him, he'd run away and hid from everyone until he managed to sort himself out. Cathy hadn't been able to do that with two small children to worry about, having their tiny intimate world turned upside down. She'd had to deal with that, along with her own heartbreak.

His already high opinion of her soared, and from each passing minute he spent with her, his admiration for her personal strength grew. No, she didn't deserve the deal she'd gotten, and that made him want to show her what a good relationship could be like. He knew he could do it, and if it worked out, he'd be the one she could learn to trust again with.

When they got to the club, he arranged them all at a table halfway between the stage and the bar. Tucked away to the side, it was close enough to the stage to see the acts, but far enough away to allow them to chat while the other acts played.

He sat close to Cathy, resisting the urge to kiss her, taking her hand instead and rubbing a thumb over her soft skin. So soft.

Tom amused them all with stories from his job as a fire fighter. It was stressful, and on many occasions tragic, but countered by the best of Dublin wit.

Sam noticed how Byron watched Tom as he held court, and it was obvious to the world and its mother that she was crazy about him.

*

Around 9.30, the other members of Sam's band joined them. Cathy, shy as ever on first meetings, smiled as Sam introduced her to Sean and Brian, the lead singer and drummer respectively. Both seemed like nice guys and she soon relaxed into the easy conversational flow around the table. A short time later the MC called for the guys to take to the stage, leaving Cathy full of nervous excitement. Sam kissed her on the brow before following Sean and Brian backstage to get ready. Surprised by his intimate display, but not the hot flush burning across her face, she looked anywhere but at Byron, who she knew was sitting open-mouthed and wide-eyed, glaring in her direction.

"Well, I think you're on a winner there," Tom said, oblivious to *the Oh, My God* looks she was getting from Byron. "He's sound as a pound."

The vodka and close attention from Sam were having an effect on Cathy. Finding the ability to talk again, she pulled Byron close. "I can't believe I'm here with him. Sam O'Keeffe. He could be out tonight with any number of beautiful women, but instead he chose me."

"For God's sake, Cathy, cop on," Byron said, not hiding her frustration. "He hasn't taken his eyes or his hands off you since he arrived. The guy is nuts about you. I'm well jel!"

"Hey, I'm sitting right here," Tom said, pouting like a hurt lamb. "But, yeah, Cathy, you should go for it. Sam is a sound bloke. I can officially confirm, as your unofficial bodyguard for the night, that you will have no worries there." He raised his glass in salute, then drained its contents.

"Okay, Tom," Cathy said, rolling her eyes, "the Guinness has spoken, so it must be true."

They ordered another round just as Sam appeared on stage with Sean and Brian. The band played some classic rock, with Sam on lead guitar and Sean on the mic. Cathy couldn't believe how good they were. She remembered Sam telling her that he played in the band as a hobby, but that the two other lads were trying to make it a serious career. They played at open-mic nights and in pubs, trying to get their name known in the right circles.

The crowd in the club took notice. Their music grabbed you and pulled you in, giving you no choice but to like it. Cathy watched as Sam worked his guitar, playing with energy to the rhythm of the drums, his long nimble fingers dancing over the frets, making the complex cords look like child's play.

"Wow," Byron mouthed over to Cathy as a song finished and they'd clapped and whooped in the band's direction.

For the last song, Sam passed his guitar to Sean and took up position at the mic. A spotlight lit him as his bandmates played in the shadows. A haunting melody came across the speakers and Sam's soulful voice flooded the room. Cathy's breath caught and her heart thumped so loud she feared they'd hear it over Sam's beautiful voice. It was like she was alone in the club, eyes locked on Sam, and he was singing right to her. At her.

"Fuck's sake!" Tom's voice shattered Cathy's reverie. "Is there nothing this guy can't do?"

Cathy continued to stare at the stage, falling deeper under the spell that was Sam O'Keeffe.

6th September

Friday

Sam rang the local florist first thing that morning to place an order. He wanted to send Cathy flowers, do the whole romantic thing, but realised he didn't have her exact address. Though he knew where she lived, having dropped her home in a taxi last night, she'd directed the driver. He hung up, telling them he'd call back, and rang Tony. His brother could get Cathy's address from Gary's HR file.

"Actually, while I have you, can you set up a meeting with our security company? I'm going to need a bit of surveillance and someone to go over some old footage of the pub."

"What's going on over there?" Tony asked.

"Ah, I've been going over the accounts," Sam said, stretching a pinch out of his shoulders. Too much stress with all this. He took a deep breath. "There are a few holes in the figures. I've narrowed it down to specific days over the past month, but I didn't go back any further. I want to check this bit out first, before I do any more digging."

"Sounds serious. How much are we talking?"

Sam rubbed the tiredness out of his eyes. "A couple of thousand so far, although that's not the point. Nobody steals as much as a cent from here and gets away with it. Not if I have anything to do with it."

"Okay, I'll email you the when and where for meeting up with Sheppard Security. We'll get some advice, see what we can find out. Talk later." Tony hung up.

Sam rang the florist again, giving them Cathy's address for the delivery. He didn't want a bog-standard bunch of roses, so instead placed an order for the autumn bouquet. From the picture on the website, this was much more exotic, with rich brown, earthy colours intertwined with berries and green foliage. This was a first for Sam, caring about the type of flowers he sent someone. He had to do something special for this girl. Something that would count. It might take a few days to organise, but it would be worth it to show Cathy how he felt about her.

In many ways, last night had been an eye opener for him, too. Since his return to Ireland, it had been difficult to blend into the background, especially when he was out and about. Having a socialite on his arm every time he went out didn't help, but last night had been different. Such a relief just going out and relaxing with a few drinks and good company.

Playing his set with the band was another buzz for him. That was the way he liked it, no pressure to perform or act one way or the other. Being out with Cathy and her friends had brought back memories of his college days. Back then there were no high expectations, no pushing from his parents or family to get his face known in the right social circles. In fact, it was the opposite, his family had almost shielded his existence, allowing him to attend school and college with a degree of anonymity.

And then Sinead arrived on the scene. Sam had met her in the UCD bar one afternoon. They'd dated, slept together, and fell in love. He'd never known anything like it. Sinead was an angel, until she proved that it was all an act. From the way Sam remembered it, she changed almost overnight, doing a number on him, taking full advantage of his impressive pedigree when she realised how cosy her life being attached to a man like him could be.

She wanted the life, and it didn't matter who it was with. Dollar signs popped up in her eyes and the focus shifted from being with Sam and loving him, to being with whoever was able to offer her the best deal. Sam's world fell apart with one final blow, forcing him to leave Ireland straight after graduation. He ran away and took shelter in a foreign climate, allowing him time to lick his wounds.

After seeing at first-hand how money could change someone in such a disgusting manner, he shunned all of his family's fortune and vowed to make his own way in the world. Of course, he kept in touch with his family, but insisted on working hard to pay his way in the new life he'd chosen.

While earning a living in various bars across the Balearic Islands, he'd kept himself busy and worked his way back to at least resembling a normal person again. It took time, but he reached the stage where, as he saw it, he was no longer vulnerable to being used by anyone.

He had regrets about aspects of his relationship with Sinead, but time helped him come to terms with decisions he had made. When he recalled the ways in which Sinead had hurt him, it was no surprise that he hadn't trusted another woman since their split, or that he'd kept all subsequent relationships casual and fun, never letting himself get to the stage of loving someone again.

Returning to Ireland had been a huge upheaval for him. Due to the recession gripping Ireland over the past few years, business had taken a nosedive. His father had approached him with a job offer in the family business. They needed to restructure, and fresh blood was required to look at things in a new way. Sam worked out the details of the job and, within a fortnight, returned to Ireland.

Something he hadn't expected, though, was the media attention his return attracted. All of a sudden he was the mysterious middle son of the O'Keeffe Empire, back from foreign lands. Tabloids couldn't get enough of him and glossy magazines portrayed him as *Ireland's most eligible bachelor*.

Every sequined dress from Dundrum Shopping Centre had been trotted past him, draped over daughters of Ireland's rich and famous, all competing to catch his eye. Sam hated all of it, but accepted that the press coverage could only be good advertisement for the family's business, and the priority now was to ensure their business survived.

*

Cathy collected the children from school at 1.30. She was well rested after a lie-in and relaxing shower, and decided to treat the kids with a baking session. Millie and Jack loved baking, but things tended to get messy when the whisks came out, and as a result it didn't happen often. Today would be fun.

Right now, as far as she was concerned, life couldn't be better. She hadn't felt this good about herself in such a long time. Her thoughts kept wandering back to last night, after the gig. Sam and his band had returned to join them for last orders. Having Sam sing so intimately to her had rocked her to her core, and she was shaking with a desire she hadn't experienced before.

She'd joined in the light-hearted banter around the table, but couldn't wait to get Sam on his own. Her confidence soared and she knew without a doubt that any fears or preconceived notions she had about this man were unfounded. She fancied him, wanted him, so why was she denying herself? It's not like she was twelve years old, trying to let on she didn't fancy the guy who'd sent his mate over to ask her out. She was an adult. True, she didn't have much in the way of experience, but that didn't matter, so she needed to cop on. What was she being so coy about? He fancied her. Sam O'Keefe fancied her. And she fancied him, so why not let it happen?

Gary, on the other hand, had treated her disgracefully, shattering her trust, making her feel unworthy of anyone else's love.

"No! It's been too long," she'd said into the club's bathroom mirror. "I so want this. I need this!"

"What?" Byron slurred from behind a cubicle door.

"I'm going for it, By. I like him, I really do. I should go for it, right?"

Byron exited the stall after flushing, washed her hands, and reapplied her lip-gloss. "Just take it slow, babe." She blinked a few times, as if to clear her vision. "Sam's a great guy, but you need to set the pace. If this is just a fling, then go for it. Although I don't think that's what you want. Is it? You're not a fling sorta gal. Are you?

Cathy didn't know what to say to that. Was this a fling?

"I don't think you've ever been flung," Byron continued, smiling to herself. "Is that even a word? Whatever, never mind. The point is, Babe, you need to take it slow. Sam's a good guy, who obviously wants you. But you've got to set the pace. Do whatever you're comfortable with. If he's willing to let you control the pace, then he understands."

She smiled and twirled her forefinger at Cathy, as if she could see her words. "That, my dear, is gold dust. If he's right for you, let it happen. Let yourself be happy for once." Like an actor after an award-winning performance, Byron bowed, so low she nearly fell face first onto the tiled floor.

"Oh Jesus, By." Cathy howled with laughter as Byron tried to stand straight. "I think it's time to go. It's getting late, and I've got a man and a plan."

She looped Byron's arm and guided her back to the table, then whispered in Tom's ear that it was time to take his pissed fiancé home. It was also time to be alone with Sam.

When Byron and Tom left, Sean and Brian made their excuses and went back to the bar, not before telling Cathy to come again soon.

"I've never heard Sam playing as good as he did tonight," Sean said, winking at Sam. "You're a good influence. Next time I'll pay to have an A&R man here, so he can sign us up at our finest hour."

When the lads left, Cathy and Sam looked at each other, but she didn't know what to say, overcome by a shyness she hadn't expected. Her throat went dry, so dry that gulping the last of her vodka and coke didn't help. Sam must have sensed her discomfort, holding out a hand to her. He stood and invited her up with him.

"Let's get out of here," he said, his voice firm and strong. "Somewhere a bit quieter, where we can talk."

This guy was so smooth. Gorgeous. Cathy grabbed her coat and bag and followed Sam outside, gasping when the cold air hit her face. She shrugged into her coat and Sam took her by the hand, his grip firm, leading her in a brisk walk down the street.

She struggled to keep up with his long strides. Another wave of nerves rushed over her. Where was he taking her? Was he bringing her back to his apartment? Was she ready to have the *Sorry, not tonight* conversation with him if he tried it on?

Her mind raced, struggling to come up with a cool way of getting out of it. She wanted to take it slow, follow Byron's advice, but she hadn't the chance to discuss it with Sam yet.

Relief flooded over her when he led her into an all-night café and found a secluded table by the back wall. He settled her there and headed up to the counter. Cathy mulled over this latest turn of events. So he wants to talk. Actually talk. Phew, they were on the same page. Who knew?

She watched him as he ordered. Could he read her mind? He was doing all the things she wanted him to, without having to be told, including treating her with reverence and respect, almost like he was afraid to push his luck until she gave him the green light.

They spent hours in the cafe, drinking coffee and talking. She couldn't believe how well it was going. This was the good part of a new relationship; the getting to know each other part.

But it couldn't last forever. Late into the night, she nearly locked her jaw with an enormous yawn and decided it was time to go home. She didn't want to, but knew she would need a few hours' sleep if she was to function at all the next day.

"I'll see you home," Sam said.

"Ah, no, it's okay. I'll be fine in a taxi." She was sure Sam could see the panic in her eyes. Did he know what she was thinking? God! Stop thinking. Stop thinking.

"Stop panicking," he said, running the tip of his finger down her cheek, his touch so light. "I'm not after that. Not tonight, anyway."

Soft lines crinkled at the sides of his eyes as she looked at him through her eyelashes, torn between wanting to give him what she thought he wanted, and what she knew she should be doing for herself. She saw desire in his soft brown eyes. There was no doubting it. What would it be like to kiss the worry lines along his temple? What would it be like to run her fingers through his untamed hair? Or feel the pulse that thumped below his open shirt collar.

A crash of dishes from behind broke the spell and they leaned back from each other. Sam cleared his throat, shaking his head like he was trying to clear a fog. "If you think I'm letting you go home in a taxi on your own, then think again, Missy."

"Missy?" Cathy laughed out loud.

"Yeah, Missy!" Sam laughed too, but then leaned closer, his dark eyes taking her whole face in. "It's all up to you, Cathy. I'm not in the driving seat here, you are. We'll do this your way or not at all."

She recognised sincerity in his voice and knew she had to try to believe him.

Sam continued. "I just want to see you again. That's enough for me right now." He reached over and took her hand in both of his. Cathy leaned over the small table and kissed him on the lips, light and soft.

"Thank you," she whispered against his mouth, her warm breath bouncing back at her. She hoped with every ounce of her being that he might turn out to be her knight in shining armour after all.

*

When they left the café, Sam found a quiet doorway nearby. He pulled her into the shadows and wrapped her in his arms. She leaned into him and tipped her head back, looked straight into his eyes. Sam lowered his head and kissed her full on the mouth, testing with his tongue until she opened her lips and let him in.

*

A thrill of spice ran through her body as she raised her hands to Sam's hair, and with her fingers entwined in his silky strands, she drew him closer and returned his kiss with a passion she didn't know she'd possessed.

Her stomach quivered as Sam ran his hand under her coat and caressed her back. So soft. Every muscle dissolved into jelly as she worked her way up to a frenzy, threatening to take her over a wonderful brink. She broke the kiss, panting, with Sam leaning his forehead against hers. An unspoken question in his eyes needed to be addressed, the same question any red-blooded male would be asking, no matter what he had just promised about taking it slow.

"Sorry, Sam," she whispered, "it can't go any further tonight. I'm sorry. I just need time." How would he take it? She'd kissed him like that and now wanted to send him home. Okay, she knew it wasn't fair, but she had to do it her way. As Byron had said, if he understood, he'd wait for her. But would he?

Sam's answer came as he pulled her tight against him, placing a gentle kiss on her brow. "We'll take it slow, Cathy. As slow as you need. Once I know you're interested, I'll wait."

She lay her head against his chest and snuggled into his warm embrace. This man can read my mind. I like it. I like it a lot. I like you, Sam O'Keefe.

"I'll take you home," he said.

She looked up at him. "Thanks, Sam, but first, can I have another snog?"

Sam smiled, his beautiful teeth gleaming through the shadows. "Certainly. No complaints here." He leaned down to make Cathy's toes curl again.

*

Back in the present, Cathy was elbow-deep in chocolate-brownie mix when the doorbell rang. Knowing it was a bad idea to leave the twins alone with the electric mixer, she unplugged it and brought it with her to answer the door. Her heart leapt when she saw the beautiful bouquet.

Balancing both mixer and bouquet, she pressed her face into the cocktail of colour, breathing in its sweet fragrance. The earthy colours, mixed with exotic foliage and berries, made for a stunning display. A burning desire overwhelmed her, and she knew there and then, without having to read the card, who the flowers were from. She'd spent the day thinking about Sam and it warmed her to know he'd been thinking about her, too.

Returning to the kitchen to find the bowl of chocolate batter upended on the floor, Cathy couldn't even muster a flicker of annoyance towards the twins. She didn't care. They could start again, both on the brownies and on the rest of their lives. She read the card attached to the bouquet.

Thanks for last night. How about dinner tomorrow? We'll take it slow. Sam.

She pulled out her phone and texted him. *Overwhelmed by the flowers, by you, by us. Dinner sounds great (pending availability of babysitter). Looking forward to it. C x*

Her phone beeped a return message almost instantly.

Great, will pick you up at 7.30. Is Italian ok? Somewhere local? Sam.

Cathy hit reply: *perfect, see you then. X.* She floated through the rest of the day.

7th September

Saturday

Cathy's sister, Becky, got to the house around six. Cathy had pleaded with her on the phone earlier that morning, begging her to babysit that night, even though she knew her sister was suffering from being out the night before.

"Okay, Okay," Becky said, "but give me a few hours to sweat this alcohol out of my system before letting the terrible two loose on me."

Now safely arrived, Cathy had left her in the kitchen where she helped herself to a recovery-snack of rasher sandwich and a strong cup of tea.

"Beck?" Cathy shouted down from the bedroom. "Beck, leave the twins watching the cartoons and get up here."

When Becky arrived, sweat on her brow from the climb up the stairs, Cathy took a deep breath and let it all out. "I'm so nervous, Beck. What if we've nothing in common? What am I talking about, we *don't* have anything in common. Look at him. Look at me. How can this work? What if he wants more than I do? I'm mortified, Beck. What'll I say?"

"Sit," Becky ordered, pointing to the bed like her sister was a wayward puppy. "Breathe. And stop it now with the self-doubt.

72

You've been there a million times, and it's so not true. Gary was a shit, and believe me, he's lucky to have his balls still dangling as far as I'm concerned."

Cathy went to interrupt, but Becky held out a hand. "No, Cathy, Sam is not Gary. You told me that yourself less than half an hour ago when I fell in the door. Look at the way he's already treated you, how patient he's been. You said it was like he could read your mind. Let him, for crying out loud. Let him show you how he's going to treat you."

She walked around the bed, shaking her hands, eyes to the ceiling, as if looking for the right words. "Look, there are hundreds of Garys out there, but believe me, there aren't too many diamonds like Sam. You struck gold, Sis, so don't knock it. Don't question it, and most of all, don't doubt yourself. You're so much better than that, and you deserve a break. You do! So please calm down, get your shit together, and take the man by the horn, no wait, the bull by the horn. Oh, whatever, either works." She winked and laughed at her own joke, then sat on the chair, out of breath.

"Thanks, Beck. I needed that cheerleader pep talk." Cathy hugged her close, wincing from the stink of stale alcohol. She stood back. "The state of you. Are you even in a fit state to mind the children?"

Becky got up and flopped onto the bed. "Don't worry about those two, Sis. And as for me, party hard, play hard, that's my motto."

Cathy shook her head. "Yeah, and die hard." She had no choice at this short notice but to trust Becky not to burn down the house. She did, however, make a mental note to ring every half hour while she was out, just to be sure.

"Millie and Jack are washed and fed. Just give them some hot chocolate around 7.30 and off to bed they go. They're wrecked so it shouldn't be too hard to get them to sleep."

"Yeah, yeah," Becky groaned from the bed. "Hot chocolate, then bed. Got it. I'll have a glass of wine once they're asleep. Hair of the dog. Mark is coming over, anyway, after his late shift, so don't worry about being late." She waved her hands above her. "It's all cool."

"It'd better be."

"Aw, Sis, will you stop worrying." She sat up, the action an obvious struggle. "You look hot, by the way. That dress is something else. I can borrow it, right?"

"No," Cathy said, knowing if Becky got her hands on it, she'd never see it again. It was a black sleeveless above-the-knee, lace-skater, dress. The fit-and-flare design, clenched in at her waist, then flowed over her hips. Flashes of delicate lace gave a gothic feel to a classic evening look. And great care had been taken with her black silk stockings, making sure the seam ran straight at the back of each leg. She wore the only high heel shoes she owned, black and simple. A fitted black blazer completed her look.

She'd styled her hair into soft blonde curls that fell in waves around her face in a ruffled look that she loved. Once again, keeping her makeup simple, she'd reapplied one last swipe of lip-gloss before finishing with a squirt of her favourite perfume.

Right. Time to go. Don't be nervous. Don't be nervous. She took a deep breath, pushed a snoring Becky off her bed, and went downstairs to wait for Sam. Her legs shook. Her stomach did its usual flip, and no amount of deep breaths quelled the jitters running through her. I'm doing the right thing. Byron said it. Becky said it. Now I'm saying it. Time to give Sam O'Keefe a chance.

She didn't want the kids to see Sam in the house so she went outside to meet him when his taxi pulled up.

"Hi," she said as she settled in beside him on the back seat.

"Hi, yourself." He leaned over and kissed her cheek. So soft. "You look amazing.

"Why, thank you," she said, heat rising through her neck and into her cheeks. Maybe he wouldn't notice in the gloom of the cab.

*

Having got on so well on their previous date, it came as no surprise that things went as well this time around. Dinner was delicious, but finished early after they had dessert when they decided to grab a taxi back to Cathy's house to let Becky go home.

Pausing, her hand on the handle of the taxi door, Cathy turned to face Sam. "I know this sounds kind of lame, especially when we're going back to my place, but I don't think this should go any further tonight." She looked through her eyelashes, almost as protection, and wait for his reaction. "Look, Sam, I still barely know you, and I'm not that comfortable hopping in and out of men's beds, or my own, as the case may be."

Sam's crooked grin sent a sweet shiver down her spine. Leaning closer, he stroked a finger along her cheek, then in a slow arc down across her jaw. "Take your time, Cathy. I told you already, I'm not in any rush. Just getting you to come out with me tonight was enough for me." He cupped her face and pressed a light kiss to her forehead.

She inhaled the sweet mix of beer and aftershave. Gorgeous. She kissed his warm neck, her voice soft against his skin. "It's still early. Come in for coffee. No more, though." She smiled up at him, amazed that her natural shyness wasn't getting in the way. "Let's get to know each other better first. Then we'll see how it goes."

*

Cathy let them in the front door, and motioned for Sam to go on through to the kitchen. She popped her head around the living room door, checking to see if Becky was still alive. "Everything okay, Becks?" She couldn't keep the grin off her face.

76

"Sis, I didn't think you'd be home so early. Are you okay? Did it not go well?"

Becky looked worried. Cathy slipped into the room and shut the door behind her. Sitting on the sofa beside Becky, she took her hands and giggled like a teenager. "It was great, Beck. Really, really, great. He's such a nice guy. I didn't know him at all. Everything I thought about him was wrong. I was too busy looking at the outside and the media crap to look at the man right in front of me. Sounds a bit soft, doesn't it?"

"Oh, snap!" Becky said, clapping her hands. "You got it, girl. You've got it bad. And he is so hot. I've seen all the photos." Becky hugged her. "How did you get so lucky?" She took Cathy's hands in hers. "That's not the way it's supposed to go for you, remember. You were all set up to hate the guy and all the stuff that goes with him. Less than three hours ago you wanted to cancel the date, ready to run back into your hermit cave. What happened? God forbid you actually listened to your little sister."

"Cheeky mink," Cathy said, giving Becky a playful shove. "To be honest, I don't know what changed. I opened my eyes, I suppose, and saw the real Sam." She thought about that, remembering his gorgeous chocolate-brown eyes. "Yeah, I let him talk and I listened to what he was actually saying, instead of relying on those preconceived ideas rolling around in my head. He's a nice man, Beck, really nice." She sat up, relishing her next words. "And, he's waiting for me in the kitchen."

"What, he's here? In the Kitchen? Oh, my God, Cathy, what a turnaround. You brought the man home." Becky did a little dance in the middle of the living room.

"Shush, Beck. Calm down, for God's sake. It's not like that. I just don't want the night to end yet, so I asked him in for coffee. Just a coffee," she stressed, as Becky raised a sharp eyebrow.

"Well, what are you doing standing here talking to me? Go into him, for God's sake. Go have your *coffee*. Get to know him better. But be careful." She wagged a forefinger. "And please wait 'til Mark collects me before you start ripping his clothes off. I don't need a performance like that tonight."

"Becky, stop! It's not going to happen. Just coffee, a chat, and perhaps a goodnight snog. That's as far as it's going tonight. It's way too soon, right?" Cathy hugged herself, enjoying the warmth and fuzziness she suspected may have come from the wine she'd had during dinner. So worth it.

"Go! Go on," Becky urged. "Tell Mr Hot Stuff I said hi. And don't worry, I'll be out of your way soon. Just don't jump him 'til after I'm gone"

"Wouldn't dream of it." Cathy grinned as she went to find Sam.

She found him in the kitchen, leaning against the counter with his strong arms folded across his chest. His lazy smile made her want to run and wrap herself around him, have those arms around her, his warm hands caressing her, and being devoured by that mouth. That mouth. The effect Sam was having had her wet between her legs. For God's sake, Cathy, Reign it in. Slow down. Then she noticed the two cups of hot steaming coffee on the worktop beside him.

"Make yourself at home, why don't you?" she said, pointing at the coffee.

"Well I didn't know how long you were going to be, so I thought I'd make myself useful." Sam stared at her, his brow creased, as if waiting for her to reveal that she was only joking.

"Have I crossed a line somehow, Cathy?" He stood away from the counter. "It's just coffee. Everything was close to hand so it's not like I took a cheeky snoop through your cupboards." He shrugged. "I just wanted to show you that when you said 'Come in for coffee', I understood that it meant *coffee*, and nothing more." He stepped towards her, one hand on the counter. "I want you to be comfortable with me, Cathy, and if that means taking it slow, then that's what we're going to do."

Cathy let out a long silent breath. She smiled, lifted her mug, and sat at the kitchen island, aware that Sam was waiting for her response. "Sorry I snapped at you, Sam. It's not you. I'm just a little touchy. I've been on my own and looking after the children for a long time now, and I'm not used to people. Men. I'm not used to men." Goodness, Cathy, get it straight, will you.

She sipped her coffee, which was just how she liked it. How did he know that? "Look, Sam, I'm not used to having a man around, especially one who wants to do stuff for me out of the goodness of his own heart."

The heat from the mug seeped into her hands, reminding her of Sam's touch. "You have to understand, Sam, it was always about everyone else before. It takes getting used to having someone care about how I'm feeling, what I'm thinking, and what I want."

She took another sip of Sam's wonderful coffee, calculating just how much of her life she should reveal at this early stage. We're here now, aren't we? Why not everything? "With Gary, things were one-sided, in every way, especially his. As far as he was concerned, the whole world revolved around him. Where we lived, what I drove, when we went on holidays, when we went out together, everything."

Sam went to touch her hand, but she shifted it out of the way. "All the daily decisions in a relationship that should involve compromise and cooperation were taken by him. I was the quintessential little woman, stuck at home rearing the children, grateful for any snip of affection or respect thrown my way. Finding out he'd been putting it into anything in a skirt was the best thing that ever happened to me. I woke up, freaked out, and kicked his arse out of my house."

She took another sip of coffee. "This is so good, Sam. Anyway, I pulled myself together, took a good look at how things were, and finally started living the life my children and I deserved.

On our own. Doing our own thing, when and how we wanted. It's been hard, believe me, but we're getting there. I suppose I didn't realise how strongly I felt about it until I walked in and it looked like you'd taken over."

She looked into Sam's eyes. Can you read my mind now, Sam O'Keefe? Do you think I'm crazy? Are you going to bolt? She needed to relax, because he was so easy to talk to when she wasn't stressed. It was all about her and her stupid preconceived ideas that he was nothing but a player, with all that represented. Well, he'd proved her wrong each time, showing what a great guy he was: kind, funny, generous to a fault, and always charming.

Most of all, she realised now that he was doing everything to make her happy, to make her life easier, to make her want to be with him, not because he wanted to control her. He was fascinated by her and her strong will. She remembered him saying it. He loved to see her challenging him and not take everything for granted. What a guy.

Sam moved over and stood in front of her, looking hard into her eyes. "I can only imagine the head-wrecking stuff you've had to deal with over the past year. I'm sorry that had to happen." He smiled as he ran his fingers through her hair, pushing it off her face and tucking it behind her ear.

Cathy relished the contact. She stood and looked up at him, recognising the sincerity in his eyes. Relax, girl. This is Sam O'Keefe, not Gary. He wanted her, he'd chased her, and now he was here, making coffee for her, because she wanted to take it slow. No pressure.

She tipped her head back and drew Sam's face down to meet hers. "No, I'm sorry." And with that she kissed him.

*

Letting her set the pace was new for Sam, but he knew this wasn't going to work any other way. It had to be her choice, her pace; her want. And he wanted her. That was clear by his hard-on threatening to explode in his jeans. He accepted Cathy's kiss, savouring her soft lips, massaging her lower back the way he knew she liked it from their time in the doorway.

*

Shaking under Sam's touch, and so turned on, Cathy leaned into his arms and opened her mouth, allowing him take full advantage as he backed her up against the wall. She reached up and ran her fingers through his hair, pulling him as close as possible, drinking him in, his tongue, his taste, his breath.

He held her head with both hands, his strong tongue exploring her mouth in soft gentle probes, their lips crushing, his teeth nibbling and drawing desire-laden moans out of her. Too much. She shoved him away, his gaze one of confusion and torment.

*

Sam knew he'd pushed too far, but he was so damn hot for this woman. He wanted her. Needed her. But on her terms. It was difficult, but he had to respect that slow was the way she wanted it, for now. She entranced him with those ice-blue eyes. Her beautiful hair. That stunning body. No one had come this close to undoing him with one single look. Cathy lit the fuse of the firework inside him and he was about to explode. One look from her, no matter how innocent, was all it took.

Knowing she needed to take back control, and not wanting to scare her, Sam backed off. He'd taken a risk kissing her like that, and now his breath burned in his chest while he watched her reaction. What would she do?

*

Cathy gasped for breath, and then looked at him, into those gorgeous eyes. All she could see was hunger, red-hot longing, and at that moment she knew she couldn't resist. Didn't want to. She stepped forward on jelly legs, connecting with him again, pulling his face down to hers again, locking onto him again, with a passion and longing she'd missed for so long. So long.

"Please," she groaned, pushing him away again, then pulling him back, laughing out loud at the absurdity of her actions.

Sam laughed, too. "Jesus, Cathy, you're killing me."

"I'm sorry, Sam. I'm feeling so self-conscious. Except for Thursday night, it's been a while since I had a snog like that. It's curling my toes."

"Mine too," he said, his grin lighting his face up.

"God, I so want to take this straight to bed right now, Sam, and my body is yelling *yes, yes, yes*, but my head is screaming *slow down*." She gripped the front of his jacket and pulled him to her, willing him to understand that she did, and didn't, want this to happen tonight.

"Which one is shouting louder?" he asked, smiling as he slid one hand around her back, keeping eye contact all the time. "Because I know which part of my body is doing all the talking."

Cathy nearly melted on the spot. I can feel that part against my hip. She groaned and rested her brow on his shoulder as he wrapped both arms around her and skimmed his lips across her temple.

"Don't moan like that," he whispered. "It'll undo me, and I'm having enough trouble holding on as it is. If you don't want to go any further tonight, I understand, I really do. It's up to you, Cathy."

She took that cue to look deep into his eyes, to gauge if it was a line, or if he was genuine and really cared about her.

"Really, Cathy, you've had a bad run of it. I don't want to make it worse. The last thing I want this to be is a quick lay, a one night stand. I don't want to be the reason for a month of sleepless nights for you, beating yourself up for doing something you didn't want to do. You mean more to me than that, Cathy. More and more every time I see you. I want you, but only if you want me, guilt free, and only when you're ready."

"I want you now, Sam," she whispered, her body signalling its true feelings, making the decision for her. "Guilt free." Just knowing that he wasn't forcing her, knowing that he was willing to wait, made her so hot that she was afraid she'd burst. Knowing that the control was hers, that it wasn't a line, made all the difference. She gave him what she hoped he'd see as a wicked smile.

"Give me a minute," she said, untangling herself from his arms and backing her way to the door. "Just need to get rid of the babysitter." She made her way upstairs to check on the children, willing herself to calm down at every step. In Jack's room, she sat on the edge of his bed and brushed back his hair from his forehead. My beautiful boy. She kissed him goodnight without waking him.

In Millie's room, she repeated this routine with her daughter and made her way to her en-suite bathroom, taking fresh panties out of a drawer on the way. She changed the damp ones, splashed cold water on her face, and gave her teeth a quick brush. On her way back downstairs, she crossed her fingers and wished that Becky's boyfriend would hurry up.

When she stepped into the sitting room, she saw that Sam had made himself comfortable on the couch and was chatting to Becky about the different clubs and pubs his family owned. He promised to put her on the VIP list for the next big after-concert party they'd be holding in a couple of weeks' time.

"Sweet," Becky said, smiling like the cat that got the milk. She did a victory wiggle in her chair, rolling her arms and shoulders. "I can't wait. I'll be dressed with the best and ready to *party!*"

Cathy stood by the fire, keeping an eye on the window and willed Jason, Becky's boyfriend, to get a move on. If she didn't get on top of Sam soon, she was going to explode. Every now and then Sam would look over at her and smile that gorgeous crooked smile of his, his eyes leaving her under no doubt that he couldn't wait to get her alone.

All the while, he entertained Becky with stories of superstars and legends who frequented his pubs and clubs. He was the perfect gentleman and kept the conversation flowing between them, ensuring Becky didn't feel like a gooseberry in their company.

Becky's phone beeped with a message that Jason was outside. She bounced up, grabbed her bag, kissed Cathy goodnight, and saluted Sam as she made her way out the door, letting them know in no uncertain terms that she was going to her own night of passion.

*

Cathy and Sam sat at opposite sides of the room, staring into each other's eyes, neither willing to make the first move, but both aching for each other.

Sam crossed the room and pulled Cathy to her feet, kissed her hard, and in one quick motion swung her up into his powerful arms. Cathy wrapped her arm around his neck and showed him how aroused she was by clamping her legs around his waist, clenching him between her thighs and grinding herself into him.

Sam took her to the large L-shaped couch and eased her down. She was surprised that he hadn't taken her upstairs, and said as much.

"This is your house, Cathy. Your children are asleep upstairs, and I don't want to disturb them. Let's take it slow and keep the hot kinky bedroom stuff for a night when we're a bit more comfortable. For now, I just want to be with you, hold you, kiss you, eat you, and hopefully, satisfy you. I so want you."

Sam's words squeezed Cathy's inner core and made her squirm in his arms. This was going to be so good.

His expression turned serious. "What are the chances of the children waking up and coming to look for you?"

While moved by his concern for her children, she couldn't hold back her smile. "No chance. I walked the legs off the two of them this afternoon to make sure they'd be wrecked tonight."

"Oh?" He looked straight into her eyes. "Did you know this was going to happen, Missy? Did you know I was going to end up here tonight?"

"Don't flatter yourself, Casanova. It was more for Becky's sake. I knew she was hungover." She squeezed Sam between her legs. "It just so happened that it worked out well for you, too." She pressed her lips to his mouth, hard, holding tight as he lowered himself to her. "Take me," she whispered. "Whatever way you want."

As Sam kissed her deep and slow, she curled her hands into his hair, moaning into his mouth and growing hotter by the second. He broke away and sat up. She reached forward and opened each button on his shirt, slow and seductive. At least she hoped that's how it seemed. As each button opened, it revealed a hard, strong chest and torso. A fine sprinkling of dark hair covered his chest, with a sensual and inviting line running from his navel, down beneath the belt on his jeans.

Tracing her finger around his tight abs, his muscles quivered at her touch. Sam sucked in a sharp breath and peeled off his shirt, then eased Cathy's legs from around him and rose from the couch. Within seconds he'd released his belt buckle and removed his jeans, then knelt back beside her.

She ran her hands up and over his chest, feeling her way around his body, wanting to savour this as much as she could, needing to see him naked, in all his glory, because this man was nothing less than glorious.

*

For Sam, it was all about Cathy. Every move would be at her pace, even though he was about to erupt. He knelt back as she stood, and watched amazed as she unzipped her dress and let it fall into a silky shadow on the floor. Still in her heels, she stepped out of the fabric and pulled Sam from his knees.

He drank her in as he straightened. She wore a black lace bra with red trimming, a black silk thong below a black suspender belt, with sheer silk stockings covering the length of her endless legs from mid-thigh to spiked high heels. If he'd known that body, with that lingerie, was hidden beneath that dress all night, he wouldn't have made it through dinner in once piece. "Jesus, Cathy, you're stunning."

He adored the way she looked at him under her lashes, shy and inviting all at once. What a woman. He pulled her close, and she crushed herself to his hard body, and when he lifted her, she once again wrapped her legs around his waist, squeezing him between those wonderful thighs.

Buried in a ferocious kiss, they fell onto the couch, Cathy's hands roaming all over his body, across his chest, over his abs, until she found the bulge in his shorts. Sam was desperate to be released. He growled into her mouth when she took him, her grip strong, running up and down his length in slow, teasing movements.

Freeing the clasp on her bra, he dived south to her now-released ample breasts, taking an erect nipple into his mouth, sucking and nibbling, her breast soft against his cheek. Cathy groaned and tightened her grip on him, and he suspected she was near the edge. Way too soon. He eased off, kissed her collarbone, her shoulder, her neck, drawing it out, making it last, though he wasn't sure how much longer he could hold himself. The way she held him threatened to send him over the edge, too.

Her eyes sprang open and sought his, her breath hot on his mouth. "Take me, Sam. Please. Now. I need you inside me. Now!"

Sam ground against her, kissing her hard, and being kissed as good in return. She wanted him. She wanted him now. He dragged himself off her and removed his shorts, then pulled at Cathy's thong, snapping the seam and letting the small triangle of black silk slip away. My god. Where has this woman been all my life? He touched her, slid his fingers through her wetness, pressed against her button, and almost came there and then knowing that she wanted him as much as he wanted her.

"Hold on," he said, praying this wouldn't ruin the magic. He lifted his jacket off the coffee table and took a condom from his wallet.

"Oh, my God," Cathy said, her hand to her mouth. "A condom." She laughed and threw her eyes to the ceiling. "I completely forgot. It's been so long since I needed one. How scary is that?"

Sam kissed her, nibbling her lower lip, their breath mixing in sound and scent. "Relax, Cathy. Don't worry, I'm clean, but until I can show you, let's be careful. Okay?"

*

Taken aback by his utter respect for her, Cathy felt at that instant closer to him than she had ever been to another man. Not wanting to think about her rat of a husband at this time, she put her total focus into the moment and let Sam enter her with everything he had.

Taking it slow at first, they soon found a sensual rhythm, but it wasn't long before things got faster, hotter, harder. With one easy motion, without pulling apart, Sam flipped her up and on top of him. Cathy rode him, pawing at this chest, his hands holding her by the hips, moving with her as she rocked up and down, grinding into him, bringing him closer and closer until there was no return. He threw his head back, his grip tighter, trusting into her until he had no choice but to release, his teeth clenched, eyes shut, coming hard like it was his first time.

Without pause, he dropped his hand to find Cathy's sweet spot, rubbing her just right and rocking his hips, still inside her.

Cathy hadn't known what to expect, but almost as soon as Sam touched her button, she came in the most delicious way, biting her lip to stifle a scream. She fell onto his chest, panting and sweating, taking deep breaths to ease her thundering heart. Lying in Sam's arms made her feel as secure as she'd ever been. He rocked her, his hands caressing her back, until both their breathing returned to normal.

Sam kissed her mouth, gentle and tender, just as he'd done earlier. Cathy liked gentle, but she also loved what he'd given her, and there was nothing gentle about that earth-shattering orgasm. Feeling respected and cared about, she returned his thank-you kiss, willing it to last forever.

*

With her head still resting on his shoulder, Sam shifted her to the side and slid out of her. He removed and knotted the condom, wrapped it in a tissue, then leaned up to the back of the couch and tugged a blanket free. No point catching a chill after such a hot experience. After setting the alarm on his watch for an hour's time, he rocked Cathy into a gentle post-coital slumber.

8th September

Sunday

Sam unwrapped his arms from around Cathy's sleeping form and got up from the couch, trying hard not to wake her. He got dressed and made his way to the downstairs bathroom, where he splashed water on his face and scrubbed his wet hands through his hair.

Staring at his reflection in the mirror, he ran over what had happened; how Cathy had initiated proceedings, giving the green light that ignited the passion he knew was already there, just waiting to be released. Wonderful. Even so, he would have waited, and had expected to wait a lot longer until she'd felt comfortable enough to sleep with him.

Yes, he'd been prepared enough to have protection with him, however, he felt a bit disappointed, for Cathy, about the where and when it had happened. He was happy with the why. It meant she was one step closer to trusting him, but he wanted the next time to be special. Next time would be so much better, with no need to worry that the kids would wake up and find their mother in a compromising position.

That's why he'd got up and dressed, before he was tempted to jump on her again. He was more than ready to bang Cathy into the middle of next week, but it would have to wait. Tomorrow was another day. He rang for a taxi, then returned to where his sweet lady lay snoring on the couch. Caressing her shoulder with gentle strokes, he woke her and let her open her eyes fully before speaking.

She smiled and moaned in a drowsy half sleep, but the smile disappeared when she took in his clothes. Sam didn't expect the shocked reaction as she pulled the blanket around her. She sat bolt upright, swinging her legs down to the floor. Sam reached to take her in his arms, but she struggled free, sprang up, and stood by the darkened fire, the blanket pulled tight around her.

"Cathy? What's wrong? It's not--"

"Not what? That you just got your bit and are heading for the hills? Job well done!" Her words spat out, her lips pulled tight, her eyes like darts, directed straight at him. "It doesn't look like you wined and dined me, screwed me, and now that you got what you wanted, leave me hanging here in the middle of the night?" She pulled the blanket tighter. "How could you, Sam? Jesus, I really am a dumb-ass blonde for thinking it was ever going to be any other way."

"Cathy, for God's sake, calm down," he whispered. "I'm not running. I swear." He moved over to her, glancing back at the sitting-room door. "You'll wake the children." He led her back to the couch and pulled her down beside him. "You've got it so wrong. Please, try to think straight and listen to what I'm saying. What happened tonight with us was...unbelievable. Incredible. I can't even put it into proper words." He ran his hands through her hair, then rubbed her shoulders.

"The way you make me feel, Cathy, trusting me, wanting me, being able to give yourself the way you did, that doesn't happen to me. It just doesn't." He held her shoulders, willing her to hear him, to believe him. "I'm not using you as a quick shag. Believe me. You're worth so much more than that." He leaned his forehead against hers. "Please believe me."

"I thought… When I saw you dressed. Leaving. I didn't know what was going on. You woke me as you were about to walk out the door, Sam. What was I supposed to think?"

"Ah, Cathy, the plain and simple truth is that I'm mad about you. If I was letting the lad down there do the talking, I'd be in you right now, and again before the morning." He grinned and moved her onto his lap. "I want you more than you know."

"Then what's the problem? Why the early exit?"

He shrugged and sighed. "It's just, I'm afraid the children will wake and come looking for you. I don't want them seeing that. A strange man in their house in the middle of the night. Do you?"

Her eyes lit up. "Then let's go up to bed."

"No, no, no. If I stay 'til morning, you're going to have to deal with me and the kids over breakfast. I want them to get to know me first, Cathy, before they have to share their cornflakes with me. I'm serious, babe, I'm in this for the long haul, and I don't want to do anything to jeopardise it."

Her reaction was immediate, and he let out a long sigh of relief as she relaxed in his arms. "Next time it would be better if we were somewhere else. Not on a couch, for example, and preferably somewhere we can wake up together in each other's arms, and not have to worry about the rest of the world while we're there."

"I'm sorry," she said, her voice soft, her eyelashes low. "Again." She brightened, then looked at him. "I'm so happy you're taking my babies into account. It says so much about you. I didn't realise… I thought the worst and…attacked. Gotta stop doing that, it's going to piss you off so bad."

"You're a bit of a drama queen, that's for sure." He smiled, hugging her to his chest, then kissed her, a long solid one, letting her know all was forgiven.

The expected beep outside brought a groan as he tore himself away from her. "I'd better go. I don't want to, but I have to." He leaned down and deposited a kiss on the tip of her nose.

Straightening his clothes, he turned to leave. "Listen, I have to work for a while today, but I'll be finished around six. Would you like to come over to my place later? We can hang out and see what happens?" He remembered that Gary would have the children later, so Cathy would be free for the evening, all night, and most of Monday morning. It was exactly what he wanted, this woman in his bed, unrestricted for 24 hours, or as much of it as he could get.

She paused a moment, which left him thinking he was pushing her too fast. He watched the struggle going on in her eyes, hoping beyond hope that she'd weigh things up in his favour.

"I'd love to," she said, her reaction sending a wave of relief over him. He held her shoulders and smiled. Yes, they were on the same page. A whole night alone with this sweet lady, with nothing else to do but roll around in his big bed.

"I'll drop the kids off, then head on over to your apartment," she said. "I'll text you this afternoon to get directions and see what time suits."

"Wonderful. See you later, so." He kissed her once more, then left to get his taxi.

*

Cathy's spine tingled and her mind sprang to life with images of Sam. Wrapping her arms around herself, she flopped back onto the couch and let herself dream of the things she'd like to do with Sam O'Keeffe when she got him alone in his apartment.

*

She woke with a little face pressed against each cheek. Giving the twins her warmest smile, she wrapped them in a giant bear hug, then, without mercy, tickled them senseless.

After a lie-in with her precious children, she bundled them all downstairs and into the kitchen for breakfast.

"Where did you go last night, Mammy?" Millie asked as she climbed onto a stool at the kitchen island. "Auntie Becky said you were out looking for the man who sells oats, for horses." Her manner was so matter of fact Cathy struggled to hide her smile. She could only imagine the flippant remark Becky had made under her breath, forgetting that children had hearing that would put Superman to shame. With two bowls of cereal prepared for the twins, she told them she'd had dinner in a fancy Italian restaurant, and that she'd had the yummy spaghetti they all loved.

"Oh, can we come next time?" Jack asked, bouncing on his chair, not about to miss out on the chance of his favourite dinner.

"Not next time, love, but I'll bring you both there again," Cathy said, then added "sometime soon" before she was bombarded with any more questions about when this super treat would happen.

"You looked really pretty when you were going out last night, Mammy." Millie frowned. "Where are all your curls gone? Did the rain wash them away?"

"Eh, yeah, the rain did that." Cathy hid her blush behind her mug. These kids are way too bright for their own good. "Come on, you guys, hurry up with your cereal. We need to root out your schoolbags and get your uniforms sorted. I'll be dropping you over to your dad's this afternoon and I need to get to a supermarket first."

She tried to convince herself that she wasn't rushing them so she could get to Sam's place quicker. He was working this afternoon, so she decided to treat the children to an hour at the playground before dropping them to their dad's. With a quickening pulse and images of what lay in store for her this evening, she went in search of Friday's mouldy lunchboxes and the ever-elusive elasticised school ties.

Before leaving the house, she sent Sam a text. He lived somewhere in Dun Laoghaire, but she'd no idea where. She would do some shopping in Bray before bringing the children to the playground, then on to Gary's. After that she could head to Dun Laoghaire to find Sam's apartment. At least if she knew the address she could choose her route and maybe pick up some takeaway food on the way.

Hey you! How's Work? ☺ Just leaving to do some errands and drop kids to G's and will head to urs then. Is that OK? Whats ur address, kind sir? Cx"

Sam replied, letting her know he'd be done in work within the hour. He supplied directions to his apartment complex, telling her to ring when she arrived.

Tackling the shoppers in Tesco's, Cathy organised a simple lunch to put in the kids' schoolbags for tomorrow. She didn't trust Gary not to send them to school again with crisps and Jaffa cakes. Jack had let this little gem slip during the week. It was time to have a chat with their father, and also make sure he was giving the twins a proper breakfast whenever they stayed with him. As an afterthought, she put an extra box of cereal and another sliced pan into her trolley.

99

She could do without the expense of having to provide shopping for Gary as well as herself, but she would never let the twins go without, so he could have the groceries this one time. The best thing was to monitor and question the children to ensure they were being properly cared for. They didn't show any obvious signs that they didn't enjoy being with their dad, often treating it like a big adventure. Sometimes, though, innocent remarks would slip out, making Cathy question the current custody situation. She vowed to keep a close eye on things.

Millie and Jack squealed with delight when Gary came out to the car to help bring the twins' stuff inside.

"I didn't pack any PJ's, or anything," Cathy said. "You have all that stuff already, right?"

Gary picked up the children's schoolbags and their small overnight bag. "Yes, I just need their uniforms for tomorrow, and I'll hang onto the clothes they're wearing for the next weekend I have them."

"I put some lunch in their bags for tomorrow, Gary, so you don't have to worry about making any. Also, I got cereal and bread while I was at the shops. For their breakfast?" Gary had the grace to at least look guilty. She silently dared him to blame the children for telling on him, even though they had once told her they preferred their father's lunches to hers.

"Eh, right, sorry about that. I just realised too late in the evening that I'd nothing in, and had to buy them something in the petrol station on the way to school." He shrugged, bags in hand. "Sorry."

"It can't happen again, Gary. I need to know the children are being looked after when they're here. It's hard enough having to leave them, without thinking they're being filled with crap twice a week. I do my best to get them to eat healthy, and it doesn't help if you pile them with rubbish.

"Okay, all right," he snapped, "I get it. No more junk food. Are they allowed Mc Donald's, or is that off the menu too?"

"Stop being an ass." She kept her voice low so the twins wouldn't hear. "You know what I'm talking about. Mc D's is fine, every now and then. A few sweets, chocolate, crisps, are grand, as a treat, in moderation, but please, Gary, not for their school lunches, or breakfast." She kissed and hugged the twins goodbye, telling them she'd collect them from school the next day, then she drove off in the direction of Dun Laoghaire, to an apartment that had Sam O'Keeffe's name on it.

*

After picking up some Chinese food, she drove to Dun Laoghaire and found Sam's apartment complex. She called him to say she was looking for a parking space.

"Go on down into the underground car park," he said, "and park in any of the spaces marked PH. I'll meet you there in a minute."

She found a line of at least six empty spaces marked PH. A brand new BMW coupe was parked at the end of the row, with a beautiful Range Rover glinting next to it. Pulling her car into the space beside the jeep, she looked around, hoping this spot was okay.

When she opened her car door, she was careful not to hit the mortgage-on-wheels. Whoever owned it wouldn't appreciate a whopping big dent in their passenger-side door. Just as she had the bags of Chinese food in her arms, she saw Sam exit the lift and stroll towards her, his gait as casual as could be. Nerves that had been doing a samba dance all day now kicked into full motion as she watched him approach.

He looked delicious in kaki combat trousers, a navy polo shirt, and a pair of converse trainers, his hair still wet from the shower. Sam kissed her, taking her in his arms, his touch so gentle. Cathy dropped the bags of food and snaked her hands up over his chest and around behind his head. She guided him down to her. After a long, passionate kiss, he broke contact, his mouth still against her lips. "Hello."

"Hello, yourself," she replied. He kissed her again, sweeping his tongue over and around hers. She had to grip onto his shoulders as blood rushed to her head, threatening to off-balance her. My goodness, if I fall, I'll melt into a puddle on the ground. When Sam released her mouth, he continued to hold her while retrieving the discarded food bags.

"Is my car okay here?" she asked, her voice strained. She needed to calm herself before she dragged this man into the back seat of her car and made a holy show of herself.

"It's fine, Cathy," he answered, caressing her lower back. "It'll be quite safe here."

She smiled, stepped out of his embrace, and leaned in to get her handbag from the passenger seat. "That's not what I was worried about. Judging by some of the models on display, I reckon there's a SWAT team patrolling a 24-hour security here." She threw her eye at the BMW and Range Rover.

"Perks of the job," he said, shrugging, as if to let her know that he could do nothing about it. "I needed a car when I got back to Ireland, and this is what they gave me. They're a bit flash, not really what I need or want, but they'll do until I can sort something a bit more practical." He took her hand and weaved his fingers through hers.

Cathy nodded as she looked again at her Micra, parked beside the big boys. She pressed the central locking on the key fob. You're in serious company tonight, little lady. Enjoy your luxury stay with Mr Flash and Mr Cash.

When they arrived at the waiting lift, Sam pressed a code into the keypad underneath the row of buttons, then hit the top button marked PH. As the lift rose, so smooth and silent, he chatted about work that day. Cathy wasn't mad about the enclosed space, and having Sam stand so close didn't help. It was a sweet relief when the lift reached his floor.

Expecting to exit into a corridor lined with doors, she almost fainted when the lift opened onto the living area of the penthouse apartment. "PH. Doh!" How could you be so stupid, girl?

"Oh, my God," she gasped as she stepped out. "Look at this place, Sam. Why didn't you warn me?" She looked at the plush white carpet that dominated the living area. Should I remove my shoes? Even standing just outside the lift, she couldn't ignore the opulence and expense in the way the place had been decorated.

Sporting a big grin, Sam guided her into the living area. As he went to put the food in the kitchen, she walked over to the wall of windows that made up one side of the penthouse. The view was outstanding. In the early-evening light, she looked out onto the Dun Laoghaire marina that housed hundreds of sailing yachts and motor boats. Seagulls swooped all around the west pier, begging for scraps from the fishermen. Off in the distance, the Irish Ferries' catamaran, which sailed between Dublin Port and Holyhead, negotiated her way home through a rift of sailboats.

She opened a glass door and stepped outside onto a wraparound balcony. The cool air hit her while the smell of sea salt tickled at her nose. Ropes and tackle jingled on the moored boats, and the screeching gulls had her laughing to herself. Was it possible they were the same ones from Wicklow who'd taken her anger and cries away all those months ago? A loud horn blast from the ferry made her jump, and she jumped again when Sam slid his arms around her waist from behind.

"This is some place you've got here, mister," she said, leaning back against him. "You really should've warned me."

He kissed her neck. "It's a bit much for me, to be honest. Too much like a museum for my taste."

"Another perk of the job?"

"Actually, no. It's my sister's. Sally and her husband are in New York for the winter, looking after some business. While they're there, this place is free. It made sense to stay here and keep an eye on things until they get back. I'll be looking for my own place after Christmas." He chuckled. "Something a bit smaller and easier to keep clean."

Cathy looked up at him, unable to hide her smile. "I'm not sure I can see you in the marigolds, scrubbing the toilet and mopping the floor."

"Hey, it's been known, though not here. A company comes in twice a week to make sure I'm not wrecking the antiques, but when I lived in Spain I looked after myself. I'm not afraid to admit that I've cooked and used a washing machine on more than one occasion."

"Oh, you are wonderful," she said, her words coming out in a teasing drawl. "You certainly are the whole package. He cooks, he cleans, but can he dance?" She turned and eyed him in silent challenge.

"Let's find out." He led her back inside and pressed a remote control. A slow Michael Bublé toe-curler filled the room. Sam reached out an inviting hand. Cathy took it and he spun her in a gentle twirl before pulling her close. With one hand pressed on her lower back and the other holding her hand at his shoulder, he moved them in an easy swirl around the living room. The sensual movement had her turning to mush, right there in his arms. She was on fire and couldn't believe how arousing such a dance could be. What a guy. Where have you been, Sam O'Keefe?

She leaned right into him, his hips hard against her. He wanted her, she could feel it, and she wanted him, too. Running her free hand up into his hair, she lifted onto her toes and kissed him. His lips parted to let her in, and she wove her tongue over his, leaving a trail of flames in her wake.

Swaying to the music, Sam took her into a full embrace, crushing himself against her. She stretched and wrapped her arms around his neck, immersing herself deep into his presence, his aura, his all.

"Wanna go to bed?" he whispered. "I'm about to get you on the floor, right now, but the bed would be more comfortable."

"Bed sounds good," she replied, nibbling on his lower lip. "But what about dinner?"

"Don't worry, I also know how to use the microwave." He swept her into her arms and carried her into the bedroom.

*

Sam told Cathy to make herself at home. She wandered into the kitchen, wearing one of his t-shirts, while he went down to get her overnight bag. Not wanting to be presumptuous, she'd left it in her car. She emptied the food into bowls and re-heated them in the microwave.

When he returned, he opened a bottle of wine and poured two glasses. Cathy brought their dinner to the kitchen island and asked him where she could find plates and cutlery.

Sam pointed across the room. "That press and that drawer."

She opened the drawer. "Fork or chopsticks?"

"Definitely a fork for me," he said, laughing, "unless you want to see me dribble dinner all over myself."

"Chopsticks it is," she said, hoping he'd see the glint in her eye. She laid out their forks and plates, and once they started on the food, she realised that she was starving. The thought that she'd probably burned off like a million calories in the past hour had her smiling to herself.

Not that she was complaining. Sam was a man who knew what he was doing, and it was obvious that her pleasure was equally important to him as his own. The first time in his bed had been a rush of hands, clothes, tongues, and then a quick climax. The second, they'd taken it a lot slower. He'd explored every inch of her body before willing her to come at the same time as him in a powerful, almost heart-stopping, orgasm.

Her world had been well and truly shaken, never mind stirred. She'd never enjoyed as much pleasure from sex before. With Gary, it was more like, *wham, bam, thank you, ma'am.* Looking back, how he'd managed to bed so many women was beyond her. But he wasn't her problem anymore, and he was not the man responsible for dissolving her bones, twice already, tonight. Sam O'Keefe was.

He was also the man, sitting across from her at the kitchen island, with a wondering look on his face.

"What are you thinking about, Missy?"

"You, me, everything. I'm happy, Sam, don't worry about that. I'm happy I listened to my friend and gave you a chance. I'm happy you didn't give up your chase. I'm a little concerned about my ability to walk tomorrow, after those bedroom gymnastics, but I'm happy I'm here. There is no one, bar my children, I'd rather be with right now."

Sam smiled and let out a long breath. "Thank God. You had a look of deep contemplation and I felt a bit like you must have felt last night. You looked like you were about to run. I hope it's not all a bit too much, too soon."

"No, Sam, it's not. I didn't realise how much I was missing out on. I know we've only been out a couple of times, and this is only our second night together, but--"

"It feels right!" he said. "Right?"

"Right." She smiled. "Another cliché, I know, but it fits. You and I, together, Sam. We fit."

"I think the cliché fits, too." He reached for her hand. "And if that's the way your life is running, let me get a book on clichés and see how many more I can make right for you."

He leaned across the counter and cupped her face, then brushed her lips with his. They left the food and headed back to bed to see how many more of her clichés they could fit into their lovemaking before the sun rose.

9th September

Monday

Spending the night together had been a rollercoaster of emotions for Cathy. She wanted to be with Sam, so much she had to pinch herself to make sure she wasn't dreaming. Were things going too fast? She wasn't blaming him. No, he'd been the perfect gentleman at every turn. In fact, he'd surprised her by being the complete opposite of the man she expected him to be. True to his word, he'd let her set the pace, and now she was acting like a woman let loose. She couldn't get enough of him. He thrilled her to the core, and while she relished their amorous lovemaking, the strong feelings she was developing towards him scared her.

The pull he had on her whenever they were near each other was like nothing she'd experienced before. It was as if the universe had weaved a tapestry of their lives and, until they met, there was this big gaping hole waiting to be filled. Now that they'd found each other, the cosmos was working overtime, stitching them both together and entwining all their colourful threads as fast as it could so they'd be complete, tight-woven, and incapable of being unravelled.

Of course, there was still so much they didn't know about each other, but that would come with time. She feared the unknown, but even after this short time, she trusted Sam enough to know he felt the same way about her. All his actions up to now had been unselfish and genuine, and as far as she was concerned, he had no intentions of hurting her or allowing her be hurt.

As they lay in bed, she opened up about her disastrous marriage to Gary, revealing how foolish she'd felt when she found out what he'd been up to.

"It's funny," she said, her head on his shoulder, "you often hear how such and such's husband is having an affair and be thinking to yourself, how did she not know? All the signs are there. Is she blind, or what? But you know, looking back, all the signs were there for me. I trusted Gary with my whole heart, and never imagined all the lies and excuses he was feeding me weren't the truth. I blamed myself for such a long time."

Sam squeezed her and rubbed her arm. "Poor doll."

"It's true, I trusted him without question. I thought I had the most wonderful husband on the planet." She cringed at the memory. How had I been so trusting? "I think the worst part was the realisation that he'd made a complete fool out of me. Him thinking he could do whatever he wanted. 'Ah, sure, good old Cathy, she'll never know. She's not capable of figuring it out.' And he was right. I didn't. I didn't figure it out. I had to be told to open my eyes and smell the coffee."

"You don't have to talk about it," Sam said, brushing loose strands of hair from her face.

She sighed. "I know, but I want to. Along with the trust, the love, the heartbreak, the jealousy, I think it was my self confidence that took the worst hit." Heat built in her eyes as it all came rushing back. "All the bashing to my ego came from me. He betrayed me, but I blamed myself."

Sam tensed beside her. He took a deep breath before pulling her closer. Cathy knew he would try to sooth her hurt and pain, protecting her in his strong arms, like nothing could ever hurt her again.

He kissed the top of her head and nuzzled her hair. "Don't ever feel that way with me,. Please, I couldn't bear it. I know it's only been a week, but from the second I saw you..."

"...across a crowded room," she said, laughing out loud.

"Another cliché, right?" Sam raised an eyebrow. "But, seriously, Cathy, we're going to be so much better than that. You and I are equals in this, whatever this turns out to be. I'll try my hardest never to cause you an ounce of pain. I can't promise I won't fuck up – but it won't be over another woman. That I *can* promise." He moved back and looked into her eyes. "Can we be exclusive?" This said with his American drawl.

"Oh, my." Cathy fanned herself with one hand, maybe like a southern belle, then turned to kiss him, slow and tender. When they moved apart, she caressed his face. "Yes, I want to be your girlfriend, Sam. We'll work all the other stuff out as it happens." She knew this was right, and she was looking forward to enjoying a relationship with her new man.

She snuggled back into his arms and rested her head on his chest, his heartbeat steady against her face as he took a deep breath. "Tell me about all your exes so. I'm gonna need full disclosure if we're to make this work"

He trailed his fingers down her arm. "There isn't much to tell. I know you're thinking that my number must run into triple digits, but really, there was only one girl who had any lasting effect on me." He kissed her head. "Before you, that is."

"What happened?" she asked, sensing from his voice that this girl had been a serious contender.

"Don't get the wrong idea, I haven't lived the life of a monk. I've had a few short flings over the years, but Sinead was my only serious relationship."

"When was that?" What if she's still around?

"I met her in college. She was beautiful. Stunning, actually. A real natural beauty, who had no idea how gorgeous she was. We were together for about two years. Things were pretty serious, and I'd say the next step was an engagement. As a student, I was sheltered by my friends from the press and photographers. Because of who my family is, and their connections, the papers loved having a juicy scoop on anyone connected with me or my family. During our last year, I was encouraged to spend more time socially with the big boys of the business world. It was all set up that I'd take a prominent position in the family business, and it made sense to get my face out there and be known about town."

"A bit like what's happening to you now?"

"Exactly, but at the time I was younger, inexperienced, and not really able to hold my own at the big social functions. More often than not, things got messy. Sinead was with me through all of this. I started sinking under the pressure, and instead of Sinead throwing me a lifeline, she rowed in the opposite direction. Actually, in a zig-zag direction."

He wove his hand in and out. "She made pit-stops along the way to pick up every well-connected kerb crawler and sugar daddy she could, using her position as my girlfriend to discover the best catches. It was obvious that her current boyfriend, me, was going down on a sinking ship."

Cathy kissed his chest. She knew how difficult it was to talk about this kind of thing, and could tell he was embarrassed at the way Sinead had treated him.

"Sinead turned dark and ugly, obsessed by money, the silver circle, who was who, and who knew her."

"I'm so sorry this happened to you, Sam. Nobody deserves to be treated like that." His pain was evident. Encased in his embrace, she rubbed his forearms and encouraged him to go on, sensing there was more, and that perhaps he was trying to find the right words to release all that buried pain and hurt.

Her phone rang on the bedside locker. She'd left it there in case the kids needed her during the night, or if Gary had to get in touch. "Shit. Sorry, Sam." She grabbed it and, with relief, saw Byron's name on the screen.

"Hey, By. How's it going?" She held out a finger for Sam to give her a minute.

"Cathy, where are you?" Byron sounded odd. "I'm outside your house, Cathy. Where are you? Are you out running, or what?"

"No, I'm not, By. What are you doing in Wicklow at 8.30 in the morning? What's wrong?"

"Everything. Everything is wrong. Tom had a huge fight with his mother yesterday. Cathy, I need to talk to you. Where are you?"

Cathy listened, doing her best to make out Byron's words between her sobs. "Oh, no. What happened?"

"My bitch of a mother-in-law happened." Byron's sobs grew louder. "She ruined it all, Cathy. My blood is boiling just thinking about her. Oh, Cathy, where are you?"

"Okay, calm down." Cathy ran scenarios through her head. "I'll be home by 9.30. Get yourself down to Halpin's café now. Have a strong coffee and I'll meet you back up at my place. We'll talk then, okay?"

"Okay," Byron said, her voice a low groan.

"And, Byron, don't worry, we'll get it sorted. Whatever it is, we'll work it out."

"Okay."

"And, sure, if nothing else works, we can have a good old bitch about your mother-in-law-to-be from hell. I'll get her ears burning, don't you worry."

"Okay, Cathy. See you soon." Byron sniffled and hung up. Cathy turned to Sam, his eyebrows raised in question.

"I'm sorry." She pouted at him. "I'm afraid my sista needs me. Trouble is a brewing with the In-laws." She fixed the pillows against the headboard and sat back into them. "Tom's mother is some piece of work when the claws are out. It sounds like she got a good swipe at Byron last night."

Sam folded her into a strong hug. "Go. Deal with the crisis. I suppose I'd better go to work, anyway, if I can stay awake, that is. I didn't get much sleep last night, someone kept swiping at me, too." He swatted her on the behind as she turned to get out of bed.

"I didn't hear you complaining too hard?" she said, climbing back into bed and straddling his lap.

"No complaints here," he said, turning her over onto the bed and proceeding to finish what she'd just started.

*

Byron's car was parked outside Cathy's house. She pulled into the driveway and waved over to Byron who was locking her car. The woman looked a mess. Her t-shirt and tracksuit did nothing to complement the streaky face and knotty hair. Byron's tears ran down her face as she rushed to be enclosed in a hug.

"Aw, what happened, By? Come on, it can't be that bad? We'll get it sorted out, whatever it is." Cathy led her inside the house.

With Byron sat at the kitchen table, Cathy filled the kettle and put some bread in the toaster. Her groceries were still in the boot of her car, but they could be dealt with later.

"I'm not joking, Cathy, that woman is the devil in human form. Her cloven hooves are well hidden in her Hush-Puppy Mary Jane's, and her tail is curled under her designer outfits, but I swear it's there. I know that if you rooted hard enough in her perfectly-coifed hair, you'd find the nubs of two horns, too." Byron's tears had stopped but the venom in her voice spat out every word. Cathy made the breakfast as her friend told her what happened the previous day.

"We were over at Cindy's for dinner. You know yourself, the token meet-up once a month just to keep everyone happy. Anyway, we got talking about the wedding. Tom was saying how we'd found the most gorgeous singer for the church and how we had to pick some songs for during the ceremony. Of course, your wan starts up, saying it should only ever be hymns that are sung in a church. If we couldn't, and by that she meant *me*, respect that tradition, then why were we getting married in a church at all?"

Byron let out a long sigh and shook her head. "I bit my tongue, Cathy. I swear, I didn't let her rattle me with that one." After a bite from the toast, she continued on. "She then started talking about my bridesmaids, saying how she thought it was a bit one-sided, that I didn't choose anyone from Tom's side to be in the wedding party even though Tom is having his own brother as a groomsman. She called the wedding the *Byrne Show*, making out that it was all about my family."

Cathy didn't interrupt, letting her get it all out.

"So anyway, at that point Tom started to defend me and told Cindy to butt out and mind her own business." Byron smiled at this, her delight that Tom had stood up for her against his mother obvious in her eyes. It made a nice change from him trying to keep the peace all the time.

"That's awful, By." Cathy buttered another slice of toast. "I know Cindy is high maintenance, but for crying out loud, it's her son's wedding. It should be all about you and him."

"Exactly! But, you see, Cathy, that's her problem." Bryon slapped the table. "It's *her* son who's getting married. *Her* son's big day. And *her* son who should be calling the shots. She's always getting a dig in about Tom having to wait three years to get married, because of what I wanted. I swear, if it could be *her* and *her* son having their special day, she'd be like a pig in shit."

"God, By, what are you going to do?"

"Wait, I'm not finished with the crazy yet. It gets better. After Tom told her to butt out, the old cow turned on me, shrieking and roaring that I have him the way he is, that I did this to him, and that her Tom would never speak back to her with such disrespect if it wasn't for me. I swear, Cathy, I was shaking. It just escalated out of nothing."

Cathy laughed at the absurdity of it all. The notion that Byron had changed Tom into anything but a better man was crazy. They were like two peas in a pod - Torville and Deane; even Tweedle Dum and Tweedle Dee. You'd be hard pressed to find two people better fitted to each other, like two halves of the one heart.

Byron flopped back into her chair. She probably hadn't slept the previous night and Cathy imagined her tossing in bed, reliving every hateful word that had been flung at her, multiplying the feelings by ten.

She related how Tom had taken her home, bitching about his mother the whole way; how this time she'd gone too far. Being as comforting as he could, he'd tried to make Byron believe that none of his mother's spew was worth a crap, and how none of the erratic feelings she had against Byron held any merit. His mother was

119

wrong, and bang out of order for taking her menopausal temper tantrums out on them, especially Byron.

Cathy knew that Byron had taken Cindy's words to heart. Byron always saw the good in people. It went against the grain that someone might fire vile thoughts at her without any merit. She would go over every single word, wondering if Cindy was right, thinking that she was the diva, turning Tom against his mother.

"I can see your mind whirling," Cathy said. "Do not believe one word of the crap she threw at you."

"I know. I'm trying not to, Cathy. I really am. It's just, you know what they say about there being no smoke without fire. She must be seeing something in the way I'm acting to come up with that sort of stuff. She couldn't be making it all up."

"Of course she's making it up." Cathy wasn't going to allow her best friend fall victim to her mother-in-law's feverish blather. "She's a witch. You said it yourself, she's the devil reanimated, trotting around on cloven hooves, looking to see who else she can make miserable. She knew where to hit you, with maximum damage. Bitch. Don't for one second think she's right in anything she said."

Time to make this girl see sense. She pushed her toast aside. "Everybody knows that the wedding and Tom are the most important things in your life right now. You always dreamed of the big white wedding, and Tom was well aware of that when he asked you to marry him. He makes no bones about giving you exactly what you want. The man adores you, Byron, and I adore you too." She gave Byron a huge hug, kissing her head and stroking her hair. Byron started bawling again, leaning deeper into Cathy's embrace.

"Come on, let it all out." Cathy rocked her friend like she would rock Millie or Jack. The girl was too stressed for Cathy's liking. The fact she hadn't gone to work was way out of character for her. Also, Byron hadn't quizzed her about where she was this morning, and that was so unlike her to let something like that slide.

"Come on, By, go upstairs and get into my bed. You need to sleep. You're exhausted. I bet you didn't sleep a wink worrying about it."

"No, I didn't. Tom was so good trying to talk it all out. To be honest, though, I think he'd be happier if I just forgot the whole thing. He's caught between me and his mother, and he knows what she's like, but she's still his mother. I know he's loyal to me, Cathy. I saw it in the way he defended me and then marched us out of her house, but still, I know Tom, and he's no good at conflict. By this morning he was telling me to forget about it, and not let it bother me. But how can I do that, Cathy? It was all too personal."

"It sounds like it was personal towards Tom as well," Cathy said, "but I know what you mean. Men don't like having to deal with stuff like this. Gary was a great one for burying his head or looking the other way. You're tired, Byron, go on up and get into bed. I'm not saying a good sleep with fix everything, but I bet you'll feel at least a little better."

Byron put her hands to her face. "I don't think I can sleep. My head is spinning in a hundred directions."

Cathy got up, went to the fridge, and rummaged around on the top shelf. "Here, take two spoonfuls of this."

"What is it?" The doubt was obvious in her deep frown as she looked at the medicine bottle.

"It's something I give the kids to help them sleep." Cathy filled a teaspoon with the amber liquid. "I use it all the time. Don't worry, it's herbal and organic. You won't overdose."

Byron swallowed the liquid and stood. "Thanks, Cathy." She sniffed and wiped her eyes. "I can always count on you to be there for me." She opened her arms for a hug.

Cathy held her and patted her back. "Go get yourself to bed. There are PJ's in my drawer. Try to relax, clear your head, By. We'll work this all out, I promise." She released her and watched her disappear upstairs.

She returned the glass medicine bottle to the fridge, hoping the placebo effect would work on Byron the way it did on the kids. Fixing the plastic label back onto the bottle, she smiled at the knowledge that she'd given her best friend the children's multivitamin, not some magical herbal sleeping formula; a trick she'd learned from her own mother, only then it had been a teaspoon of cod liver oil.

She was just about to go and unpack the groceries from the car when Byron's phone rang. Tom's name flashed on the caller ID.

"Hi, Tom, it's Cathy."

"Oh, hi, Cathy, is Bryon there?"

"Yeah, she is, but she's gone up to bed for a while."

"I suppose she told you all about yesterday?"

"Yes, and I'm really sorry, Tom. It sounds awful. But look, I don't want to get involved in your personal stuff. I'm here for Byron as a sounding board, someone she can blow off steam with."

"Thanks, Cathy, I know that. Thank God Byron has friends like you and Annabel. I'm hopeless at all this stuff. I couldn't get her to calm down last night. My mother really did a number on her. I'll be having it out with her as soon as I can."

"Well, that's between you and Byron." She didn't want him to think she was taking sides. As far as she could see, Tom was doing all the right things. He just needed to put his mother back in line and things might calm down again for them all.

"Cathy, can I ask you a favour? I'm on 24-hour call today and won't be home until tomorrow morning. Could you keep an eye on my little lady for me?" He let out a heavy sigh. "I don't want her at home on her own."

"I'll get her to stay here with me tonight, Tom. No worries, I'll keep an eye on her. I'll see if Annabel can come over later, and we'll take her mind off things."

"Sound, that's great. Thanks again, I appreciate that."

Cathy heard the relief in his voice. The last thing he needed was the worry that his partner would be tying herself up in knots at home on her own. No, she'd have the next best thing to him with her two friends.

"Okay, Tom, I'll have her call you when she wakes up." She said goodbye and hung up, not envying his impending confrontation with his mother. Thank God it's nothing to do with me, this time. Now, time to bring in yesterday's groceries.

*

She called Sam while she waited outside the school for her children. Though she couldn't wait to see Millie and Jack, she wanted to get in a quick call to Sam first. He answered on the second ring.

"Hey, you," he said, his voice deep and soft over the phone. "How did things go with Byron?"

"Hi to you, too. Byron's a mess. Her bitch of future mother-in-law did a dance on her yesterday, but I'll fill you in on the details another time. I'm sorry I had to leave so early this morning, Sam. I could have stayed there with you for the day."

124

"Yeah, it's a shame, but what about your poor children? Are you sending them to boarding school, just so you can have sex morning, noon, and night with me?" He laughed at the other end. "Ah, no, I didn't want you to leave, either. You looked delicious lying naked in my bed with me wrapped around you." He groaned into the phone, sending Cathy on a welcome journey of recall.

"Are you still there? What's the plan for the rest of the week? When can I see you again?"

"Well, it looks like I've got Byron staying with me tonight. She needs all the cuddles she can get at the moment. After that, I'm not sure. I don't know yet what days Gary has off, so I'll have to let you know." She wasn't too happy about their situation, but there wasn't much she could do about it.

"I'll miss you tonight," he said, his soft voice caressing her ear. "I've got something on tomorrow night that I can't get out of. A fundraiser thing, but how would you feel about me, you, and the twins going out somewhere on Wednesday?"

The twins? Was he testing the waters to see what her reaction would be? Of course, they already knew him from being at the pub with Gary, but they'd never seen him with their mammy before. "Em, that sounds okay." The words came out slower than she'd intended. "Millie and Jack have drama after school until 4 o'clock, but we could meet you after. What were you thinking?"

"Probably Eddie Rockets, or something. Somewhere casual, easy, and we can fill them full of ice-cream to make them like me."

"No ice-cream." Visions of Gary's feeding habits jumped into her head. "You're not the one who has to go home with two hyped-up five year olds. Anyway, you won't need bribery, they'll love you--" She stopped before she blurted out *just like I do*.

Whoa, girl, where had that come from? She looked around at the other waiting mothers. It's not like they could read her thoughts, not the way Sam could. Love, though? She filed it away for later when she'd have more time to think about it properly. "--but Eddie Rockets is a great idea, Thanks for doing this, Sam."

"We can sort out the rest of the week later, but I have to warn you, I can't wait to get you back in my bed."

Her eyes squeezed shut with the memory of all that had happened the last time she was in his bed. She couldn't wait to be there again, and told him so, turning her back on the waiting crowd outside the school, sure that her flushed face would give away the erotic scenes whizzing through her head.

"Sam, I've got to go, the kids are coming out. I'll call you later."

"Later, bye."

*

Cathy took Millie and Jack out for a treat to a local café, where she ordered hot chocolate and coffee. The longer Byron slept undisturbed the better. She'd left a note telling her where they were, and to ring if she was up before they got home. Millie shared a small leather couch with Jack, while Cathy settled into a comfy armchair. They filled her in on their night at Gary's.

"DVD's, popcorn, bath, and then bed," Jack told her, leaving Cathy relieved that it had gone well enough.

"We were even early for school today," Millie added with delight. Cathy knew she was guilty of getting the children to school late on the odd occasion, so she couldn't apportion all the blame to Gary on that one. Still, it was good to hear he was making an effort. Perhaps her little talk had gone in through his thick skull and stayed there.

Millie clapped her hands. "Great news, Mammy. We need to bring in a sock for school. Jack has the note about it. I think it's for doing Art with--"

"It's for *making* something with," Jack corrected, and with both of them eager not to be wrong, Cathy read the note and told them they were both right. They needed to bring in odd socks, and during art class they'd be making sock puppets.

"I'm making a spotty dog," Jack said, "with long ears and a tail, and everything."

"Brilliant. That sounds amazing, Jack." Cathy smiled, tickling him under the chin as his eyes glowed. Cathy looked at her daughter who, as usual, was deep in thought. "What about you, Mill?"

"I don't know yet," she answered, her expression dead serious. "I'll have to see what else there is."

"Oh, right. Well, I'm sure it will be fabulous." Cathy suppressed a laugh, knowing her daughter would give the whole project infinite consideration until she decided on the best possible sock puppet the world had ever seen. God help their teacher, Ms Delaney. It was going to be a long day for all concerned. When she got going, Millie wouldn't stop until she deemed her endeavour perfect.

When they arrived home, Byron was in the kitchen, on the phone with Tom. She flicked the switch on the kettle when Cathy and the twins entered. Cathy fixed a snack for Millie and Jack and set them at the kitchen table to do their homework. Byron finished her phone call and joined them, kissing the children hello.

"How are you feeling now?" Cathy asked, although she could see that the sleep had done Byron the world of good.

"A lot better, thanks. I really needed that. I was out for the count as soon as my head hit the pillow." She turned her attention to the children. "That homework looks good, you guys. I love the colouring-in you're doing, Jack. Very good keeping inside the lines."

"I'm the best at colouring in the whole class," Jack said, a proud grin lighting his face up. "My teacher told me to use lots of colours and not to scribble." He showed Byron his page, pointing out how he'd used every crayon in the box to colour his picture.

"And what's your favourite thing to do, Millie?" Byron asked.

Millie shrugged. "I don't really have a favourite, Aunt Byron. I'm good at everything."

Bryon raised an eyebrow and looked at Cathy, then leaned over and hugged Millie. "Don't let anyone ever knock that self-confidence, baby girl."

Millie told her that a few boys had already tried to knock her over in the playground, but none of them could.

"Good for you, Mill. That will do for starters." Byron laughed and shot Cathy a look that told her everything would be okay.

*

Annabel wasn't available for their impromptu girls' night in, so after dinner, when the children had gone to bed, they climbed into Cathy's double bed with two cups of tea and a packet of biscuits.

"Rough day, By?"

"I'll get over it, I always do. You know this isn't the first swipe Cindy has taken at me, and you can bet your ass it won't be the last. In fact, I'm thinking of growing a pair of balls. I think I'm going to need them before this wedding is done."

She spoke with such passion, it left Cathy with no doubt that the kid-gloves were off. If there was ever a next time, Byron would come out of her corner fighting.

"Good for you. Give as good as you get, girl. If you ever need me on your tag team, count me in. I wouldn't mind getting that old crow in the ring for a couple of rounds." Cathy could reel off a list of things she'd love to say to her friend's nemesis, but would hold her tongue, for Byron and Tom's sake. Unless they gave her the thumbs-up, of course, then it would be handbags at dawn.

"Oh, I've a bone to pick with you, Ms," Byron said, wagging a forefinger. "As soon as I cleared all the muck from my head, I remembered that you weren't here when I called this morning. I know you didn't have a school run, coz Gary had the kids, so spill it, sister." She arched that eyebrow again and dunked a Hob-Nob in her tea.

"I stayed at Sam's last night," Cathy said, as casual as she could manage, acting like she always stayed over with her lover. Where else would she have been, if she wasn't here?

"Oh, my God, you dirty stop out!" Byron squealed, letting the other half of her biscuit fall into her tea, then shoving Cathy like it was her fault. Cathy laughed and shoved back, spilling some of her own tea onto the duvet.

"Shit, damn!" they both said together, then laughed again.

"Tell. Me. Everything." The urgency in Byron's voice told Cathy there was no getting out of this, so over the next two hours, and two cups of tea, she filled Byron in on all that had happened with her and Sam.

Byron interrupted her towards the end. "Why didn't you tell me all this first thing this morning? It would have blown all this crap with Cindy right out of the water. This is mega huge."

Cathy had told her about the previous two nights with Sam, leaving out some of the technicolour details, but giving Byron a fair idea of where she and Sam now stood.

"I can't describe it, By," she said, almost afraid to say the words in case she'd jinx it. "He's charming, and kind, and thoughtful--"

"And sexy as hell," Byron cut in, both eyebrows raised. "Don't forget sexy as hell."

Cathy smoothed the duvet. How could she explain the strength of her feelings for Sam after just a few dates? "It's not just that, though, Byron. I know we've only known each other for just over a week, and I know I had all these reservations about him at the start..."

"But?"

"But he's so different to what I thought he would be like, and from the way the papers and media portray him. It's like there's the public persona, which he hates, and the private man behind it all, who I love."

"Love?" Byron gasped, both hands to her face. "Have you told him that?"

"No, I don't mean I love him." She paused to give clarity to her thoughts. "I'm not in love with him, but I love the man he is, and the way he's treating me." She looked at her best friend. "I don't want to be hurt again, Byron."

Byron squeezed her hand. "No one does, honey."

"I have this feeling that with Sam it isn't going to be an issue. I don't need to be worrying about things like that. The way he talks to me so openly, like there's nothing to hide." And there isn't. She knew that she and Sam shared the same feelings about each other. "We can't keep our hands off each other, By. Give me a couple more weeks of this, and I'll be best part of the way towards a happy ending."

"Well, thanks be to Jaysus someone's life is running smoothly for a change." She winked at Cathy as she snuggled down under the duvet, settling in for a long night of girlie gossip.

One week, two dates, one coffee break, and a night in the sack was all it took to have Cathy falling head over heels for Sam O'Keeffe.

10th September

Tuesday

Bryon borrowed clothes from Cathy so she could go straight to work. She kissed everyone goodbye and headed back up to Dublin in a much better mood than she'd left it yesterday.

*

Cathy dropped the children to school, then sent a quick text to Sam. *Morning sexy. What you doin? Miss me? C x*

As always, Sam's response was more or less instant. *I miss your body in my bed. When can we do something about that?*

She sent off a reply, blushing and squirming at the thought of what he would be doing to her if she was in his bed right now. *How about now? You free for a booty call in Wicklow? X*

What felt like a long moment later: *Aaaaaggggghhh, am tempted to ditch very important meeting and road race down N11, but no can do, sorry babe. Stop teasing x*

Disappointed that her impromptu invitation wasn't accepted, she replied: *Ditch the meeting and I'll leave the door on the latch, my knickers on the floor, and me naked on the bed. C*

Sam didn't reply. After a couple of minutes, her phone rang.

"Jesus, Cathy, are you trying to kill me?" Sam's voice was a deep growl. "I nearly crashed the fucking car after that last text."

"Bold boy. You shouldn't be on the phone while you're driving."

"Oh, it's Garda Cathy now, is it? Anyway, I was stopped at lights. My foot slipped off the clutch when your message was read over the Bluetooth speaker in the car."

Laughing so hard that she snorted, Cathy tried to get the sexy back into her voice, enticing Sam to come and join her.

"I can't, babe. Believe me, if I could I would. Any other day I'd be there already, but I've got this meeting I can't get out of this morning."

She groaned. "I guess it's just me and my Bob so."

"Who's Bob?" Sam's voice was sharp as a tack.

"He's not a who, he's a what, and he'll have to do now that I'm all turned on with nowhere to go."

"Jesus, woman, you're trying to kill me."

"I'll let you go," she said, smiling to herself and hoping Sam got the message. "Call me when you're done in your very important meeting and we'll talk about bringing Bob out on our next sleepover."

*

The rest of Sam's journey to work was somewhat uncomfortable. Damn, she could turn him on. He'd missed her last night, and had caught his mind drifting to her more than once. There was only one thing for it, he'd check the bar-staff work rota when he got in, and maybe do another re-shuffle of Gary's days off. But for now, he had to concentrate on driving the car, focus on this damn meeting that was preventing him from being with Cathy right now, and think about Enda Kenny in the hope it would quell his erection.

Once in work, he took a quick look at the week's rota. Gary was due two days off on Thursday and Saturday. Thinking ahead, he worked out if the days would suit his plan. Today was out. He was meeting Cathy and the children tomorrow, so Thursday would be perfect for another all-night session with his woman.

His woman. It was a long time since he'd considered anyone his, but he liked the sound of it. He was serious about Cathy, and if all the other areas of their lives fell into place, he could see this relationship being a long-term affair. The important thing was to keep his eyes open to head off any issues that might get in the way. He knew how reluctant she'd been in the beginning, but he was sure those feelings had passed and that she now felt relaxed and safe in their relationship. He'd go as far as to say she was downright adventurous when it came to playtime in the bedroom. Why would someone who had any reservations about him initiate or encourage some of the things they'd done on Sunday night?

"Shit." He realised he was aroused again just thinking about her. There was no doubt he was going to be late for this meeting if he had to keep stopping to think about Enda Kenny every few minutes.

Tony, along with Pat Sheppard from Sheppard Security, were already in the pub when Sam left the office. He waved over to them, then went to organise some tea and coffee to be brought to their table.

"Pat, how are you? Thanks for coming." He extended a hand to their security consultant, then slapped Tony on the shoulder before sitting beside him. "So, Pat, what did you find out from the old surveillance recordings? Anything concrete for me?"

Pulling out papers from a folder, Pat relayed his findings. "I've had one of my lads go back across the whole month of August, like you asked. There was a lot of footage, obviously, of the various tills being operated. Far too much to pinpoint anything specific. However, when we focused on the individual dates you gave us, we discovered a trend."

He spread several pages out. "There were a number of employees and regular customers in the pub on those dates. Deliveries from different suppliers were also made during that time, but the bar was never left unattended. This would rule out a rogue delivery person slipping out a few quid, or a customer seeing an easy opportunity."

"So that leaves staff." Tony said, looking sideways at Sam.

"Yes, staff," Pat agreed. "One member in particular."

Sam looked straight at Pat, knowing the answer, but needing it confirmed. "Who?"

"This guy here." Pat showed them his phone and played a short video of a man taking money from the till and putting it straight into his pocket.

"Fuck it, anyway," Sam said, anger bubbling through his veins. He knew it had to be Gary; that the incident he'd witnessed hadn't been a once-off. Now he had the proof. But now that he knew for certain, he was stuck between a rock and a hard place. He clenched his hands into tight fists, wanting so much to tear Gary's head off and kick his scumbag ass out of the pub. It's what he deserved, what would be done if he'd caught any other employee ripping him off. They'd be gone in an instant.

But how did he deal with Gary without it affecting Cathy and the kids? He knew she relied on the fucker for the bulk of her money, and if the bollox had no job, she'd also be screwed. This meeting confirmed what a personal mess this was turning out to be. He turned to Tony.

"Can we do another week of surveillance, focusing just on this guy? Make sure we have the right man. Try to get a bit more footage to confront him with when the time comes."

Keeping his emotions in check was difficult. The surveillance wasn't cheap, and he knew Tony would question him later on the need for it. This wasn't the first time someone had been caught with their fingers in one of their tills, but never before had they given anyone more than one chance. Normal practice saw the culprit identified, then fired, no questions asked. They owned a chain of pubs, and two clubs, employing more than four hundred staff, and wherever there was money there was also temptation. Staff needed to be aware that there was never a get-out-of-jail card available to anyone caught thieving.

Finishing up with their meeting, he thanked Pat for the information, telling him he would be in touch. Walking him out to his car, he chatted about a mutual friend's wellbeing. When he re-entered the pub, Tony was still at the table, with two fresh cups of coffee and a couple of sandwiches. The pub was now open, and a few regulars trickled through the door looking for an early pint to get them started on their day.

Sam sat opposite Tony and waited for his brother to speak. He knew what was coming, but how much could he reveal about his relationship with Cathy? Did Tony need to know everything? Always believing honesty was the best policy, he launched into a long explanation of what was going on.

"Under any other circumstances, it wouldn't be a problem getting involved with a staff member's ex-wife," Tony said. "In fact, I'd nearly do it just to piss the prick off. But this case is different. Awkward."

"Yeah, damn awkward," Sam said, wishing again that the whole mess was someone else's problem. "And none of this is mine or Cathy's doing. I can't let the little bastard get away with it, but I can't see a way to deal with it just yet. Cathy would never accept financial help from me. It's too soon for anything like that. If this was six months down the line and we were a bit more secure about things, I'd insist she move in with me. Then I could tell Gary to go to hell. But I can't do that yet, can I? Not that I don't want to, but she'd flip. No way would she go for it. I swear, she'd go on the game before allowing me to support her."

"It's bad timing, all right," Tony said, tapping the table with his pen.

Sam scratched his fingers through his hair, as if trying to satisfy a nasty itch in his brain that just couldn't be reached. He sensed Tony was holding back on telling him to quit while he was ahead. *Never mix business with pleasure* went unsaid between them.

Tony looked around the pub before laying both hands, palms down, on the table. "Best thing to do for now is leave it another week. Let Pat concentrate on the surveillance. You keep an eye on the books, and I'll make discrete enquiries into any other problems we might have had with our boy wonder here."

Sam knew it wasn't the ideal situation, letting this go on longer than it had to, but he was grateful that Tony was willing to give him time to sort out the personal stuff. He could tell Tony didn't envy his position, probably wondering if Cathy was worth it. Sam had been hurt in the past. The last thing he needed was a big mess like this, just when he'd found someone he trusted.

"One week," Tony said, gathering his stuff up. "We'll meet again next Tuesday with Pat and take it from there." He clapped Sam on the shoulder and left.

With a mood rivalling a pre-menstrual woman, Sam returned to his office to figure this stinking mess out.

11th September

Wednesday

Cathy brought the children to drama class after school. It was their second week, so they were more familiar with the teacher and other pupils. She stayed for the first half hour, delighted to see that Millie was in her element, joining in with the others during the warm-up games, and putting her hand up to sing a solo when the teacher requested a volunteer. Millie was a natural, mixing well and enjoying every minute of the performance atmosphere the class created.

Jack, on the other hand, was reserved, struggling to mix with the other kids, except when he was with Millie and she was doing the talking. When the teacher split them into separate groups, poor Jack looked lost. He fidgeted and danced like he needed to pee. Cathy didn't know whether to interrupt the class and ask him if he needed to go, fearing he'd embarrass himself right there on the floor.

She held off, though, figuring that if he needed to go he'd ask someone, or at least come over to her for help. He was almost six years old and had never had an accident before, not even while he was being potty trained. Cathy watched the class until the break, then approached the teacher.

"Hi, Mrs Campbell, I'm Cathy Byrne, Millie and Jack's mother."

"Delighted to meet you," Mrs Campbell said with a flourish. "Please call me Magda. Your children are delightful."

"Thank you, but I'm a little concerned about Jack. He doesn't seem to be mixing well. It's like he's not comfortable. What do you think?" She always sought the advice of the professional, whether it was a teacher at school or in a class like this. They had a lot more experience dealing with all sorts of kids and personalities than she had. She'd bet Magda had seen it all before.

"He is a quiet little one, no doubt, but I think he'll be okay." Magda made a soothing noise that reminded Cathy of her grandmother. "Even since last week, he is mixing more with the others." She paused and looked around. "One suggestion I have is that you don't stay in the room while they are in class. Sometimes children can be self-conscious performing in front of people they know. Until they are able to block it out, it can make things difficult for them. I see it all the time with my own son. He plays junior football, and is a great little striker, scoring goals all over the place when I'm not there. As soon as I put a foot near the side-line, his game goes to pot and the manager is screaming at him to wake up." She chuckled at herself.

"You might be right, Magda. Maybe Jack is feeling self-conscious with me here. I'll slip out for a while, see if it's any better without me. Will you keep an eye on him?" She knew she could trust this sweet woman with her children.

143

"Of course, he'll be fine and dandy here. If he starts to fret at all, I have your number. Anyway, Millie will be here. I'm sure he is more than reassured by that."

Cathy told the twins she had to go for a message and would be back to collect them at the end of class, just like school. Jack looked a little uneasy but didn't protest. Millie just waved and went back to eating her snack.

In a nearby café, she ordered a latte and put her phone on the table in case Magda rang. Even though it was only the second week, she worried about Jack, but knew she should give him a chance to find his own way. He was naturally quiet and reserved, and perhaps with encouragement from Magda and the rest of the class, he would develop his own awareness. As well as boosting his confidence, she hoped the classes would highlight his sensitive side and help him focus on the fun aspect of learning with games, singing, and dancing.

At ten to four, she made her way back to the hall and stood with all the other yummy mummies. That made her laugh to herself, as did the theme song from the Muppets being sung with gusto behind the closed door. A few minutes later, a stream of hyped-up ankle biters burst out of the room. Millie and Jack sought her out and raced over.

"How did you get on, guys?" She smiled, reassuring Jack with a hug that she was there for him.

"I got a jelly, Mam. Look." Jack opened his mouth to display the half-chewed Jelly Baby between his cheek and back teeth.

"Well done, big man." Cathy was so proud. Looking up, she saw Magda give her a thumbs-up. Things had gone well.

"Okay then, because you both did so well, and Jack got the jelly, I've got a nice surprise for you."

Millie screamed. "Is it a puppy?"

Cathy laughed. "Try Eddie Rockets." They all raced to the car, scrambled in, and had their seatbelts fixed in record time.

"I love Eggie Rockets," shouted Mille

"I love Eggie Rockets," repeated Jack.

"Okay, shush, you're hurting my ears." Cathy drove north along the N11, towards Eddie Rockets and Sam.

*

Sam sat in his car, watching in the rear-view mirror for Cathy and crew. He couldn't believe how nervous he was. Sure, he'd met them before, he'd even helped Jack out with a scrape on his knee, but this would be different. Last time they'd been with their dad. He didn't have a lot to talk to Gary about so any conversation had always been brief.

It was important to get Jack and Millie onside if his relationship with Cathy was to move in the right direction. Having them in the mix wasn't a problem for him. He had a few nieces and nephews of a similar age, so kids were not such an alien species. Cathy was a good mother. She talked about the twins all the time, relaying funny stories of things they'd said or done. He'd sat through some boring one-sided children conversations with friends or family, but Cathy was different. Her children were her life and passion and he knew they idolised each other.

Cathy's bitterness towards Gary was obvious. She'd confided that she did her utmost to shield the twins from the nastiness of the situation. Thankfully, like most five year olds, they'd taken it in their stride. He hoped that introducing himself into the mix would create a nice fluffy batter, not a floppy mess.

*

Cathy parked the car and texted Sam. Before she could put her phone in her bag, she saw him approach from a short distance away. She turned to the children and told them they were lucky, as she'd just spotted a friend of theirs, and maybe he would join them for dinner.

"It's Sam from Daddy's work," Millie said, pointing out the passenger window. Waving in his direction, she unbuckled her seatbelt and let Cathy open the door for her.

"Hi, Cathy. Hi, Millie and Jack. How are things?" Sam smiled like an idiot on Prozac.

146

"We're going to Eggie Rockets, and Mammy said you can come, too. If you want?" Jack added, hiding his shyness behind Cathy.

Keeping the face-splitting smile in place, Sam told them there was nothing he would love more than to have dinner with the Dude and Dudette, and their gorgeous mammy. Millie and Jack giggled at the thought of their mammy being gorgeous. Cathy rolled her eyes, then told Sam to relax his face before the wind changed and left it like that. With the ice broken, they made their way to the fast-food restaurant.

Finding a table and ordering their food was the easy part. For the next hour the twins held centre court with stories of school, friends, likes and dislikes, all with a bit of sibling rivalry thrown in for good measure.

"Do they ever stop talking?" Sam asked when he could get a word in.

Cathy laughed. "Not between the hours of 7.30am and 8pm."

Millie wanted to know if they could come to Eggie Rockets with their dad sometime, and maybe Sam could be there, too.

"No, I don't think so, Sweetie," Cathy said. "Sam will come and see you whenever you're with me."

"But we already see him when we're with Daddy," Jack said. "Why can't he come to Eggie Rockets with us?"

"Daddy works in the pub with Sam, and that's how you see him there." Cathy didn't know how to finish. She looked to Sam.

"I'm your mammy's boyfriend," he said, as if it was the most natural thing in the world, "so you'll only see me with your mammy when I'm not in work."

Cathy's mouth opened and closed like a fish on steroids. Jack and Millie seemed satisfied and went back to seeing who could finish their cheesy fries first.

"Was that wrong?" Sam asked under his breath, looking almost afraid to make eye contact with her. Cathy ran over what he'd said to the twins. Either he *was* as serious about her as she was about him, or else he was the biggest dick going, saying something like that to her five-year-old children.

"Is it true?" Cathy looked at Sam, knowing she would get a straight answer if she asked.

"*I* think it is," he answered. "In all honesty, I haven't been this sure about anything in a long time." He squeezed her hand. "Sorry if that was the wrong thing to say to them." He eyed Millie and Jack.

Cathy grinned. "No, Sam, it was exactly right. You are my boyfriend." She squeezed his hand back, the most affection she could show him in front of their two young chaperones.

She could have sat there all night. The children were enjoying the unexpected treat. Millie filled Sam in on the average day in the senior-infants' class, and in fairness to him, he made easy conversation with them all. As time ticked by, Cathy watched as he got to know the two most precious people in her life, confident that she'd made the right decision letting him become involved with them. The time came, though, when she had to make a reluctant effort to get Millie and Jack ready for the journey home. Sam handled the bill after a minor scuffle, pointing out that he'd invited them out, so he would pay.

"Well, next one's on me," Cathy said, sterner than intended.

After a quick bathroom visit, Sam walked them to their car. He helped with the seatbelts and hi-fived the little ones, promising to see them again soon.

"Thank you for tonight." Cathy pulled him to her and kissed him. "It was perfect. How did you get to be such a nice guy?"

He slid his arms around her back. "Years of practice."

"Well, it's paid off. You're one fine catch."

Sam smirked, lowering his head, as if inviting her in for a kiss, but then turning to whisper in her ear. "You need to get those children home now, or I won't be responsible for my actions. Between yesterday's message and now this, I'm in agony, ready to take you into the bushes."

She pressed against his hardness, the movement unseen by anyone, including the twins. "Follow me on down to Wicklow." Her face flushed at the thought of it. "The kids will be asleep by the time we get home."

Sam's eyes glinted at the invitation and he kissed her before shoving her towards the driver's door.

"What are you waiting for, woman? Drive!"

12th September

Thursday

Sam didn't spend the night, which Cathy knew she just had to accept for now. After the children had gone to bed, and she'd assured him for the tenth time that they were asleep, he'd taken her to the couch and made her body quake. It delighted her when his orgasmic release left him spent and shuddering, and he'd wrapped her in his arms as she too found her release.

Still uncomfortable at having the children upstairs, he'd dressed and settled back on the couch, with Cathy curled against him, a position she was growing fonder of each time she got to do it. They talked for hours; silly childhood stories remembered and relayed, until around 3am when he told her he had to go home.

"Gary has the children tomorrow, right?"

"You better believe it," she said. Tonight with Sam had been unexpected and wonderful, more-so because she'd been counting the days since Sunday until Gary's next day off. She had to admit to feeling guilty wishing her children out of the way, but then she cast her mind back over the past year to when utter loneliness had engulfed her every time the children were absent. This was a better way to be, and she deserved it after everything she'd been through. The children would always have days away from her, so it was only right that she enjoy that time, rather than sitting alone feeling sorry for herself.

Sam squeezed her hand, bringing her back to the moment. "I'll be home from work around six. Do you want to come for a sleepover?"

"I'll be there, but can't promise you'll be doing much sleeping." She gave him a preview of her intentions by dropping to her knees, unzipping his jeans as she went.

*

After picking the twins up from school, she dropped them to Gary's flat in Bray. She waited until they ran inside and she had him alone. "I wanted to tell you, before you heard it from the kids. I've started seeing someone and they met him last night."

Gary shrugged. "Okay, thanks for letting me know."

His blasé reaction surprised her, but she knew the next bit would shock him. She took a deep breath. "You should know that it's Sam that I'm seeing."

"Sam who?"

Cathy held her head high and looked him straight in the eye. "Sam that works with you."

A red flush crept up his neck as he folded his arms across his chest. "You're joking. For fuck's sake, Cathy. Sam O'Keeffe? What are you doing hanging around with him?"

"We met a couple of weeks ago, while you were with me, actually. You introduced us," she added, like it was all his doing.

"I remember, don't push it down my fucking throat."

She watched him brood, his little brain in turmoil. Then he grabbed the children's bags up and made to go inside.

"Millie, Jack, your Mam's going. Come and say goodbye."

Though he made no further comment to her, Cathy knew he was holding back on a full-blown row. She didn't need a crystal ball to know that he wasn't happy with the situation. Something wasn't right, though. Instead of the expected fight, he'd walked away, which was not like him at all.

She kissed and hugged the children. "See you guys tomorrow after school. Have fun."

"You too, Mammy," Millie said, blowing a kiss before speeding back inside to watch the telly.

If looks could kill, Gary's spearheaded assault would have had her gasping for breath. With her bubble pricked by his cold reaction, she left and headed to Dundrum Shopping Centre for a spot of retail therapy.

An hour rooting around Penney's department store always lifted her mood. She treated herself to new underwear, picking out some sexy lace tongs and a red plunge bra. The process of choosing and buying even these few items did the trick.

In Starbucks, mood much improved, she sat at a window seat and watched the world go by. What's Gary's problem, anyway? Unlike him, she'd not been involved with anyone since their breakup. He'd continued to hop from bed to bed whenever the mood took him, so he'd no right to have a snit on with her. Why couldn't she move on, too? Tough nuts if her new guy just happened to be his boss. Gary was a big boy, he'd have to grow a pair and get over it.

For once, she had the upper hand, and it wasn't such a bad feeling making Gary's life a bit more difficult. She had no intention of using Sam to get back at him, but if their new relationship made Gary uncomfortable, she could only see that as an added bonus.

She phoned Byron. They'd had a quick chat each day since Tuesday, her way of checking that everything had settled down and there was no further fall-out after Cindy's meltdown. Byron's phone went straight to voicemail so she left a message. "Hi, By, Just checking to see how you are today. Kids are with Gary, so guess where I'm heading tonight? Anyway, hope things are still okay. Call if you need me. Also, I'm free Saturday day if you want to do something. If not, I'll just chill, Okay, talk later. Bye, bye, bye, bye, bye." As she hung up, she spotted two teenage girls laughing at her extended salutation. She laughed, too. Jesus, she was turning into her mother.

She rang Annabel. Rumour was she'd also caught herself a new man and, according to Byron, was the reason she was so under the radar all week. Cathy wanted to find out all the hot gossip.

"Cathy, I'm up to my eyes, Love, but I've time for a quick chat. How are you and the kids?" Ever the businesswoman, Annabel was direct and to the point.

"Tell me about your new beau," Cathy said.

"Oh, you know, he's rich and handsome, a bit like your fella. Just a bit of fun really. Nothing serious. Sex and work. That's how things are at the moment, not that I'm complaining. Work pays the bills, and sex…well, good sex is something every woman should treat herself to as often as possible."

How Cathy and Annabel were friends was beyond her. But in truth, she was glad they were. Chalk and cheese had nothing on them, but somehow their friendship worked. Annabel brought the reason and structure to Cathy's life, being sharp as a tack. After the breakup, they'd fallen out for a while. Not that Annabel had taken Gary's side in the whole debacle, but she hadn't fully accepted that Cathy wasn't aware of what was going on. She also didn't feel it was her responsibility to reveal what was happening when she found out. As far as Annabel was concerned, shit happened and you should move on.

There had been sympathy and understanding, of course, but Annabel's patience soon ran thin. She was one in a million, though: different, hardnosed, cut and dried, but when things sorted themselves out, Cathy was glad their friendship had survived. She'd missed her straight-talking friend who told her things as they were, whether she liked it or not.

"Look, I'm heading into a meeting," Annabel said, "but can we catch up next week? I'm dying to hear all the news."

"Sure, I'd love to. I'll text you over the weekend and get a night sorted with Byron too."

"Okay, see you soon." Annabel rang off.

Cathy ordered another coffee and rang her mam.

"You sound very chirpy," her mother said. "Is everything okay, Love?"

Cathy rolled her eyes as she stirred the new coffee. "Yes, great, Mam. How are you and Dad? When are you coming down to see your grandchildren?"

"Oh, you know how it is with your dad's back, and then me with my cold. It's impossible to plan any tournament with this Irish weather, we just have to play one day at a time."

Cathy knew her mother. As captain of the ladies' golf club, her everyday life would be put on hold until whatever tournament they were playing finished. "Well, give me a shout if you're around on Sunday, and if not, I can drop up with the kids some day during the week."

"Lovely. We'd love that. How are they getting on back at school?"

Cathy chatted with her mother for a few more minutes. She'd expected to be quizzed about Sam, knowing Becky would have given a full report. Then again, she also knew that until this golf tournament was over, anything said would have gone in one ear and out the other. She'd talk to her next week when she visited. They could have a good catch up then.

"We'll see you next week, Mam, if not before."

"Bye, Cathy, love to you, darling, and love to Millie and Jack."

"Bye, Mam. Love you, too."

Realising it was almost half five, she finished her coffee and made her way back to the car park. Sam phoned as she was paying the parking ticket. She shoved the phone between her ear and shoulder and fed coins into the machine.

"I'm leaving the pub now," he said.

"Good timing, Batman. I'm just leaving Dundrum."

"You know the code for the lift at my apartment, right? Come up when you get here. I should be home before you, though."

"I'm on my way," she said, unlocking her car and flinging her bags onto the back seat.

She was relieved to see Sam's car already parked. Though he'd said to go on up, trusting her with the lift code and direct access to his apartment, she didn't know if she'd the nerve to do it if he wasn't already there.

Her fingers buzzed as she punched in the code, and a wave of excitement bubbled up inside her as she waited for the lift to reach the top floor.

"Hi, I'm here," she said, as she stepped into the spacious penthouse.

"In here," he called from the kitchen. He was still in his work clothes, minus the suit jacket, which had been discarded onto the back of a high stool. His broad shoulders rippled under a crisp white shirt. She spied a fine sprinkle of hair at the V of his neck where he'd unbuttoned the top two buttons and loosened his tie.

He stooped and kissed her as she joined him at the cooker. "I'm doing some dinner."

"It smells lovely, whatever it is." Her mouth watered at the array of ingredients spread across the counter top.

"Chicken Satay salad. Quick and easy."

"A bit like yourself." She smiled and slid an arm around his waist.

"Oi! You promised never to mention that 'quickie' incident again. Anyway, didn't I make it up to you for hours afterwards?"

"That you did." She reached up and kissed his nose. "Let's hope the dinner is as delicious as you are so. I'm starving."

He swatted her away, telling her to make herself useful by opening some wine. "I thought we might go out tonight," he said, chopping herbs. "Up into the town to a great little pub I found."

Cathy didn't answer. She'd prefer to be staying in alone with Sam, not share him with others in a pub. She poured two glasses of wine, then propped herself onto a stool at the kitchen island.

"I told Gary about us today," she said to his back, sure she saw his shoulders tense.

He didn't turn around. "What did he say?"

"He wasn't impressed. Asked me what I was doing going out with you. Didn't really say anything else, but I could tell he wasn't happy."

"Maybe he was just surprised," Sam said, his voice calm, "like he wasn't expecting it, or something?"

"Perhaps, but it had to be done. After meeting you yesterday, the twins were bound to say something to him. They loved you, by the way."

He turned, holding two plates of the most delicious-looking salad Cathy had ever seen. How come her dinners didn't look like that? Might be the soggy lettuce she produced. Mental note - buy a salad spinner to make excellent dinners.

"I enjoyed being with the kids, too," he said. "My poor ears were ringing all night, but they were a pleasure to be with."

"Well, your ears will be burning tonight, too, because I bet Gary will quiz forty questions out of them."

He looked uncomfortable. Was he annoyed that she'd told Gary about them? He had to understand that there could be no secrets when children were around, especially when they liked someone and couldn't stop talking about them.

They ate in silence for a while. Cathy enjoyed every bite, but the awkward silence drove her nuts. In an effort to steer conversation back into the room, she asked him about work.

"It's a headache. There's crap going on that for the moment is beyond my control."

His words left her with the sense that there was more to it than he was letting on. She didn't want to pry, so let it drop, for now.

After a couple more minutes of silence, he stacked their empty plates into the dishwasher. The mood over dinner had taken a nosedive and Cathy couldn't take any more of it. "Is everything okay, Sam? Is it a problem that Gary knows about us? Is that it? Because, I'm sorry, but he was bound to find out from the kids."

"No, it's nothing to do with that. It's just...well, look, grab your coat and we'll go have a drink and talk about it then." He finished tidying the kitchen while Cathy slung her jacket over her shoulder and grabbed her bag.

They went down in the lift in silence, but instead of going all the way to the basement they got out at the pedestrian entrance on level one.

Sam held her hand. "We can walk to the pub from here. It's a beautiful evening for a romantic walk by the sea."

This left Cathy even more confused than she'd been before. "It's a beautiful night to be rolling around in a king-size bed."

"Patience, my pretty." He kissed the top of her head and led her up the Marine Road and into his local pub.

Once seated at a small table near the door, Cathy had to admit that this was a real gem of a find. Tucked between two shops, The Weir was full of life and bustle. People milled around, but the lounge area was big enough to absorb everyone, leaving each table with enough privacy from its neighbours.

She watched Sam as he waited at the bar, observing a myriad of emotions creep over his face, as if he was having a full-blown argument with himself. What was bothering him? She was dying to know, but accepted she'd just have to wait it out and see what he had to tell her.

He set down a glass of white wine for her and a pint of Guinness for himself. "I like this place," he said after taking a lengthy draft of his stout. "It's a real locals' pub. Traditional."

"It's nice, all right," she said, wanting him to get to the crux of his Jackal and Hyde mood swing.

"It's so unassuming from the outside. You wouldn't even realise it was here unless you ventured inside."

Cathy nodded in agreement. More small talk. She sipped her wine and waited for him to say his piece. She didn't have to wait much longer. He put his pint down and leaned forward, his eyes pained and his face tense.

"There's something I need to tell you about Gary."

She stared at him. "Like what?" What could he have to say about her ex?

Sam took a sip of his pint and placed it back on the table. He coughed into his hand and looked at her. "There's money missing from the pub. It seems to be going on for a while, but we only discovered it recently. I've been doing a bit of investigating, and it looks like Gary's the one with the sticky fingers."

Cathy felt the life drain from her face, then rush back up her neck to flood her cheeks. Her mind ran blank as she struggled to make sense of what had just been said. She grasped for words and kicked her mouth into gear.

"No way, I don't believe it. The stupid thick! What's he playing at? How much?"

"I don't know for certain yet. We have a guy working on it at the moment, gathering evidence."

Her mind raced. Gary wasn't her problem anymore, but it would have a huge effect on her life if he got fired. The children. "Oh, God. I can't believe he'd be so stupid." She rested her head in her hands, then came up for air and took a huge gulp of her drink. "How do you know? How did you find out?"

"Actually, you tipped me off."

"Me. How?"

He tore a used bar receipt to shreds, his embarrassment obvious in the way he averted her gaze. "I saw him on the CCTV one day taking money from the till, then going outside and giving it to you. I followed him out, and spoke to you. Remember?"

Realisation hit like a ton of bricks. Her brain spun and her stomach lurched. Sam thought she was involved in Gary's scam. He'd been checking up on her that day, trying to find out if she was in on it. Did he think she was Gary's partner in crime? Was that why he was with her all along? Getting close to her, making her trust him, gathering evidence so he could find out the dirt on Gary and bring them both down together?

"I'm going to be sick." She grabbed her jacket and bag and ran for the door before Sam could stop her. Once outside, she turned left, then left again, heading towards the seafront, away from Sam's apartment. She ran all the way to the pier, only stopping to catch her breath. Unable to hold it in she raced to the side of the pier and vomited into the water. Tears streamed down her face, as the phone in her pocket rang non-stop. She walked the length of the pier and sat on the last bench.

Was that the reason Sam was with her? Was what they had all too good to be true? The rich playboy and the single mother. She knew it didn't add up, and now she could see what the attraction for him had been. Evidence; getting close enough to find out what was going on, to see if she was involved. She had to hand it to him, it was a good way to get the inside track on Gary's scam. Gain her trust and hope she'd let something slip.

And now her world once again crashed down around her. She'd trusted Sam. He'd worked hard to gain it. And it made perfect sense now why he hadn't mentioned the missing money. He'd kept his friends close, but his enemies closer.

An elderly gent walking along the pier approached her, asking if she was okay.

Cathy ground out a weak smile through her tears. "I'm fine, thank you. Just having a bad night, that's all."

"Well, don't stay on this pier too late, my dear. Get yourself home and open a bottle of wine. It will all look better in the morning." He tipped his hat and continued on his walk.

She sank lower onto the bench and brought her knees to her chest. Why was this happening to her? Again. What was wrong with her? Sam had seemed so perfect, so nice. *It's the nice ones you have to watch,* the devil on her shoulder whispered in her ear. Cathy shook it out of her head. Her heart felt like lead, and she wanted to crawl into bed and sob, knowing that she'd been made a complete fool of, again.

But why had he decided to tell her now? Had he realised she knew nothing useful about Gary's antics? Did he think she was of no further use to him? Maybe that was the reason he seemed annoyed that she'd told Gary about them. For him it wasn't real. It was all an act. He was damn good at acting the smitten boyfriend for as long as he was using her. Until he had enough evidence against Gary.

Drying her eyes on a sleeve, she registered the phone ringing in her pocket again. There was a list of missed calls from Sam. She expected that, but she had to check none were from the children. Fifteen missed calls – Sam. Fifteen voice messages – Sam. She listened to the first message.

"Cathy, what the fuck? Where are you? Why did you run out like that? Ring me." Then the next one: *"Cathy, where are you? I'm back at the apartment, but you're not here. Ring me. What's going on? We need to talk."* Then the next: *"Cathy, come on. What's going*

on? We need to talk about this. This stuff with Gary has nothing to do with you. I just thought you should know about it...try to warn you, or something. Ring me, please. I'm worried." Then the next: *"Cathy, Jesus, will you let me know you're okay? I'm walking the streets here looking for you. You're obviously pissed at me about something. Fine, whatever it is. Just let me know you're okay. Please."*

She heard the panic in his voice during the last message and without listening to the rest, dialled his number. He answered on the first ring.

"Cathy, thank God. Where are you?"

"On the pier."

"Stay there. I'm coming."

It didn't take long before she saw him approach, his stride fast and strong, his face red from running so hard, his hair wet with sweat. He reached for her, but she pulled away.

"What the hell happened, Cathy? One minute we're sitting there talking, the next you're up and out like an Olympic sprinter. What did I say?"

She couldn't talk, so he continued. "Cathy, I'm aching to touch you, wipe away your tears. I want to make it right. But first you need to tell me what I did wrong."

His words sent her into a tailspin. She didn't know what to think. Was she right, or had she made a huge mistake and jumped to the wrong conclusion? Her heart pounded so hard she feared it would burst from her chest. She would have given anything for things to work out with them. The only reason she'd revealed her location was because he'd sounded so frantic on the phone, so worried. It was only fair to let him know she was safe. Not okay, but safe.

They sat in silence for a while. She tried to regain her composure enough to speak and find out for better or worse what was going on with them. "Is that the reason you're with me, Sam?"

He looked confused, his brows knitted into a deep frown. "What? Is what the reason?"

"Are you with me simply to get the dirt on Gary? To see if I'm involved? To get my guard down so you can get the evidence you need to nail him to the wall?" She looked straight at him, her heart breaking at the horrible reality that everything was lost.

"What?" Sam blanched. "Jesus, Cathy, where did this come from?"

She didn't trust herself to speak, so she remained silent and let him figure it out on his own.

*

Sam groaned as he realised what had happened. Between their conversation in the pub, and his reaction earlier to her telling him about Gary, Cathy had put two and two together and come up with fifty-seven. So far outfield it was unimaginable, but looking at it from her perspective he could imagine how she'd made some sort of connection between their relationship and Gary's problems.

He kicked himself inside. Because her conclusion was so far from the truth in his mind, he hadn't realised that telling her about Gary would send her running, thinking it meant something else. Not one thing she'd asked him could be further from the truth. How could he think that of her? He was besotted with her, and had been from their first meeting. He had to make her see that, make her believe.

She looked so hurt and vulnerable, he just wanted to wrap her up and take her home. He understood now whey she'd taken off. If that's what she thought was going on, he didn't blame her. He needed to fix this, and fast, before she let any more mad ideas ruin the best thing that had ever happened to him. To them.

He scooted closer, slipped an arm around her shoulders and pulled her to him. She resisted at first, but he persisted. Even then, once she'd allowed his arm to remain at her back, she sat ramrod straight.

"Cathy." He wiped tears from her cheek. "The answer to all of your questions is no. No, I am not with you to get the dirt on Gary. No, I don't think you're involved and, no, I'm not trying to get your guard down to gather evidence against that scumbag. I'm sorry you have to be involved with him at all."

After a long moment, her rigid posture softened and she sat back against his arm.

"Use your head, Cathy. I asked you out way before I even knew what was going on at the pub. From the moment I saw you, I couldn't stop thinking of ways to get you to go out with me. I texted you that Monday. We were all set to go out with each other before I caught Gary on the CCTV."

He held her hand, relieved that she didn't push him away. "Okay, I admit that for about thirty seconds, between the time I saw him hand you the money and when I spoke to you, I had a bad feeling that you could be involved, but as soon as I talked to you at your car that day, I knew it had nothing to do with you. I was so relieved, so happy that my initial attraction to you had not been tainted. I knew the truth the second you told me Gary had just given you money for the children's drama class. You would never have said that if you were in on it."

He took a deep, steadying, breath and rubbed the back of her hand. "I'm mad as hell that all this shit with him has to touch your life in any way. The only reason I told you at all was because things will probably get ugly between me and him. Even more so now that he knows about us. My security guys will be talking to him next week about the money, so I just wanted to warn you. I didn't think it through. I never looked at it from your point of view."

He brushed stray blonde tendrils from her face. "I never imagined you could think I was using you to get information."

*

Cathy had the grace to look guilty, knowing now that her thoughts and actions were nothing less than irrational. Silly girl. How could she have thought the worst of him? Her Sam.

He leaned closer. "Seriously, Cathy, after all we've spoke about, everything we've done over the past few weeks, can you not feel how much I care about you? How could you think it was all an act?"

She knew she'd hurt him. Sam wasn't a cad. He didn't treat women like playthings, just to get what he wanted. She was in the wrong here, and she needed to fix it.

"I'm sorry." She squeezed his hand back. "Sorry for running away like that, for scaring you. I should've stayed and let you know what I was thinking, instead of freaking out." She took his free hand, warming it between her own. "All the time you were telling me about Gary, one image kept rolling around my head, snowballing. I don't really think all that stuff about you, Sam. Please believe me."

She touched the crinkled anguish lines across his forehead, ashamed for helping put them there. "You're a good man, Sam O'Keeffe. I'm sorry."

He let out a long sigh, then kissed her and hugged her close.

"You're a good man," she said again, burying her head into his chest. "Too good for me."

"No, not too good for you." He smoothed damp hair away from her face. "I'm just right for you. We're the perfect fit." He kissed her forehead, causing Cathy's tears to brim again as she thought how close she'd come to ruining everything.

He placed a finger under her chin and lifted her head so they faced each other. "You need to trust me, Cathy. This is for real. Me and you. I would never do anything to hurt you. And you? You just need to get all the crazy out of you so you don't have to run away every time I say the wrong thing."

Cathy groaned. "I know. I'll try. Thanks for being so understanding. I know you were worried about me. Where I was. That's why once I heard the panic on the voicemail, I rang to tell you I was safe."

"I was everywhere looking for you," he said, "I hated thinking of you wandering around Dun Laoghaire on your own at night."

"It's hardly the Bronx, Sam, and it's not even nine o'clock." She straightened, squared her shoulders and pushed out her chest. "I think I'd be okay."

"Still, no more running. If you run we can't talk and sort things out. See how stupid this whole thing turned out to be. A complete misunderstanding that had both of us going out of our minds."

They cuddled together until it grew too cold to stay, then they walked, hand in hand, back to Sam's apartment.

"What are you going to do about the Gary situation?" she asked after they'd warmed up and were sitting on the couch with a glass of wine.

"I don't know yet. I've a meeting early next week about it. We'll decide then what's going to happen."

Cathy was quiet for the rest of the evening, mulling over events, about how she'd acted earlier, and how she'd hurt Sam. She trusted him, but he needed to know that. Looking back, none of her thoughts made sense to her, either. She needed to make things right.

Later that night, as they climbed into bed, she took a deep breath and turned to him. "Sam."

He looked up, holding her gaze with a questioning look.

"I think I love you."

He smiled and moved across the bed, laid her back against the pillows and climbed over her, resting an elbow on each side of her head. "I think I love you, too, Cathy Byrne."

13th September

Friday

Friday the 13th, a notorious day of bad luck around the world. Not for Cathy, though, and definitely not for Sam. After their emotional evening dodging the bullets that could have killed their relationship, she realised that the only way she could show her man how she really felt was to show him.

She'd told him she loved him, putting every drop of emotion she could into her words. Then she'd shown him just how much, using every part of her body to make sure he got the message. They made love throughout the night, exploring new ways of pleasing each other, all the time learning about and deepening their mutual desire.

At five-thirty, she got up to get a drink. Wrapped in Sam's bathrobe, she made her way to the kitchen, her legs like jelly, her muscles aching, though all in a satisfying way. She told herself she'd go for a run later on, but wasn't convinced she'd meet that goal, not after the athletic workout they'd just finished. I think I've had enough exercise for one day.

As she walked back through the living room, light filtering in from a gap in the curtains caught her eye. She drew back the drapes and gasped at the incredible view of Dun Laoghaire's harbour and marina that lay before her.

Morning dew hung like tiny rainbows to bare trees, backlit by the rising sun peeking over the horizon. This lifting light cast sparkles across the Irish Sea, each ripple turned into a million shards of broken glass, twinkling to the tune of the early-morning breeze.

Seagulls swooped and squawked above a returning fishing trawler. The sky shone a clear bright blue, with orange and red clouds masking the outline of the yellow ball of fire rising like a precious gem. Hugging herself, Cathy drank in the spectacle. Maybe there were only a handful of humans witnessing this glorious moment. What a privilege it was watching Mother Nature wipe yesterday's canvas clean, then setting up brand new one for the day ahead. She prayed her canvas would sparkle as well as the scene before her, and sent a silent whisper into the wind that she would not screw it up.

*

Gary was still bulling. "Smarmy rich bastard," he snapped, over and over until he started to annoy himself. He dropped the children to school, then returned home to consider again what Cathy had told him. Her words rattled around in his head, blackening his mood by the minute. He'd known this day would come. She was a good looking woman.

For him, the real surprise was that she hadn't become involved with someone earlier. A lot of his friends had the hots for her, even knowing she was married. Yes, he was well aware of what a good catch she'd been. He only had himself to blame, acknowledging that his own stupidity and sloppiness had ruined their marriage, failing to realise what a good thing he'd had until it was gone.

However, now that he didn't have her anymore, he didn't want anyone else to have her, either. He could warn his friends against making a move on her, but there was nothing he could do about his boss.

"Fuck him, anyway," he said. Unable to sit easy, he made a sandwich to have before going to work, and while pulling ham and cheese out of the fridge, he tried to focus on why he was so annoyed. His anger had many splinters and he wasn't sure which bothered him the most.

First was the reality that Cathy was dating someone. His wife was with someone else. Yes, he knew the irony of what he was thinking. He'd cheated on her for their whole marriage, treated her like dirt and expected her to act like it was no biggie. The fact was, Cathy wasn't cheating on him. They were separated. She was to all intents and purposes a free agent. She could do whatever she wanted. It stopped being any of his business the second she'd thrown him out and filed for a legal separation.

Of course, the way his children were being treated in this new relationship was his concern. This was the second thing bothering him, as well as the suspicion he'd not find any dirt to cry about there. Cathy had always been a super mum, and he'd no doubt Millie and Jack would feel no negative impact from her and Sam's relationship. If anything, their lives might be better because of Mr Moneybags.

That led him to item number three: Sam O'Keeffe. Why did it have to be him who Cathy hooked up with? Gary didn't know him well, but in his mind, Sam was everything he wasn't: Good looking, rich; from a wealthy family, with secure job prospects. By all accounts, he was even a decent-enough bloke. Rumour had it he'd hooked some of the lounge staff up with digs when they'd got cheap last-minute flights to Ibiza during the summer, making sure they had access to all the best pubs and clubs while there.

Gary knew Tony, Sam's brother, and their dad, having worked for the family for years, but up until now he hadn't had much dealings with Sam. Before yesterday, he couldn't fault the bloke. The guy had never been anything but professional to him, never causing him a second thought. But now, this was personal. He was after his wife. Okay, ex-wife, though the *ex* didn't make the pill any easier to swallow. Why in the hell was this swanky rich man moving into his territory? What annoyed him most, was knowing Sam was probably going to make a better job of it than he had.

Last, and by no means least, Gary's extra cash-flow source was now in jeopardy. He couldn't be seen splashing it at Cathy, making out to be the big man. Not while Sam was on the scene, anyway. He knew how much Gary earned, and it didn't take a rocket scientist to figure out that his wages alone were a tight stretch with a house mortgage, rent, Cathy's allowance, plus his week to week living.

There was another debt to worry about. He'd become involved in on-line gambling, operating several accounts with bookmakers and casinos that were barely in the black. His credit card and loans from friends kept it that way. Damn it, why had he been stupid enough to rack up so much debt? He'd been trying to make a quick buck, but ended up bursting his overdraft, maxing out two credit cards, and hitting his friends for a couple of hundred each.

For some time now he'd been skimming the tills at the pub. A few months, at least, ploughing the extra few Euro into the horses in the hope of winning back big to clear some of his debt. As a barman, he'd spent years watching racing fanatics sit at the bar and turn over hundreds, if not thousands while downing a few pints.

At the beginning he'd used whatever spare cash he had and took advice from the veterans who knew the sport. He'd won as much as he'd lost, somehow always managing to break even. Because he wasn't losing money, he used this new addiction as a way of making ends meet from week to week; using Peter to pay Paul. It didn't take long before things took a bad turn and the shit hit the fan.

Never one to admit defeat, he ignored advice from the old lads at the bar to give it up for a while, and went on to place bigger and riskier bets. Convinced that the horses and dogs were a poor man's game, he'd set up an on-line casino account that he could play at night after work. The stakes were bigger but so were the rewards.

He needed funds fast. In a moment of insanity, he bet a full week's wages on a casino site in one night. Clicking the mouse each time to make a bet, he couldn't believe his luck when the money started adding up and the cards in every game fell his way. Thinking he was the master gambler, he varied his games, outwitting the computer-generated odds at every turn. With a beaming smile on his face, he logged off his account that night in credit to the tune of €7,000.

His memories of that night were vivid. He'd sworn to use the money to pay off some of his debt, but he'd fallen behind with Cathy's maintenance and knew she would be after him. The credit-card statements burned a hole in his wallet, and rent was due in the next few days. There was only one thing to do - clear the casino account and take the money and run.

But he didn't. Still on a high from his big win the previous night, he logged back onto the site, intending to double his previous windfall. Before he could blink, his money was gone. He'd lost everything - €7,000 worth of winnings, plus his week's wages. He was potless, slipping from one extreme to the other in less than 24 hours. In a fit of madness, he'd smashed his fist into a wall and wrecked furniture, then sat and shook with the realisation of what he'd done.

At work the next day, in the most desperate state known to him, €20 notes started disappearing from the tills. He knew he was skating on thin ice, and if caught he'd be screwed, but he saw no other way out. Times were desperate. He didn't even have money for petrol to get home from work that night.

Solid in the belief that it was only short term 'til he got sorted again, he used the tills at work like an ATM, topping up his wages each week, endeavouring to get his head above water and the debt off his back.

Back in the present, he thought again about Cathy hooking up with Sam. This was too close to home for his liking. Way too close. After his sandwich and coffee, he tidied the kitchen and got ready for the late shift at work. He'd have to be careful, keep his eyes peeled, his actions guarded. It was important that he not draw unwanted attention to himself, which was why he'd have to be at least civil to his boss, the fucker.

That annoyed him. He wouldn't be able to cause a stink about Cathy's new relationship because it might put Sam on the defensive and start him snooping around. No, he'd need to be careful how he played this one. He didn't like it, though, having to pretend to be okay about another man taking his wife, letting on that he couldn't be happier for them. But he'd do it, because he had no other choice.

"Fuck's sake." He grabbed his keys. "What did I do to deserve this shit?"

179

14ᵗʰ September

Saturday

Sam couldn't figure out where the queue for the tickets started or ended. It didn't help that he was surrounded by hundreds of wayward kids. "Whose bright idea was this?"

"Yours," Cathy said, laughing at his bemused look. "I did try to warn you."

He held a hand out in a silent plea for help, but she just shook her head and gestured for him to enter the lion's den while she stood to one side with the children.

It was Saturday morning at Movies @ Dundrum, slap bang in the middle of the Kids Club screening of the latest Disney animation. Hundreds of children milled about, with frantic parents trying to keep some sort of order in the mayhem. Birthday-party groups mingled with stressed-out chaperones struggling to supervise children hyped up on sugar. Kids of every shape and size, some dressed in Disney outfits, spilled popcorn and fizzy drinks all around them.

Sam had no idea that taking the children to the cinema would be such a stressful ordeal. Thank God there were only two of them. He looked around at other adults who had the misfortune of involving whole school classes of eight-year-old boys in their adventure. Why someone would bring thirty-odd, pre-pubescent boys into an enclosed space, with popcorn, was beyond him. Crazy.

181

He was having problems juggling two kids' meals, with extra drinks and sweets, along with their tickets, and still maintain a grip on his sanity. Cathy would have to get their coffees, there was no other way around it. With the tickets held firm between his teeth, he carried the boxes of popcorn and drinks over to where she stood waiting with the kids, just about avoiding the helter-skelter of youngsters racing around the foyer.

"We tan det de goffe ater," he mumbled, indicating his full hands. She picked the tickets out of his mouth.

"Sure we can get something now. We're in screen 3. That's right over there." She pointed to the end of a corridor, which to Sam may as well have been thirty miles long. No way could they make it through this tornado with two children and refreshments intact.

"Come on." She held Millie and Jack's hands, side-sweeping and shimmying her way through the mass of bodies ahead of them. Keeping close behind, balancing his trays as best he could, Sam was grateful that Cathy was parting the Red Sea for them. When they entered the cinema and located their seats, he let out a breath he hadn't realised he'd been holding. Not for the faint-hearted.

Settling the children onto booster seats, Cathy organised their popcorn and drinks with the precision of a seasoned moviegoer. Then she sat beside Sam and relieved him of a steaming cup of coffee she'd stopped for on their way through the madness.

Sam sipped his coffee, but didn't dare get too comfortable. They were only in and people were already making their way along the row. He had to stand again and again to let others to their seats. Cathy and the kids only needed to move their legs to one side to allow someone pass. When he'd attempted that, he'd ended up with a face full of arse and a hand in his groin when the person tripped over his legs. It didn't help matters that he'd grabbed the woman's boob to stop her falling. His nerves were gone.

The sooner this film started and everyone sat down the better. He soon found out this wasn't an ordinary screening of Ice Age 2. This was Kids Club at 11.30 on a Saturday morning, when adults brought their monsters out, hooked them up with sugar and fizz, then brought them into a darkened room with flashing images. Whether it was seizures the kids were having from the sickly-sweet products, the high-singing voices, or the fact that some cartoon creature was finding it hard to contain itself with all the snow and ice, Sam knew that whatever marketing genius came up with the idea of Saturday-morning Kids Club had to be related to Hitler.

No adult in their right mind could welcome this activity with open arms and rise on a much-longed-for weekend morning and shout, "I know, let's go to the cinema! Let's fill our little darlings full of crap, then expect them to sit and watch computer-animated slop for ninety minutes. So what if they want to run up and down the aisles, in and out of the bathroom. So what if others want to watch the film and our little ones want to stand in their seats and scream at their friends at the other end of the row." He looked around the madness. Who were these outer-space adults who considered this to be acceptable behaviour?

Then he looked past Cathy to where Millie and Jack sat, glued to the screen, with a look of pure magic on their faces.

His heart melted. He squeezed Cathy's hand, urging her to check out the twins, but she was as into it as they were. So what if he was uncomfortable. Three faces, so pure and innocent, believed this was the best thing since sliced bread, and that was good enough for him. He sat back and did his best to enjoy the spectacle, and was nearly there until the little bollox behind upended his juice box down the back of his shirt.

Escaping intact at the end of the film was a damn sight easier than when they'd arrived. Sam breathed a huge sigh of relief when they emerged into the sunlight. It was clear from their excited and nonstop chatter that Millie and Jack had loved the film and were no worse for wear after their Kids Club experience. In fact, it looked like something they would enjoy on a regular basis.

That thought caused him to pause. Hmm, maybe I'll leave that up to Cathy. Maybe bungee jumping or rock climbing would be a less-dangerous activity to try them with the next time. They went to Pizza Hut for lunch before the twins were to be dropped to Gary's for the evening.

"I love pizza," Millie said.

"I love pizza, too" echoed Jack, as they scampered towards the lift.

Cathy laughed. "They only love it because they get a little pizza each and don't have to share."

"But we love them, Mam," Jack said. True to their word, every bit of pizza was demolished. Sam noted how their consumption of *real* food pleased Cathy.

"Do you mind if we head into House of Fraser for a minute?" he asked, his skin sticky from the back of his neck down. "I just need to get a few shirts for work while I'm here. I'll get something to change into later, too." Though he knew he was spending the night in Wicklow, he hadn't factored in being assaulted by a variety of snacks and drinks.

"Don't *touch* anything," Cathy hissed at the children as they made their way through the posh shop. Sam chose two shirts, one light blue and the other a pale lilac with a small cheque pattern. He also picked out a navy Ralph Lauren rugby shirt that would go well with the jeans he was already wearing.

*

Cathy couldn't believe her eyes when the figures added up on the till. Not batting an eyelid at the eye-watering total, Sam handed over a gold credit card while they waited for his clothes to be wrapped and bagged. When he turned to her and smiled, her heart lifted, but then his smile disappeared and his eyes widened.

185

She looked over her shoulder to see what had stopped Sam in his tracks. Behind her, making a bee-line in their direction, came a beautiful woman laden down with designer bags and shoes. Cathy caught Sam's frantic reaction, his eyes shifting from side to side, as if looking for a hole to dive into. What the hell was going on? Then the penny dropped. This woman strutting towards them, with the Hollywood smile and the supermodel body, had to be Sam's ex-girlfriend, Sinead. She bypassed Cathy and the kids and planted herself in his path, with poor Sam looking like he was about to be shot.

"Sam, darling. How are you?" Sinead leaned in, placing a hand on his chest before air kissing the side of this head. A second kiss was directed straight to Sam's mouth, lingering far too long for Cathy's liking.

"Sinead," he said, his tone sharp

Cathy pulled the children closer. Why was Sam acting like he'd been caught in the lights? And why was he avoiding eye-contact with her? Maybe because he's too busy untangling himself from that woman's claw-like grip on the front of his jumper. He'll have no choice but to change it now.

Sinead flung her dark hair behind her shoulder in a giraffe-like flourish. "Sam, I heard you were back on solid ground. I expected a phone call. All my friends have seen you out and about these past few months. How are you settling back into working life?"

"Fine. I've been busy since I got back. How are you keeping?"

"Oh, you know, same old, same old. Victoria is married, Sophie got a brilliant promotion, and Susan is ready to drop baby number three any day now."

"Great." Sam looked anywhere but at Sinead, or Cathy. Cathy sensed his utter distaste for Sinead's friends, but why was he so shocked at his ex turning up like this?

Sinead broadened her smile, her teeth pristine. Then she batted her false eyelashes at him. "Oh, Sam, can we meet up soon? For a catch up? I've missed you. I really was expecting at least a phone call when I heard you were back." She brushed a hand down his arm, letting it rest just above his wrist.

Sam flinched. "Why would I do that?"

"We could paint the town red, just like the old days. Celebrate your return to civilisation. I don't know how you lived over on that island for so long."

He untangled himself for a second time and reached around Sinead to clasp Cathy's hand, pulling her to him, with the children in tow. "Sinead, I'd like you to meet my beautiful girlfriend, Cathy. These are her lovely children, and my friends, Millie and Jack."

Sinead's eyes narrowed as she looked from Millie and Jack, then to Cathy, then to Sam, and back to the kids. Cathy spied something flash across her face, but couldn't quite place what emotion it was. Was she hurt? Shocked and awkward for sure.

Sam smiled at Cathy and gathered up his bags. "Sinead, good to see you again. Take care."

"Yes. Nice meeting you, Cathy." Sinead shot a glance at the children again, then with even more urgency than before hugged Sam goodbye. "Perhaps I'll see you around town sometime. Call me?" She turned to walk away, but Sam stopped her.

"Sinead. It was good to see you, but you won't be seeing me again, either in town, or anywhere else. I'm done with all the fake pompous crap. It's not my scene. It never was. You more than anyone should know that. Things haven't changed. I'm with Cathy now and the quiet life suits me just fine."

"Yes," she said, drawing out the word, looking Cathy up and down. "Well, if you're happy with the simple life, who am I to argue?"

"Enough." Sam stepped between them. "Goodbye, Sinead".

Sam led Cathy and the children out and back into the mainstream shopping centre. He was almost jogging by the time they got outside and the kids were finding it difficult to keep up. Cathy panted several steps behind him. "Sam, slow down. Wait for us. I know you wanted to get out of there, but the children can't make a quick escape like you can." She tried to lighten the mood with a smile, but Sam's face still bore the scowl he'd left Sinead with.

188

There was no doubt Sinead's comment had been directed at her, or that it had been a cheap shot. She'd done nothing to this woman, never even met her before. If Sinead chose to be that way, there was little she could do about it. It's not like they would be running into each other every second day, or anything. They lived in different circles and wouldn't cross paths too often, if ever. The fact Sam had managed to avoid her since his return was a good sign.

The woman's beauty couldn't be denied, though. She was stunning. Would Sam be interested in relighting that particular fire? Even to the untrained eye, her clothes and accessories screamed expensive.

Catching up to Sam, she watched him take a deep breath and regain some of the colour in his face. He kissed her forehead, mumbling about being sorry and hoping she was okay.

"Sam, stop. It was nothing. She's only trying to get at you. And don't worry about me. Water off a duck's back. Honest."

She glanced around to make sure the kids were still with her. Poor Sam. He looked distraught. But what could she say to help him? He needed to cop himself on and not go to pieces over a stroppy little diva. She couldn't say that, though. He wasn't happy, that's for sure.

"Mam, when are we going?" Millie asked, her final word drawn out in a long whine.

"Look, Sam, seriously, don't worry about it." Cathy pulled Millie to her. "I have to get the kids over to Gary's, so do you want to follow me down to Wicklow, or what?"

"Yeah," he said, stepping out of his darkness. He turned to the children and hi-fived them. "Have a great night with your dad, guys."

"Thanks for the movie, Sam," Millie said. "It was brilliant."

"And the lunch," Jack added.

"You're welcome, little dude and dudette. We'll do it again soon. Okay?"

"Sam, I'll drop them off and see you back at mine later." It was obvious he was having some sort of inner battle with himself. Thing was, she didn't know how much of it involved her.

"Okay, I'll see you later," he said, then wandered off in the opposite direction, leaving Cathy standing there wondering what the hell was going on.

*

A short time later she dropped the children to Gary's flat. She was in no mood for an argument and was grateful when he took the twins without a fuss.

"I'll collect them after dinner tomorrow," she said, then returned to her car and drove home. With no sign of Sam, she let herself into the house and began tidying up. An hour and a half later there was still no sign, so she rang him. Perhaps he'd changed his mind about coming down, or maybe he got delayed.

"Hi, Sam, are you okay?"

"Grand, Cathy. I'm grand as grand can be." His slurred words were difficult to understand.

"Are you drunk?"

"Little bit."

"Where are you?" she asked, concern and frustration jockeying for position in her voice. Was this all because of his run-in with Sinead? He'd been emotional, but not to the extent he'd go to the nearest bar and get blotto. And it wasn't even two hours since she'd left him. He'd have to drink a bottle of vodka straight to be so drunk in such a short amount of time.

"Where are you?" she asked again.

"I believe I'm in…Phil Healy's."

"Phil Healy's here in Wicklow?" It surprised her that he was even in the county, never mind just down the road from her house.

"That's the one," he said. "A lovely man. Very good at pouring the pints. I'm trying to get him to come work for me, or maybe I can come work for him, or maybe we can work together?"

She didn't know if he was talking to her or someone in the bar. "Stay where you are. I'll come down and collect you." She grabbed her keys and rushed out to the car. Thank God the kids aren't here.

Having some idea what state he'd be in, she was still shocked when she spotted him holding up the bar in Phil Healy's pub on the main street of Wicklow Town. The barman was keeping an eye on him and at least had the good sense to take his car keys.

"Is this fella with you?" he asked when Cathy approached.

"Yes." She watched Sam struggle to keep his balance on a barstool. "Thanks for keeping an eye on him. He's a bit far gone by the look of him."

"A bit, all right. Won't have to worry about tonight's profit, that's for sure." He grinned, then asked if she needed a hand getting him home.

"No, but thanks for the offer. My car's outside. I'll throw him on the couch and let him sleep it off."

"That's the best thing for it." The barman hooked Sam under the arm and guided him out to the car. "Have you far to go?"

"Just up the road. I'll be okay."

"Well, ring if there's any messing and I'll send one of the lads up to you. I'm Mick."

Cathy knew that look. Mick had seen it all a hundred times before, the wife left to deal with the effects of too much alcohol on a body, even a situation turned bad. It was good to know there were men like him willing to help, even if he was responsible for providing the alcohol in the first place.

She struggled getting Sam out of the car, and had a good mind to leave him there until he sobered enough to come in himself. It wasn't too cold of a night. He wouldn't freeze to death. Then she realised the neighbours would have a field day knowing her new fella was turning out to be a raving alcoholic. A right piss artist.

Biting her lip, and pulling him by the arms, she got him out of the car and into the house. The best she could do was leave him sprawled face down on the couch. At least here she could keep an eye on him from the armchair. She placed a towel and plastic bowl on the floor in case he needed to hurl, then drew a blanket over him before settling in to wait for soberness to arrive.

*

Sam's head hurt. His stomach, too. Was he going to be sick? God, he couldn't open his eyes, he just couldn't. He needed sleep. Sleep.

*

Cathy watched Sam groan and toss on the couch, but she didn't go near him. Better to let him sleep it off. What had caused

193

such an extreme reaction? Meeting his ex couldn't have been such a big deal. Sure, Sinead had hurt him, but that was years ago.

She rubbed her face, tired from all the running around. If Sam hadn't got over his ex by now, it didn't bode well for her. He must have been besotted beyond belief with the woman, and meeting her out of the blue had seen the return of all these feelings and memories. Did he want her back? Was that what all this was about? If he needed to make a choice, Cathy didn't think she would fare well. What had she to offer Sam? There was no contest. Sinead was rich, beautiful, and socially acceptable in their group of friends and families. She knew how to hold her own in the rich world and shopped in all the right places.

Cathy, by extreme, had two children, with a rat of an ex-husband causing hassle for Sam. No money, no prospects. Sure, she was good looking and took care of herself, but how could she compete with Sinead? As far as she was concerned, there was no contest; Sinead would win out and out.

With each passing hour that Sam slept, her heart sank further. She wanted to shake him awake and get the inevitable over with. He would dump her, she was sure of it. She couldn't compete with the golden goose. Well, if that's the way it would go, she may as well head to bed. It was one thing being heartbroken, but another being cranky from lack of sleep. She locked up the house and made her way up the stairs.

Sleep wouldn't come. Her mind raced, while she tossed and turned, unable to put the horror of what was to come out of her head. After what seemed like hours, tiredness won the struggle and she fell into a restless sleep sometime after midnight.

15th September

Sunday

Sam woke scrunched into a ball, tangled in a blanket with his head lolling off the side of the couch. Where the hell was he? And how did he get here? He wiped his eyes and blinked to focus on to his surroundings, then realised he was in Cathy's living room, fully dressed and sprawled on her couch.

Where was she? He raised his head, slow and easy, uncurled out of the blanket and stood up. Desperate for a piss, he ignored the pounding in his head and went to relieve himself. The face staring back at him in the mirror was not pretty.

He had a fuzzy flashback of Cathy dragging him from the car, and another of him getting tangled in the blanket before giving up the fight. However he'd got here, or wherever Cathy was, he knew one thing for certain – he'd a hell of a lot of explaining to do.

It took him a while, and serious effort, but he managed to make two cups of coffee before going to look for the woman who may or may not still be his girlfriend.

He set the coffee cup on her bedside locker and nudged her shoulder. "Cathy."

"Mmmmmhhh,"

"Cathy, wake up."

"Hmm? Sam, go away."

"Come on, Cathy, can we talk?"

She rolled over. "What time is it?"

"It's twenty-to-four. I, eh…brought you coffee. Can we talk? Please?"

"Sam, you asshole. Twenty-to-four in the morning? Could you not at least let me sleep till morning before breaking up with me?" She rolled back over and covered her head with a pillow.

"Cathy, I need to tell you something important. Please, can we talk? I'm not going anywhere until we do. Well, actually, I can't. I've no car and I'm over the limit. But, anyway, I need to talk about Sinead."

"Sinead?" She bounced up from under the pillow. "You woke me up to talk about Sinead? What? How you're still in love with her and you didn't realise it until you saw her today, and now we're over? We had a good time while it lasted, but I'm not what you want, so bye bye, Cathy. Have a nice life. The end. Conversation over. Go back downstairs, Sam, sober up, then go get

196

your car and leave me alone." She flopped back onto the bed and pulled the duvet over her.

Sam shook his head, then regretted it because it hurt his brain more than he could've imagined. Even his hair hurt, but if what he'd just heard was right, Cathy thought he was breaking up with her to get back with Sinead. How did she come to that conclusion? He nearly puked at the thought of spending a minute with his ex, never mind the rest of his life. He knew women had a different way of thinking about things, but what Cathy thought was bordering on insanity.

Why would he get back with Sinead? Why would he not want to be with Cathy? As far as he could see there was no contest. He was happier with Cathy over the past few weeks than he'd been the whole time he'd spent with Sinead. He'd thought with Sinead it had been love, but now he'd been with Cathy he knew different. What he'd had then was nothing more than window dressing; a fancy display, something to be admired from the outside, but plain and basic once you get in.

With Cathy, he had the whole damn chocolate factory dressed up like a valentine's day: red, pink, gold and sparkly, with sweet, sweet chocolate everywhere. It was like Christmas on Prozac, the best feeling in the world, and they added to it every day to make it better and better.

Looking down at her now, he wondered what she was on about. Would he ever figure out how her brain worked? But now he

197

needed to talk, first about the crap she'd just flung at him, then about Sinead. That was a lot of stuff to get through.

He lifted the duvet and climbed in behind her, sliding his arm around her waist. She flinched, but didn't move away or shove him out of the bed. That had to be a good sign.

"Cathy, Love, I'm not breaking up with you." She didn't move, so he whispered to the back of her head. "Nothing could be further from the truth. I love you. I adore you. You're my everything, Cathy. Please listen to me."

Her pillow was soft under his head, but he couldn't be distracted from his mission. He had to tell her the truth if there was to be any hope for them. "I know I've been a right dickhead tonight. It doesn't happen that often, and I'm sorry you were the one who had to deal with it. It shouldn't have happened, at least not the way it did. I don't know what you're thinking, or why you're thinking it, but I've no interest in Sinead. There's no way I want to get back with her. I can't stand the woman, so there's no fear of me ever going near her again, or any other woman. I'm with you, Cathy. It's you I love, you mad thing. It's you I want to be with. If you can forgive my behaviour tonight, I was hoping you wanted to be with me, too."

Cathy softened against him. "So you're not breaking up with me?"

"Of course not."

"Then what was that all about earlier? After we met Sinead, you went all funny and disappeared for the best part of the day. To get pissed! Jesus, Sam, she obviously had a strong effect on you. What's going on with you?"

She turned to face him, but then sat up and leaned again the pillows. Sam did the same, even though the sequence of actions nearly blew his head open. Cathy lifted her cup of coffee and cradled it in both hands. "Okay, Sam, I'm listening. Talk."

*

Sam sat up in the bed. The hangover sweats were starting to pump the alcohol out of his system. He was such an idiot. Being a barman for so many years, he knew better than most that the bottom of a glass was no place for answers. Two or three to be social on a night out, yes, but the best part of a whiskey bottle? Never.

It raised unwanted questions like: 'I didn't realise you were an alco' - or - 'Is drink your crutch when the going gets tough?' He'd made a huge error in judgement by trying to make friends with the amber liquid. What had happened? He'd panicked. Seeing Sinead today had been a shock. He'd assumed that since he hadn't run into her up until now, she was out of the country, or had moved out of Dublin. Bitter memories shot to the surface, along with feelings he'd buried nine years ago. He'd surprised himself with his strong reaction, and was annoyed that Cathy had been there with her children to witness the display of a lover scorned. Apart from all the negativity surrounding them as a couple, something else had happened between him and Sinead that Cathy needed to know about. Now was the time to tell her.

"Okay, so it's like this, Cathy. I told you before that I was with Sinead all through college. She was always looking for something else, someone richer than I could give her."

"You told me all this. I know what a bitch she was and, to be honest, it sounds like you had a lucky escape."

"Well, there's more. During the last summer before we graduated, she got pregnant. We were still together, but only sort of. She was playing around, but we'd been with each other, if you know what I mean?"

"Sex?"

"Yes. Anyway, she admitted she'd been with a couple of others around the same time, so she couldn't be sure who the father was. She begged me to look after her. To raise the baby as my own. Even tried to convince me there was a good chance it was mine. And in her strange, warped way it didn't matter that she'd cheated. I didn't know what to do. I was twenty-four years of age, just finished four years of college, and now this happened. It was like I was being trapped into something with someone I didn't even like anymore."

He dreaded the next part, knowing he wouldn't come out smelling of roses. "I told her she was on her own. If the baby turned out to be mine I would take responsibility financially for it, but I didn't want anything to do with either of them."

Cathy's glare burned into him and he had to avert his eyes. This was the hard part - telling the woman he loved, who had children of her own, that he chose to turn his back on his own child. He knew he deserved the dirty look she was giving him. What a low-lying shit he'd been, knowing that if he threw money at the situation it would go away.

Being the man in the relationship, he could do that. He didn't need to know what would happen in nine months. Once the cheques were written and sent he could forget about the whole sorry mess, pretend it never happened.

"So, what happened?" Cathy whispered.

"Whenever Sinead copped on that I wasn't playing ball, she went running to the other two fellas, giving them the same sob story. Rumour has it neither of them were as generous with their offers and basically told her to fuck off. She came running after me again, but I wasn't having any of it. Next thing I know she's banging down my door, screaming and shouting that she'd had a miscarriage."

Cathy groaned. Sam continued, relieved to get it all out. "She stayed with me for a couple of days, but after that we broke up properly and went our separate ways - me to Ibiza and her back to her parents."

"I almost feel sorry for her," Cathy said. "It's a horrible thing to happen to anyone. Not her getting pregnant and not knowing who the father is, but the miscarriage. That's not nice."

"I'm not one hundred percent sure she lost the baby," Sam said, the thought of it still haunting him. "While she was staying with me for the few days, she left some papers lying around the apartment. One was a boarding pass for Heathrow airport, two days before she arrived screaming at my door. After asking around a bit it turns out she was in London when the *miscarriage* happened. I don't know for certain that she had an abortion, but either way, when she got to my apartment that night she was no longer pregnant."

"How did you feel about her losing the baby? I mean, I know you said you didn't want to have anything to do with it, but were you upset at all about what happened?"

"I never knew if the baby was mine or not, and once it was gone there was no way of knowing. Yes, I was upset that a life had been lost, but I wasn't ready for a baby, a family. The relationship with Sinead had dragged me down, but after the baby was gone I did feel a loss that somewhere a little soul was no more - this life was not going to be allowed to grow up and make something of itself. Even if the baby wasn't mine, it still hurt that it had happened. I asked her if it was intentional, but she maintained it was a miscarriage."

He wiped his hands on the duvet, aware that she was looking at him. "After I left, a lot of people went to town on me. Firstly, when it got about that Sinead had been pregnant and that I was having none of it, and then after she lost the baby and I left her to deal with it on her own. It was the coward's way out. I knew that.

202

Run away and bury your head was screaming through my mind at the time. I kept telling myself that even though Sinead had been my girlfriend, she wasn't at the time it happened, and the baby wasn't mine, so let her deal with her own problems. She'd ruined my life enough without taking on her emotional crap as well."

He turned to Cathy, saw her eyes glisten. "I don't expect you to understand, Love, what it was like, or how I felt. I can't say what I did was right. It wasn't. I know that now, and a part of me knew it then, too. But like everything, it was easier to run away and let others sort my problems out."

Sam's heart was beating so fast, he let out a long sigh to help slow it down. He took Cathy's hands in his. "I'm not that person anymore. I've changed so much since then. Even now, when I see you together with your children, I sometimes look at myself and think, God, I could have an eight-year-old son or daughter if things had been different." He blinked away the distant visual, his constant torment. "But it would never have been the same relationship as you have with Millie and Jack."

"What do you mean?" she asked, sitting up. "Why not? Surely a child is a child and you would love them either way?"

"Perhaps," he said, his voice so quiet he hardly heard himself, "but Sinead and I were never going to last. I'd say we would have been lucky to make it through the nine months together, and after that - who knows. I can't see myself sticking to my *not having anything to do with the child* rant, but I don't believe we could have been close. I know she would have used every trick in the book to get what she wanted. If that meant using the child as leverage then she would have pulled both barrels of the gun and fired at will. That relationship was a lost cause, and the poor child would have suffered the most, being used as a walking chequebook."

"So what was that all about today then? You going all weird when you saw her and trying to drink Phil Healy under the table this evening?"

"I thought she was out of the country, or at least out of Dublin, and I hadn't told you about all this stuff, and when she copped you and the kids were with me, I saw her face change. I knew she was capable of starting World War Three, and I needed to get you guys out of there before things kicked off."

He touched her lips to keep her from interrupting. "I didn't need her making some smart remark about me not wanting kids, especially in front of yours. When you went to drop the kids off in Bray, I panicked. I knew I'd have to tell you everything, and I was terrified of your reaction. Looking back on it, I know I was an immature, selfish, rich boy, and I didn't want you thinking that prick was still around."

Her hands were warm as he rubbed them, but he couldn't read her eyes. What was she thinking? Did she understand? He needed her to. He couldn't lose her over this. "I'm different now, Cathy. I swear I am. I nearly told you once before but we got interrupted by a Byron crisis. It's not something you just blurt out over breakfast. I needed to explain it to you properly and give you a chance to see that I'm different now. It was another world, and I'm not the guy whose girlfriend got pregnant and then ran for the hills when the going got tough. I love you, Cathy, and if the same thing happened with us, it would be different. I would be here for you, one hundred percent. I couldn't do anything to hurt you, and I want so much for you to believe that the idiot boy of twenty-four is all grown up now."

The growing lump in his throat choked his words, threatening to well up through his eyes, but he took a deep, shaky breath and blew it out. "That fool had to live with his decision for the past nine years, and will do for the rest of his life. I can't change what happened, Love. I can only try to reassure you that things are different now. With you and me, but especially with me. It doesn't change the way I feel about you or your children. In fact, it made me realise how lucky you are, having such a great relationship with them. You adore those kids and they adore you. I don't think it would've been the same with mine, but you never know." He looked away. "I'll never know."

He got out of bed and looked down at Cathy, who had not uttered a single word. "I can't change what happened. I can only look forward and try not to fuck up the future. I hope you and the kids are in my future, Cathy. I really do." He paused, letting that sink in. "I know I've hit you with a lot of stuff here. Knowing you, it's going to wreck your head. Have a think about it." He knelt at the side of the bed and took her hands in his. "I'm sorry about earlier. Being drunk and everything. I'm an ass."

*

"Yeah, you are," Cathy said. "A total ass." Then she snuggled back under the duvet. She didn't know what to say to him, but she knew she needed time to think this through. Her two best friends and a bottle of wine would give some perspective, but in the end it was up to her how she responded. It was difficult from a woman's point of view to understand men's reactions to unexpected pregnancies. She had been twenty years of age and pregnant with twins, with no job, no house, and no ring on her finger, but not once had it crossed her mind that Gary wouldn't stand by her.

She was lucky. Gary had been a shit in every other way, but as far as her unexpected pregnancy went, it wasn't an issue for him. Of course, it had been scary and daunting, and hard as hell to cope with two little babies, but she wouldn't have had it any other way. Could she now look at Sam the same way? A man who'd washed his hands of a bad situation. He didn't love Sinead, and there was a chance the baby wasn't even his, but situations like that can tell an awful lot about a person.

She could see he hadn't dealt with it well, and certainly not in the way she would have liked if it had been her. But she hadn't known him then, or what he was like in college when he was younger. Could she believe that he'd learned from his mistakes and copped on to the real world? Would he be a stand-up guy if something similar happened with them, or would he run for the hills like he'd done before?

She was tired, and much as she'd love to lay tossing and turning this over in her head all night, she needed to sleep. At that moment, she didn't care if Sam stayed or went. She needed to deal with her own feelings before she could reassure him that everything was okay.

*

Sam got the hint when she turned her back to him. He made his way back downstairs. It was too soon to collect his car; he was still over the limit, so he lay on the sofa and prayed for a forgiving hangover in the morning, and after that, a forgiving girlfriend.

*

Sunday morning was a tense affair. Cathy knew Sam didn't know how she felt about last night's revelation. He knew she needed time to think it through. Would his promise that he'd changed hold up? There was no arguing that he'd been a selfish bastard, but could she trust him now? She didn't know him inside out yet, or for that long.

It had been an amazing two weeks, but what would happen if sometime in the future something drastic happened? Would he run? Did he feel differently for her to the way he had felt for Sinead? He said he did. She couldn't deny that he acted like he did, or that he made love like he did.

That thought brought a smile. They were still in a honeymoon phase - still getting to know each other's likes and dislikes, exploring body and mind. The next phase, opening the ex-file, was inevitable. They needed to look into the past if they were ever going to move forward. Apart from silly teenage stuff, Sam knew pretty much everything there was to know about her. She had nothing to hide. Her life was out there for anyone to see. That's what happened when someone destroyed a marriage, the privacy doors were thrown open and everyone had a good look inside. Her book read like hundreds of other separated or divorced parents up and down the country. People had an opinion on the split, whether they knew the couple or not.

In Sam's situation, though, he could have kept his mouth shut and said nothing. She had to give him points for that. He could have let her fall deeper into the relationship where she would be devastated all over again. Now he was giving her all the information, getting it out in the open, so there were no surprises later on. She admired his concern about her reaction, especially when it risked her flipping out and telling him to get lost. She had to decide if he was a changed man, if she trusted him to look after her, and whether this relationship could go further.

*

Sam could see Cathy struggling with it. If only she'd talk to him, he would tell her anything she needed to know. The last thing he wanted was for this to break them up, but he was certain from the start that he wanted her to know about it. He would do whatever it took to convince her he was mad about her and the children, but it was up to her whether she could love him and trust him enough. It wasn't so different to the start of any new relationship, but he knew she had to consider her children as well as herself.

They sat in their silence at the kitchen table, nursing two mugs of coffee, each lost in their own thoughts. Then he stood, ready to go, knowing she needed time and space to work this out. Him sitting there staring at her didn't make it any easier.

"Cathy, before I go, I have to tell you one more time that I love you. I love your children." He closed his eyes. Just thinking that this might be the end hurt so much, but for now he'd done all he could. It was up to her now. Their relationship was in her hands. If she could accept his past and know she could trust him, things would be okay.

Once he'd found his car keys, he took Cathy in a hug, maybe for the last time. He didn't trust himself not to cry, so he let her go and turned for the door.

Cathy found her voice at the last second. "I'll ring you later." Then let him walk out the door.

*

She ran to the sitting-room window and watched him walk up the road away from her house, away from her. It took all her strength to fight the overwhelming urge to run after him and grab him back.

209

She wasn't angry with him. Why had she let him leave then? She should have talked to him, got this all sorted out, hating now that he'd left with this cloud looming over them. How could she do that? She wasn't someone who could keep bad feelings going for long, preferring to deal with things there and then rather than let them fester and grow out of control.

She watched as he walked away, and knew in that instant that he was the man for her. The grey clouds in her head parted just enough to let a ray of light through. Sure, all the stuff that needed to be sorted was still milling around inside her, but her gut feeling was, *do not let that man walk away from you, now or ever!*

It was right. Sam was a good man. He wouldn't hurt her. Yes, he'd made mistakes in his past. Who hadn't? Okay, this was one big humdinger, but she knew she had to trust her gut, her head, her heart, which were all breaking at the sight of him leaving. She would deal with the whys and hows later. Right now, she needed Sam here so she could tell him that she was his. Everything else would sort itself out. She was sure of it, and it was obvious that her gut agreed. Perhaps she needed some breakfast to quieten it down. She grabbed her phone and dialled Sam's number.

"I know you're the man for me, Sam," she said before he could get a word in. "I love you, too. What's done is done, it can't be changed."

"Cathy, are you sure? I've only been gone two minutes. You couldn't have done that much thinking."

210

"I don't need to think, Sam. I know. You and I are meant for each other. We deserve to be together to deal with all the mad things life wants to throw at us. I'm not angry at you. That was the old you, nine years ago. Selfish prick that you were, you needed to go through all that to make you into the new and improved Sam that you are today."

Sam laughed.

"Come back when you collect your car," she said. "I'll make us breakfast and we can have a proper talk."

"See you in ten," he said.

"Oh, Sam…"

"Yeah?"

"You do realise that now I know all your deep dark secrets, you can never leave." Her efforts to talk like an old cackling witch ended up sounding like a sixty-a-day smoker with pneumonia.

"I never had any intentions of leaving, Cathy," Sam said, his voice soft in her ear. "Even if you didn't want me, I wasn't going away."

Tears ran down her face. Tears of happiness. "Thank you, Sam. Oh, and pick up some milk and eggs on your way back, please."

16th September

Monday

Cathy felt a great deal better after their chat. It had given them both a chance to express feelings and emotions normally left unspoken. She suspected that, at the time, Sam had buried a lot of his shame and guilt, and it pleased her that he now felt comfortable enough to talk to her about that dreadful time in his life.

Even though it was nothing to do with her, she prayed for the life that had been lost. As a mother, her maternal instinct could not allow such news pass without acknowledging the little soul, and because of that, there was now peace in her heart and she was ready to move on.

As she cleared away the breakfast dishes that morning, she paused to ponder this strange feeling and how it had affected her even though she had nothing to do with it. It caused the same grief as the time she visited her granny's grave and came across the resting place of a child buried close by. That time, she'd scattered prayers into the air, wishing the child a peaceful rest. It was her way of dealing with a loss so unimaginable, it scared the living daylights out of her.

Later that night, as the children lay asleep, she sat on the floor between their beds, holding one little hand in each of hers. She connected all three of them in a human chain, willing them both to know how much she loved and needed them. Tears came as she tried

212

not to consider anything ever happening to her own children. She would never survive. Ever.

Unable to let them sleep without her that night, she moved them both to her double bed, climbed in between them, and hugged their soft sleeping forms close. She smelled their sweet breath fanning her face as she held them, never wanting to let go.

"It's us against the world," she whispered. "Now Sam wants to come along for the ride. What do you think? Should we let him?" Her words went unheard, but Millie and Jack snuggled in closer, giving her the answer she needed.

*

Leaving Cathy after revealing his bombshell had been hard. But at least everything was now out in the open. No more secrets. It would take time for her to sort through all he had told her, and it made things so much better that she was willing to try. He knew she loved him, and was willing to give him a chance to prove himself.

From now on, he was going to use one of Cathy's blank canvases to mark the start of their relationship. He wanted to splash it with as much colour and abstract madness as he could. Life was too short to waste on someone else's dull print. He needed to take charge, look forward, and start moving on. And this time, Cathy would be by his side, helping to paint their canvas together.

Once at work, his day went from bad to worse. A stinking hangover did nothing to improve his nervous mood, but the meeting with Pat Sheppard and Tony tipped him over the edge.

The security team had gained more footage of Gary's sticky fingers. There was no doubt in anyone's mind that he was their man. From the CCTV recordings, it appeared that money had been lifted each day, and now that Sam was keeping a closer eye on the lodgements, he could see how Gary was getting away with it. Numbers on the lodgement slips were being inverted. This, coupled with the fact he only took small amounts of twenty Euro or less from each till, meant that suspicions were never raised.

A general non-spoken rule in the pub was that there would always be discrepancies with the till balance and final receipts. Mistakes happen, wrong change is given; sometimes too much or too little. Anything less than a twenty-Euro difference in the bottom line is ignored, thought of as human error. Gary had known that and worked it to his advantage, some days taking a little more and perhaps blaming a new trainee for messing up the tills. It was easy for him to write such a note at the end of the ledger.

By Sam's calculations, around €2,700 had been taken over the past eight months. His head ached as he berated himself for not spotting it sooner. He vowed to go through every other aspect of the pub's running to see what else might be going astray. A couple of bottles of spirits here, a keg or two there, who knew? He had a bad feeling this wasn't the end of it.

As the manager, it was up to him to confront Gary and recoup as much of the losses as possible. Being caught between a rock and a hard place wasn't the ideal position to be in, and he needed to figure out a way of dealing with this without the results affecting Cathy.

He didn't give two shits about Gary, but if he lost his job, Cathy would suffer. That wouldn't happen. Not if he could help it. The little prick couldn't get away with it. He checked the roster, noting that Gary would be in after lunch for the late shift. Time to tackle him then.

First, though, he needed lunch; his stomach was eating itself and the rumbling was audible. He left the office and headed for the carvery. As he reached the counter, a familiar voice had him spinning around in shock.

"Hello again, Sam. Fancy seeing you again so soon."

"Sinead? What the hell are you doing here?" Anger filled his throat, choking his words. Hadn't he made himself clear back in Dundrum? Then it struck him that Sinead being here was in no way a happy coincidence. She was up to something. A horrible dread added to his already weakened state, because if he knew Sinead, whatever she was up to wasn't pretty.

"Oh, I was just out and about and thought I'd stop in for a bite to eat. I know the food's really good." She smiled at him, waving her hand about as if she came in all the time.

"Give it a rest, Sinead. You've never eaten pub-grub in your life. What are you at?"

He placed his lunch order before he grabbed her elbow and steered her out of earshot of the amused-looking chef and lounge girl. No way did he want them knowing who this woman was putting pressure on their boss. Sinead looked so out of place in a pub like this, she did nothing but draw attention to herself by being there. She also did nothing to curb their curiosity, clicking her way in high heels across the tiled floor to the table.

"I thought I made myself clear the other day. I'm with someone else. I'm happy. I'm not interest in anything you have to offer." Sam was blunt. The message had to get through this time. He didn't need Sinead popping up here and there, thinking there was still a chance of something between the two of them.

Her smile wavered as his message hit home, but it was obvious she wasn't ready to give up.

"I just need to know, Sam. Do you regret what happened with us? With our baby, I mean?"

"First off, was it ever my baby?" He glanced around to ensure no one else was near them. "And second, yes, I regret the way I acted, taking the easy way out. There were a lot of things I needed to deal with. I had a lot of growing up to do, to be honest."

His head was thumping, but he had to get through this. He looked her in the eye. "I'm sorry about what happened to you. I am.

At the time I felt relief, but looking back, I never really thought about how you were feeling, whether it was a miscarriage or an abortion." He saw something flicker across her face. Pain? Distaste? "Either way, Sinead, I'm sorry you had to go through that. It can't have been easy for you. I know that now. But, look, we've both moved on. Can't you just let it go?"

A lounge girl interrupted them to bring his lunch. Sinead ordered a slim-line tonic for herself.

Flicking hair away from her face, Sinead studied Sam, boring her eyes into his, like she was trying to dig deep for something he'd hidden from her. "That's the thing I'm concerned about, Sam. Are you happy? How can you be willing to raise another man's children when you were dead set against wanting your own? How is that fair on the way you treated me or what happened to our child."

Though she spoke without emotion, Sam noticed the hint of tears forming in her heavily-lashed eyes.

"I always loved you, Sam," she continued. "You knew that. Okay, I might have had a couple of tiny flings now and again, but it was always you I came back to. You were my rock. It was my way of getting you to notice me, to keep you interested. The others were just to make you jealous, to get you to fight for me."

"What type of twisted fairy-tale have you concocted in your head, Sinead? You were trying to get my attention?" He heard the scorn in his voice, and glanced around again to see if anyone was bothered with them. When he turned back to Sinead, he kept his voice low. "You were trying to make me jealous? You're nuts, do you know that? You say you loved me? Who does that to someone they love? Who goes out night after night, living the high life, trying to catch the eye of the richest man in the room, not even caring that their boyfriend was standing beside them at the time? You didn't love me, Sinead. You loved the idea of who I was, and what I could get you. You used me."

He paused and pinched the bridge of his nose, then took a deep breath. "When you fell pregnant, you thought I'd be a soft touch, the one who'd take the hit."

Where those tears in her eyes? Crap, why do women have to cry so much? "I can still see your face when I told you I wasn't interested in having a baby with you. To be honest, that haunted me for years, reminding me of what I'd done and the way I acted."

"Sam, please..." Sinead started, but he held a hand up to her, pushing his untouched dinner away with his other. He'd lost his appetite, but could do with a stiff drink. What was it about this woman that made him want to get plastered every time he saw her?

"Sinead, I'm with Cathy now. I love her. I love her children. We're making it work. The rest is really none of your business. What I do with my life and whoever I do it with is none of your concern. We're happy, and with you in or out of the picture, that's the way it will stay."

A tear slid down her cheek, but she wiped it away before it could leave much of a trail. Sam didn't understand her. They'd been apart for over nine years. The last year they dated had been less than a bundle of laughs, so why was she bringing this all up now, after so long? There'd been no contact after he left. The only time they'd seen each other was two days ago. Sinead had to see they were never going to be happy. Even if the baby had happened, they would not have made it as a couple or a family.

I must be missing something here. Why hasn't she moved on? She wasn't the type to sit back and let one mishap pull her down. Even while trying to avoid her, Sam had seen her face splashed across the social pages for a good few years after they'd split. Not at first, but after about a year or so, she seemed to get back out there to begin her social climb again. He'd heard she'd been engaged twice during the past nine years, but she wore no ring on her finger now. Was that what this was all about? Was she trying to get back in with him? The old reliable?

There was only so much a man could take. He needed to get out of there, before he said or did something he might regret. Whatever her reasons for turning up today, he could bet they were nothing but selfish.

"Sinead, look, I have to go. I need to get back to work." He stood.

She put a hand on his arm. "Wait, Sam, not yet. There's something I need to talk to you about." Her words came slow, and she didn't look him in the eye.

"Spit it out then." He remained standing, waiting for her to continue.

"Not here. It's personal." She glanced around. "Isn't there somewhere more private we can go?" She looked over at the office door.

"No." He had no intention of being trapped in any enclosed space with her. "What is it? Are you after money?"

"I can't go into it here, so openly." She flicked something unseen off the table. "We need to talk privately. I'll set up dinner during the week in Shanahans. We'll talk then."

"Talk now, Sinead." She was pissing him off. He didn't want to meet her again, not least for dinner.

"No, now isn't the right time, anyway. You're too wound up to listen properly. I know what you're like, remember?"

He didn't know how much more he could take. The way she spoke, it was like butter wouldn't melt in her mouth. "You know nothing about me anymore."

"Perhaps. I'll text you the day and time and we can talk then." She looped her bag over her arm. "When you hear what I need to say, you can decide whether you want to see me again. After what you put me through nine years ago, Sam, you at least owe me that much."

She leaned up, kissed him soundly on the mouth, then turned to click-clack her way out of the pub. Sam stood rooted to the spot, staring after her, wondering what the hell her game was.

He turned to go to his office and spotted Gary watching him from behind the bar, a sly smile on his face. How much of that had he seen? He stalked past him and slammed the office door shut, in no mood to deal with Gary and his crap today. Fuck it, he could wait another day to sort that scumbag out. For now, he needed to figure out what Sinead wanted and how in God's name he was going to explain this dinner to Cathy.

17th September

Tuesday

"Wow, that was a rough few days to deal with," Byron said, stirring sugar into her tea. "Why didn't you let us know sooner? We would have come down to help you out."

Cathy sipped her wine. "The shit going on with Gary is just that. Shit. There's not much I can do about it. Just sit back and see what happens. I feel a bit responsible, though. Suppose he was using the money to pay my maintenance each month? Isn't it like I'm forcing him to steal? Maybe I'm giving him no other option?"

"Are you on the stupid pills again?" Annabel asked in her usual blunt manner. "Gary's wages are adequate enough to cover the measly sum he forces you to live on each month. Okay, he probably doesn't have a fortune left after he sorts you and his rent out, but I'll bet it's enough to live on." She leaned back in her chair and shook her head. "No, there must be something else going on with him. Must be."

"He probably owes it all to the VD clinic, or something."

"Eeewww, Byron, that's gross."

"You never know, Cathy," Byron said, warming to her subject. "Some of the slappers he's been out with. Am I right, or am I right?" She raised an eyebrow. "I'm surprised his wee willy winkle hasn't fallen off by now." She looked from Annabel's amused face, to Cathy's hurt one.

"Ah, I'm just saying, Cathy. Obviously, I don't include you in the slapper comment, you dimwit." She cleared her throat. "I know this is a bit personal, but while we're on the subject, please tell me you got yourself tested to make sure Gary didn't give you the nasties? I mean, he was still bouncing you while he was at all those other ones, right?"

Cathy couldn't help laugh at Byron's way of putting things, and was quick to reassure her friends. Yes, of course she'd been tested, and no, she hadn't caught any of Gary's nasties. "I can only assume," she added, "that while his little member was leading him into all sorts of trouble, his half-baked brain had the good sense to use protection."

"Thank God he did something right," Annabel said, grimacing. "That's all you'd need. A kick in the teeth to find out your husband is cheating, then a case of the clap to top it off."

"What about Sam?" Byron asked.

Cathy laughed again. By God, she's on a roll tonight. "What about him?"

"Well, is he, you know...? *Protected?*" She whispered the last part as if the sleeping children upstairs might hear her.

Cathy pulled a face of mock horror. As if she would have it any other way. How old did her friend think she was, twelve? "Of course he's protected. Not that it's any of your business, you big nosey parker. What do you take me for?"

She wasn't really offended by Byron's question. It was good to know her friends were looking out for her. It was pure idiocy to go unprotected these days. With so many sexually-transmitted diseases being passed around, she couldn't fathom how anyone wouldn't use a condom. There was no shame in carrying one, and using one, even if was a little embarrassing buying them when you had two kids with you. But a couple of red cheeks at a checkout was far more desirable than an itchy visit to the doctor, and a lot of explaining to do.

Thinking back, it was Sam who'd reminded her on their first night together that they should play it safe. Since then, they'd both been to the doctor's and received good news."

"Better safe than sorry," Annabel said.

Byron snorted. "No, better safe than scabby."

Annabel wiped tears of laughter from her eyes. "Oh, Jesus, Byron, where do you get them from? That's even worse than the last one." She watched Cathy open another bottle of wine. "Anyway, enough about Gary and his dodgy dick. Tell us more about the whole Sam/Sinead/baby thing."

She relaxed back into the chair, waiting for the full story, but Cathy didn't want to go into all the sorry details with them. Even though she'd been over it a million times, the answer was always the same. She wanted to be with Sam and trusted that he wouldn't hurt her. This was a private matter between them. She owed him a measure of loyalty by keeping his personal life private, to a certain degree.

The girls had got the edited version. They didn't need to know all the intimate details Sam had trusted her with. They got the gist of what happened: Sam dated Sinead, she got pregnant, she lost the baby, they broke up and he moved away; end of story. She hoped they'd all be spending a lot more time in each other's company and didn't want to tarnish Sam's halo by giving the nitty-gritty on what had really gone down. When it came to Sinead, though, there was nothing preventing them talking about her. Nothing at all.

"You should have seen her in the House of Frazer," she said. "Seriously, she was like a supermodel, polished and bronzed. Not a hair out place, either. Oversized shades perched on her head, holding back her mahogany mane of extensions. Make-up perfect, teeth sparkling, clothes immaculate, manicure unchipped on the most natural set of gel nails I've ever seen."

"Easy knowing she doesn't have to wash up or clean the toilet," Byron said, keeping it real.

Cathy looked at her two friends, almost afraid to admit she'd felt about two feet tall standing there that day, even scruffy, though she was as clean as anyone else. And ugly, though she knew she wasn't. She'd go so far as to say Sinead made her feel like an old, haggard bag lady, even though she didn't come near it.

Byron smoothed Cathy's hair off her face. "Cathy, honey, don't be like that. You're worth a million of her. A million! Look at all you've gone through, and come out of. You're beautiful, funny, and smart. You have two amazing children, who want for nothing, and you do that on less than eight hours sleep every night. You don't even have a regular beautician."

Annabel leaned forward in her seat. "Yeah, Cathy, look at you. Amazing figure, even after carrying two lumps of babies, at the same time, too. Ouch!" She held her ankle and glared at Byron. "Feck off, By." She looked at Cathy. "I'm sorry sweetie, but I've never seen twins so big in all my life. What were they again?"

"7lb-9oz and 8lb-3oz." Cathy laughed, then considered what Byron had just said.

"Your right, though, By, I don't have a hairdresser, stylist, or beautician on call 24/7. I have a real life, with real children, and real stinky toilets to clean. Why should I be jealous of her?"

Byron smiled. "I can tell you one thing you do have that she would give her eye teeth for."

"What?" Cathy and Annabel asked together.

"Sam!"

"You know what, girls? Sinead can keep all the fancy clothes and perfect hair she so obviously adores. Sam is with me, and loves me just the way I am. And good thing, too," she added before they could get a word in, "I don't have the energy for anything else."

Once their laughter had subsided, Annabel tapped the table. "Speaking of getting all dolled up and beautified, I've got tickets for a charity dinner on Saturday night. A big one. Would anybody like to go?" She produced a white, gilded invitation from her handbag and handed it to Byron.

"Holy cow, Batman. How did you get invited to this?" Byron passed the invite to Cathy.

According to the gold, italic script printed on Olde-World parchment, the event was a black-tie, invitation-only, affair. Celebrities, musicians, politicians, and some of Ireland's rich list were sure to attend. Invites were at a premium and only the well-to-do and famous were considered to be good enough.

"My boss was invited," Annabel said, taking the card back from Cathy. "A whole table has been reserved in his name. I suppose the organisers thought having him there with his cronies would be a smart move. Fortunately for us, he's off to Bermuda with his second wife, and ever-so-casually passed his full-table invite on to me. Not sure that the powers-that-be will be too impressed at my presence there, but who am I to pass up a free meal?"

Cathy fidgeted with her hair. She'd just admitted how out of her depth she'd felt around Sinead. "I don't know, Anna, it looks very fancy. I'm not sure I'd be comfortable at something like that."

"Nonsense," Annabel said, refusing to take no for an answer. "With sexy Sam on your arm, you'll fit right in. Besides, I'm sure he's well used to frequenting that kind of thing, terribly boring as they tend to be. It'll be fun to have my girls with me so we can mix it up a little."

Cathy looked over at Byron, who looked in deep thought, probably cataloguing her wardrobe and wondering what would look fabulous.

"Come on, Cathy, it will be a laugh. Let's go and get pissed and make a right holy show of ourselves. It's not like we're going to run into those people again at Sunday brunch in the Four Seasons."

Cathy knew she was beaten. With both her friends in the mood to party, she didn't want to be the pooper, so to speak.

"Okay, I'll go, but only if Sam agrees to come. I'm not going on my own. Knowing you lot, you'll leave me stuck between two boring bankers, too jaded to get up off their seats. At least if Sam's there, I'll have something pretty to look at while I'm being bored to death."

"That's the spirit," Annabel said, clapping her hands. "Hunky boyfriend, plenty of booze, and perhaps a little Chanel goody bag to bring home if the night goes well."

"Will you be bringing your hunky fella?" Byron asked Annabel.

"We'll see. I've a date with him tomorrow night so I'll decide after that if he's worthy enough to meet my friends."

Cathy and Byron shrieked with delight, then begged Annabel to divulge more saucy facts about her mystery man.

"Soon, my pretties. Soon." She finished off her wine, then produced another bottle from her bag, indicating that it was going to be a long night.

18th September

Wednesday

Gary left the pub's back office, slamming the door behind him. "Shit, shit, shit, shit, shit." Each word came out louder. He needed air. Fast.

Once outside, he bummed a smoke off a regular and leaned against the wall to think. He'd just been hauled over the coals by that fucker, Sam, and was now in serious shit. Sam had recorded footage from the CCTV, lodgement slips, plus a whole damn folder with his name on it. He was screwed, that much he knew. But how in the hell had he been found out? He'd been so careful by only taking money from the till when he knew no-one was around. He didn't know that anyone actually checked the security cameras.

According to Sam, he'd helped himself to over €2,700 from the tills over the past eight months. It couldn't be that much, could it? It's not like he was keeping track of the extra twenties in a little black book. He only took what he needed, every now and again. The odd score or tenner, sometimes just a fiver.

He took a long drag on the musky cigarette, then started coughing, unused to the strong, unfiltered tobacco. Who even smoked this kind of shit anymore? Right, Gary, focus. How do you get yourself out of this mess? You're a talker, so talk your way out. No, that wouldn't work this time. The CCTV footage was there, all in black and white. He couldn't deny it. Fuck!

He flicked the cigarette butt into the gutter. Panic numbed his mind as he ran through his options. The only thing he could come up with was to plead with Sam to have mercy on him. Admit he'd made a mistake. Ask him to help him out by giving him a chance to repay the money. If only he could keep his job.

Oh, Jesus, if I lose this job, that's me done for. May as well make sure the life assurance is paid up to date, then take a long walk off a short pier. Slumping back against the wall, he wondered if this was how it felt to hit rock bottom. How had he let it get so bad? He cringed thinking of all the stupid decisions he'd made over the past few months, the past few years. How had he let it get this bad? He slid down until he rested on his haunches, scrubbing his hands over his face to help alleviate the desperation burning through him.

Damn it, he'd never felt so desperate in all his life. Not when Cathy got pregnant at 21 and they had nowhere to live or even a job between them. Not when Millie had been taken ill and spent a week in Temple Street Children's hospital. Not even when he fucked up his marriage and got kicked out of his own house. All those had been fixable. Once he had an inkling that things would be okay and the worst was over, he managed to work a way out of a crisis.

Not this time, though. He was in big trouble and he knew it. Apart from the money he now owed to the pub, he was in debt to the tune of thousands in unpaid credit cards and loans from mates. A couple of nights ago, he'd been warned by some henchmen that the local moneylender was getting antsy about repayments. By his own admission, he knew his gambling addiction was way out of control. He barely had food in the press to feed the kids when they came to stay with him. And now things had gone from bad to worse with that prick Sam finding out about his extra income.

He relived the moment his world came crashing down around him. Sam had set up a meeting to discuss deliveries, but instead had interrogated him about the missing money. Sneaky bastard. He'd all the evidence there, neat and tidy, so Gary couldn't deny it. There was no point. It galled him to stand there while that fucker tore strips off him, going on about respect and loyalty and all his family had done for him.

Sam had roared on at him about not shitting on your own doorstep, and there was nothing Gary could do but sit there and take it. In the end, he'd been informed that he was on six weeks' probation, until a full and final investigation was carried out. A decision on his future and any criminal proceedings would be made then. Sam warned him that one false step meant instant dismissal, and told him he would be watched like a hawk.

It sickened him to have to hand over his keys to the premises and safes, as did being demoted to regular barman. No more picking and choosing what shifts he wanted to work. From now on it was up to Sam to do the roster, and Gary would work the hours given to him, along with a few extra shifts at other pubs each week so he could start repaying the money he owed.

He stood and stretched his legs. The walk back into the pub was like walking to his doom. It was the last place he wanted to be right now. He wanted to turn around and walk in the other direction. For fuck's sake, he was a grown man, he didn't have to take orders or demands from anyone, not least Sam O'Keefe. He could do whatever he wanted.

Maybe he should go home, let that jumped-up little smartarse get out and work the bar for a change. I'll do my punishment tomorrow. Some time at home would do him the world of good. Give him time to think. But what if Sam freaked out? What if he sacked him outright? He couldn't afford to lose the only steady income he had. It was the only way he had of getting himself out of this mess. He was at the door when a woman coughed behind him.

"Excuse me, do you work here?"

Gary glanced at her, not interested in assisting anyone, but once he saw who she was she had his full attention. What a knockout. Wouldn't mind some of that tasty ass.

He gave her his full smile. "Can I help you?"

"Could you tell me if Sam O'Keeffe is working today?"

"Yes, as a matter of fact, he is. Are you a friend?" He remembered her from Monday, kissing the face off Sam as she said goodbye.

"Girlfriend," she said, looking over his shoulder.

"I see." Was good old Sammy boy having a bit on the side behind Cathy's back? And so soon in their relationship, too. That wasn't good. One side of Gary's brain wanted to smash Sam's face in for the hurt he would cause Cathy, but the more practical side wondered how he could use this little nugget to his advantage. Perhaps an arrangement could be made after all. His silence on the 'girlfriend' situation, in exchange for a little leeway, and even a small pay-rise to help him pay off his debt.

Giving her his most disarming smile, he held the door open. "After you," he said, guiding her with his hand on the small of her back. "I'll bring you right into his office so you two can have some privacy."

He didn't bother knocking, entering and announcing Sam's visitor with the smirk of a cat who'd got the cream. "Sam, your girlfriend is here to see you."

Sam stood, his eyes wide and his face red. "Sinead, what the hell are you doing here?"

"Sinead, is it?" Gary asked, almost bowing to her. "Lovely to meet you, but I'm sure you lovebirds have lots to talk about." He glanced at Sam and smiled, knowing he had him by the balls. Then he left, closing the door with a flourish.

19th September

Thursday

Cathy relaxed into the chair with a mug of steaming coffee. Gary was collecting the children from school and keeping them overnight. She was going to meet Sam at his place later that evening, but until then she was a free agent.

While speaking last night on the phone, she could tell Sam had a lot on his mind and that he was stressed. Things were a little shaky between them, but at least they'd spoken every day, even though they hadn't seen each other.

She couldn't wait to see him tonight. I need to touch him, kiss him, and reassure him that things are okay. They'd get over this bump in the road. They were always going to have issues, which was no surprise considering the baggage they both had. That's the way life worked, seldom running without a hiccup. A little drama along the way provided necessary spice. Sometimes she wished for a little less spice, though. When would the universe decide it was her turn to take it easy for a while?

"One of these days," she said out loud to herself, "I'll have not a care in the world. Things will be easy-peasy for us."

*

Once she pulled into Sam's underground garage, she took out her phone and rang him. She still didn't feel comfortable arriving in the penthouse unannounced, even though he'd given her the direct-access code for the lift.

"I'm just parking the car," she said, steering her little Micra in beside his two monster cars. "Will be up in a minute." What list does the universe have Sam on? Do you have to be rich or famous to be on the 'easy life' path? Sam qualified on both those counts. If being sexy and unassuming were also criteria, she'd no doubt he was in for the life of Reilly. No begging the universe for him. He was born into a family of privilege. All he needed to do was stay there and perhaps give her a hand graduating upwards.

She stepped out of the lift onto the living area's plush white carpet. "Sam?" Where could he be? She checked the kitchen and balcony, but there was no sign of him. When she got to the bedroom, she tapped on the half-open door. "Sam?" Nothing. She moved inside and heard the shower running in the en-suite. Soft steam billowed out through the doorway. She stepped forward and gasped at the magnificent sight before her.

"Holy shit. What a man." She studied him through the walk-in shower's glass door. "What a body." The other times she'd seen him naked hadn't done him justice. Rolling around in the king-size bed gave her an idea of his strength and virility, but seeing him standing tall, muscles rippling, all soaped up, left her heart pounding and her vagina aching for intimate contact.

Sam turned and caught sight of her standing there ogling him. She noticed his immediate reaction to her presence and didn't need to be asked twice when he called out for her to join him. Stripped in record time, she stepped into the shower, raising her face for a sensual kiss, catapulting her already startled senses into orbit.

Water cascaded around them as their wet, slippery bodies embraced. Sam lathered her with a luxurious shower cream from behind, sliding his hands over her full breasts, kneading them, much to her delight. She leaned back against his torso, letting his strong body cradle her as he cleansed her skin. His hands travelled lower across her flat belly, and when one hand rested on her hip, the other dipped south to the top of her thigh.

Cathy reached up behind her, knotted her fingers into his hair and pulled him down for him to kiss her neck. She gasped as he moved his hand between her legs, and almost lost her mind when he slipped his fingers between her lips. His rock-hard length pressed into her back, but being so tight against him, she could do nothing to pleasure him until he released her.

She moved her legs apart as his fingers brought sweet relief to her aching loins, crying out with pleasure, her legs buckling, letting Sam's name leave her lips in a slow groan.

He eased her forward so she had to rest her hands against the wall. She pushed her bottom out and he held her hips and entered her from behind, slow and full. Oh, my God. She leaned her hot cheek against the cool tiles and moaned as he filled her. His hands moved to her breasts, his rhythm rocking her against the shower wall. Hot, wet thrusts, building from slow and easy to deeper and more urgent, pounding into her, giving way to an explosion of power from behind that had her screaming for more as he emptied himself into her. He melted against her, his breath fast and shallow, and she knew there was no more stress to trouble her man. Not for today, anyway.

After wrapping her in a white fluffy bathrobe, Sam carried her to his bed. She closed her eyes, loving the way his muscles rippled against her as he set her down. He arranged the pillows, then helped her out of her robe and rolled her onto her belly. She glanced behind. What was he planning?

He went to the bathroom and returned with moisturiser matching the brand of luscious shower cream he'd used on her earlier. A moment later, he'd straddled her thighs and began spreading warm lotion down her spine, so soft and tender she wasn't sure if he was touching her or not. With his big, firm hands, he massaged muscles in her shoulders she didn't know she had.

Soon she was on fire. Desire rushed through her veins, causing her to squirm and buck under his rock-hard thighs. He took his sweet time, massaging every inch of her back and shoulders before turning her over to work on her front. Cathy was in heaven. All this time, Sam didn't utter a word, letting his hands do the talking, something she found so erotic.

When she could take no more teasing, she pushed him onto his back and straddled him, taking him hard and fast, letting their slick bodies mould together into a spectacular climax of animalistic love she could never have imagined with anyone else. Both of them were gasping when she collapsed onto his chest, spent, and so, so satisfied.

"Jesus Christ," Sam said, through gritted teeth. "I so needed that." His powerful arms held Cathy to his chest, her hair, still wet from the shower, sprawled across his shoulders, cooling them both down a notch. They'd barely spoken two words to each other since she'd arrived, but she didn't care. Woven into each other's bodies, she was happy to fall into a peaceful slumber with her sexy man.

*

When he woke, he stretched out to touch Cathy, but she wasn't there. What day is it? Had she changed her mind about staying the night? He didn't like the idea of her driving alone in the middle of the night any better than the thought she'd left without saying goodbye. Where was she? He pulled on track bottoms and went to investigate, checking the bedside lockers first for a note.

Relief flooded him when he found her drinking tea in the kitchen. "What time is it?" He yawned so wide he almost swallowed his own tongue.

"A little after twelve," she said, reaching onto her tippy toes and kissing his nose. She was wrapped once again in the fluffy bathrobe, and Sam's fingers itched to untie the belt and take her right there on the kitchen island. Her hair was a mass of blonde waves, having dried without a straightener to hand. He made a mental note to sort that out.

Her face glowed and her eyes shone like diamonds, and he had to take a deep breath to deal with the depth of the love he felt for this woman. This was the woman who could fix anything. How had he gotten so lucky?

He took a juice carton from the fridge and filled a glass, then sat at the island. "Hi, babe."

When he pulled her to him, she nestled her body between his open legs and wrapped her arms around his neck, ruffling his hair.

"Hi, yourself," she said. "That was some workout you gave me earlier."

"I know." He grinned back at her. "Best damn shower I've ever taken."

Cathy laughed. "It was a first for me, but something I think we should schedule in on a regular basis. I adored the heat of the water pounding us, and the smell of shower gel and shampoo mixing with the scent of our lovemaking. It was wonderful, and a million times better than a quick fumble with Gary in the hotel Jacuzzi after our wedding."

Sam had to laugh. He kissed her neck and her collarbone, heard her stomach rumbling. "Are you hungry? I forgot we didn't have dinner."

"I could probably eat something. What have you got in mind?"

"You," he said, with a wolfish growl. "Or maybe we should go for pizza first?"

"Pizza it is." Her smile broadened. "I definitely need to replenish my energy. I'm sure I'm going to need it."

Twenty minutes later they were sitting cross-legged on the living-room floor, the pizza box between them, Michael Bublé's soft voice crooning from the surround sound.

"You're quiet this evening," Cathy said. "You've barely spoken all night. What's up?"

"I've a lot on my mind at work." He reached for another slice of pizza. "And I've also had two very annoying visits from Sinead this week."

"Visits?" Her head snapped up from the CD cover she'd been reading. "What did she want?"

"I don't really know, to be honest," he said, feeling a bit guilty for not telling her sooner. He knew she was already troubled about the situation, so telling her now that Sinead had been to see him not once, but twice, was a bit like rubbing salt into an open wound.

"Well, what did she say?"

Sam recognised the tense, squeaky tone in her voice. She was liable to flip out if he didn't handle it well. "She caught me by surprise coming into the pub at lunchtime on Monday, spouting all sorts of crap about how she was worried about me taking on another man's child, and could I ever be really happy in this relationship."

Cathy's face paled, but she looked down and remained silent.

"I told her again and again that I was with you now, that I love you and wanted to be with you and the children. She has mental problems, Cathy. The words I'm saying just aren't getting through all those hair-extensions. I told her it's none of her business what I did, or who I did it with. I basically warned her to get lost and leave me alone. Leave us alone."

"So what happened, then?"

He saw that she was trying to control her breathing. "She said she had something to tell me." He held her hands. "Something important. She wouldn't say it, though, because she thought I was too wound up to listen. Either way, she wants to have dinner with me so she can give me her big news, or whatever it is. I told her it wasn't going to happen, that I wasn't interested, but she flounced out of the pub, telling me she'd arrange it all and that she'd be in touch."

Cathy rubbed her face, and it was obvious to Sam that she was shocked. She shook her head and shoulders and growled. "Who the hell does she think she is? Beyonce? What gives her the right to slam-dunk someone they haven't seen in nine years, pretend to be concerned for their welfare, then insist on an intimate dinner to discuss some nonsense that's probably all cotton wool floating around in her head?"

"Way to go, girl," Sam said. Where did this wonderful woman appear from?

"Seriously, Sam, she's some neck. I've a mind to give her a good run for her money. She'll learn she's not the only one who can play dirty."

"Don't go there, Cathy. It's bad enough having one crazy woman on the scene."

She stared at him for a long moment, like she was trying to figure something complex out. He didn't like how it made him feel in the pit of his stomach. What was troubling her now?

"You mentioned two visits," she said, her voice catching. "Did you…"

"Whoa! Don't go jumping to conclusions, honey." He lifted a strand of hair off her face and rubbed her shoulders. "I didn't have dinner with her. I didn't. And for the record, I've no intention of allowing it to happen, either."

"So what was the second visit for?" She shifted her position so she knelt instead of staying cross-legged.

"She came back into the pub yesterday afternoon, right after I confronted Gary about the missing money. I don't know why she was there, or where they met, but somehow she introduced herself to him as my 'girlfriend'. I can tell you, Gary took lots of pleasure letting me know what *he* thought was going on. The little fucker

243

tried to use the info to blackmail me into going easy on him, even asked for a raise to help him pay back the money he stole. He threatened to tell you all about me sneaking another woman into the pub for an afternoon booty call."

He rolled his eyes, remembering the accusations Gary had thrown at him after he'd managed to get rid of Sinead. "Anyway, I got him sorted. He's on a six-week probation. And Sinead, well, apparently she'd called in to tell me that our little chat would have to be postponed. Something came up and she needed to go away for a few days."

He let out a long sigh, slumping his shoulders, glad at last to get it off his chest. The stress with Gary had been bad enough, only to be made worse by Sinead bringing her trouble to his door.

Cathy's cheeks puffed up as she blew an audible breath out. "I can't decide if I'm angrier at Sinead for causing trouble, or Gary for being his usual dickhead self, trying to wriggle out of his dire straits." She leaned in and caressed both sides of Sam's face. "You've obviously had a lot on your mind. It's no wonder you didn't feel well last night."

"I know. That's why you were like an oasis in the desert when I saw you standing at the bathroom door tonight. I just needed to drink you all up after the crap week I've had. You're like a sweet, soothing elixir injected into my veins, giving me instant relief from my pain."

"Well," Cathy said, climbing onto his lap. "I'm delighted to be of use. Is there anywhere else that hurts? Perhaps I can kiss it better?"

"Oh, yeah, baby, I'm sure I'll find something you can kiss." He covered her mouth with his and held her hips as she wrapped her legs around his waist. "Midnight pizza's always a good idea, but midnight sex is even better."

20th September

Friday

Cathy was on a mission. After a night of rocket sex with Sam, she felt like she was floating on air. And he'd agreed to come to the charity dinner with her and her friends.

Okay, I have a man and a place to go. Now I need a babysitter and a fabulous dress.

After school, she called to her mother's house, hoping to catch Becky on her afternoon off. She was prepared to beg, borrow, or steal both Becky's time for tomorrow night, and any suitable dress she might have in her wardrobe. Becky, being the star-bar that she was, agreed to stay over and mind the children, but only if her boyfriend could join her.

"I don't see a problem with that," Cathy said. "Just don't do any nasty stuff in my bed."

Becky laughed. "As if. We prefer the more exotic positions and locations of the Karma Sutra. Beds are so last year. The top of a washing machine or the turn of a stairs are much more exciting. We could even take a trip outdoors. Is you grass cut?"

Cathy was only half shocked, but she wouldn't put it past her sister to get down and dirty on the patio table, not giving a hoot if one of the neighbours might cop an eyeful from their bedroom window.

"At least wait until it gets dark," she said. "I'm not fully up to speed on the indecency laws around doing it in your own back garden. I don't want a phone call from the Gardai to come and bail you out."

At least if it's dark, it would only be Becky's moans and screams the neighbours would hear. She could explain that away as a stray cat or a fox if anyone ever asked.

"So, what sort of fabulous dress have you got for me to wear?" she asked, moving on to a more important issue.

"I've a few nice ones here." Becky pulled out two black dresses and a red, glittery ensemble from the back of her wardrobe. "I'm just not sure they'll fit you, Cathy. You've lost so much weight in the past year. These'll be hanging off you."

"Crap. What am I going to do? I've only got that one black dress that I use for nights out, and Sam's already seen it. Besides, I think this charity event will be a bit fancier than a night in the local Italian restaurant."

"Don't panic," Becky said, both hands out in a soothing gesture. "I've got an idea."

Cathy waited for this idea that was going to save her, but Becky seemed reluctant to share it. "Come on, Beck. Help me."

"We need to go shopping."

Throwing her arms up in frustration, Cathy glared at her sister as if she had fifty heads for even suggesting such a notion. "Beck, if I could afford to go shopping for a fancy dinner dress, do you think I'd be here scabbing one off you? I can't afford to waste money on something that will only be worn once."

"Calm down, for God's sake. You're such a drama queen. Did anyone ever tell you that?" Becky held her head sideways, her eyes wide. "I'm going to let you in on a little secret of mine."

Cathy eyed her. God, how much time do you get for shoplifting?

Becky linked her arm and guided her out of the room. "First, let's see if Mam will mind the children for an hour. We need level heads and no distractions if we're going to do this right."

Their mother was in the kitchen. Becky twirled and clapped her hands. "We need to go out and get Cinderella here suited and booted for her big night tomorrow. Will you mind the twins for an hour, Mam?"

"We'd love to mind them," she replied, hugging her two grandchildren close until they made faces to be rescued. "We haven't seen them properly for ages."

Cathy let out a sigh of relief. "Okay. But, Dad, don't let them eat too much crap, or I'll leave them here with you for the night." She held eye-contact with her father. He was guilty on more than

248

one occasion of bringing Millie and Jack to the sweet shop and letting them run amuck.

"I'll do a bit of dinner for us all later," her mother said, then turned to her youngest daughter. "Will you be here, Becky, or are you going out?"

"No, I'll be here. My plans for having a skin-full tonight have gone by the wayside. I must be responsible. If I'm babysitting tomorrow night, I don't want to be dying like I was the last time."

"Good. About time you realised that you don't need alcohol to have a good time."

Becky rolled her eyes and made a face behind her mother's back. The children giggled so Cathy pushed Becky out the door, making a quick exit before their mother realised what they were laughing at. She called goodbye to those left behind as they barrelled towards the car.

*

Becky directed Cathy towards Wicklow Town, telling her to park along by the river. "We've a lot of shops to get to. Better put €2 in the parking meter."

Cathy looked around, astronomical cash totals racing through her mind. Wicklow had a number of high-class fashion boutiques that were miles out of her price range. No way would she find anything suitable within her non-existent budget. "I'm not sure about this."

"Stop panicking," Becky said, opening her door, "we'll find something for you to wear."

As they strolled up the street, Becky bypassed the classy boutiques, their window displays full of designer clothes. She stopped outside a little shop near the top of the town.

"It's time to let you in on my little secret."

Cathy looked up at the shop sign, then back at Becky. Was she serious? "A charity shop?"

"You're welcome." Becky laughed at her sister's bemused face. "These places are like an Aladdin's cave. We'll definitely find something for you in one of them. If not in Wicklow, Bray has about nine or ten of them."

Cathy wasn't sure. She hadn't been inside one of these shops in years.

"Look, Cathy," Becky said, putting an arm around her shoulders, "there's nothing wrong with having a look, is there? Sometimes they have the most wonderful dresses from debs or weddings. Many have only been worn once or twice, and everything's been dry-cleaned, so it's no different to borrowing something of mine or Byron's. You just need to have an open mind and keep an eye out for the good stuff."

Cathy followed Becky into the shop and stood watching while her sister rooted through a rail of clothes. She looked around. It really was like Aladdin's cave in here. Shelves and shelves of books, ornaments, bags, shoes, with household items adorning every available space on the walls. Anything you could imagine might be here, in some shape or form. All these pre-owned items looking for a new home. It was like the dog pound, only with items their previous owners had no use for any more, but that someone else might find useful.

As she flicked through a Marian Keyes' novel, she was hit with the musky smell of old paper. It reminded her of being brought to the library by her dad when she was young. The books were good value, too. THREE FOR €2, the sign read. That was a bargain if she ever saw one. So many people preferred to read a book once, having no more use for it after. Giving it to a charity shop to sell on was a far better idea than pitching it into the recycler, or letting it gather dust on a shelf, never to be read again.

An old-fashioned dining set of plates, cups, and saucers caught her attention. They were painted in a beautiful white and blue china pattern, identical to the plates and cups her grandmother used to serve them afternoon tea on when they went to visit. How had these particular items come to live in this charity shop? It saddened her to think that it might be the result of a house clearance after the owner had died. None of the family had wanted outdated cups and saucers, so had packed them up and brought them here instead. What happened to all her granny's stuff when she'd passed on? Maybe Mam would know.

Becky snapped Cathy back to the present by dragging her to the counter at the rear of the shop. Her face glowed with an excitement Cathy wasn't feeling. "The saleslady, her name is Marion, by the way, has gone to root out some dresses in the back. It's where they keep stuff that's out of season." She looked around and leaned closer. "It's really just to save room. Anyway, I asked and she said they have a couple of deb's dresses you can take a look at."

Marion returned with two full-length dresses. One was cerise pink, with diamante sparking all around the halter-neck collar. The other was a dark navy blue, similar in sparkliness, but somewhat dated. The blue did nothing for Cathy. She didn't want to look like an old frump just because she couldn't afford to be up-to-date with the latest houte-couture.

She checked the size on the pink halter-necked dress. Twelve. Too big, but she could ask her mother to take it in. It could only be described as a princess halter-necked, floor-length, chiffon dream. The skirt flowed in an A-line sheen, while the neck straps were encrusted with hundreds of diamante.

"What do you think?" Becky asked, twirling the dress on its hanger so Cathy could get a good look at the front and back.

"It's beautiful. Perfect. Do you think I'd look good enough to be on Sam's arm wearing that?"

Becky screeched, "Good enough? You'll look hot, hot, hot! He won't be able to keep his hands off you." She paused and looked up to her left, maybe trying to catch a thought. "Do you still have your wedding shoes? They'd be perfect with that dress."

"I do." Cathy visualised her beautiful wedding shoes." Never thought I'd get to wear them again. And you're right, you wouldn't get a better match."

She stepped closer to the dress and scrutinised it back and front. There wasn't a mark or a stray thread anywhere. It was like brand new. She imagined how it would look with her hair and makeup done, perhaps a splash of fake tan to take the whiteness off her back and arms.

"Beck, do you have silver clutch bag?"

Becky raised an eyebrow in horror. "No, I do not. Are you mad? I wouldn't be caught dead with something like that."

"Hang on a minute," Marion said, coming around the counter. "I've just remembered something." She disappeared behind the storeroom curtain and reappeared a moment later with a small, box-like clutch bag covered in identical diamantes to those on the dress.

"This came in with the dress. It's part of the outfit, I presume." She looked like she'd struck gold on Cathy's behalf.

Becky looked at Cathy. "So what do you think?"

"Like I said, it's perfect, and with the bag and my shoes, it will be stunning. Perfect for tomorrow night." She swallowed back her nervousness. Was it too good to be true? Would something prevent her from having this dress? The price?

"I'm not sure I can afford it, Beck. It's probably about €100. I don't have that sort of money to spend on a dress for one night."

Becky turned to Marion, looking ready to haggle a good price for the outfit. "How much is it?"

Marion put on her reading glasses and checked the price tag attached to the dress's collar. "It says here, €60."

Cathy closed her eyes and took a quiet breath. She knew it. What was she going to do now? She looked at the dress and shrugged, doing her best not to cry.

"Hold on," Marion said, looking around to check no one else was within earshot. "You only want it for one night, right?"

"Yes," Cathy answered, her mouth going dry. "Tomorrow night."

"I'll give this to you for €10, right here and now. You wear it for the dinner, then have it dry-cleaned and returned within a week.

Once that's done, everybody's happy." She smiled and placed a finger to her lips.

"Are you serious?" Cathy asked, her face tingling at the turn events had taken. "You'd let me do that?" It was the perfect solution to having the dress that would make her look stunning.

"It's a very generous offer," Becky said.

"Listen, girls, I've been working here for years. I've seen it all, the good and the bad. If you get a good wear out of this dress tomorrow night, then my job is done. It is stunning, and the colour is perfect for you. You'd be hard pushed to find something more suitable if you'd gone to one of those designer shops, or even on the internet. You'd probably have ended up with something similar, anyway. Now you have exactly what you want, at a fraction of the price."

Cathy couldn't believe her luck. "Thank you so much. I'll take great care of it. I promise."

Marion replaced the protective plastic cover over the dress, popped the clutch bag into a small, mismatched paper bag, and hung it on the hanger. Cathy paid her, then gave her hand a grateful squeeze.

"If I'm not working on the day you bring it back, just leave it here like a donation. No one will be any the wiser."

Cathy prayed the dress would fit, and couldn't wait to get back to her parents' house to try it on. There was such a lot of work to be done. Fake tan and nails needed to be sorted, hair washed, then set with big curlers to give it sleek body. And Becky's make-up bag needed to be raided to see what sort of glittery eye make-up she could find.

Becky told her she'd come and stay tonight, giving her the chance to make the most of tomorrow and make herself as beautiful as possible. She was looking forward to the gala now. A night out with her friends and her man was just what the doctor ordered.

21st September

Saturday

Butterflies flapped around Cathy's belly. Apart from her wedding day, she'd never spent so much time and effort getting ready for a night out. When they got back last night, Becky put the children to bed while she got going with a pre-beautifying routine: exfoliating, shaving, plucking, and polishing. Becky helped with the fake tan on her back and arms, then set her hair with moose and large, spongy rollers.

Cathy hung the new dress on the shower rail and sprayed it with impulse, letting the fragrance seep into the fabric. She then turned on the hot-water tap and the shower, creating a cloud of steam that would release the last few wrinkles from an otherwise perfect ensemble.

This morning, she'd kept her rollers in for as long as possible, letting Becky take the twins to the playground to entertain them for a while. Sam rang to say he'd collect her around five-thirty, and they could go for a drink before heading to the event.

"I'm so nervous," she said, feeling like a child on her First-Communion day. "I've never been to anything like this before."

"You'll be fine. Don't build yourself up too much. Most of these things are boring as hell. Full of pompous tossers taking advantage of the free bar and trying to cop a feel of anything in a skirt."

"Lovely, that makes me feel so much better." The last thing she needed was some sleazy suit chasing her around all night. She wanted to enjoy herself, not fend off dirty old men.

"Don't worry. I'll be with you the whole time. I'll be like your knight in shining armour, warding off all the fire-breathing dragons."

She laughed, visualising Sam in clinking armour. "Okay, you're hired. Make sure your suit is polished, mind. I'll need something to check my hair and makeup in."

It was amazing how a few simple words or a joke from Sam could calm her nerves. Right now, it was like it was just the two of them; that the rest of the world didn't exist, or at least didn't matter. Cathy was sure she could conquer Everest with his encouragement, or basecamp, for starters.

Sam hung up and she returned to her preparations. She texted Byron and Annabel, inviting them to join her and Sam for a pre-gala drink. Byron replied with a *Hell, yea*, while Annabel texted she'd meet them at the hotel. They were to ring her when they arrived and she'd meet them in the bar with her date.

Becky returned with the children. They'd been to the chipper and picked up nuggets and chips for the children's lunch, with a fresh cod each for the adults. Sitting around the kitchen table on a Saturday lunchtime, eating fish and chips and with rollers in her hair, no one would guess that in less than three hours Cathy would be transformed.

At five, she was almost ready. She flapped around the bedroom, spraying her hair for the hundredth time, making sure her make-up was perfect. Becky stood by the door, studying her through squinted eyes.

Cathy looked at her. "What? Is it my hair? My make-up? Oh, do I look like a slut now?" She ran to the mirror, terrified something was wrong. "What is it, Beck?"

Becky came over and turned her. "You look beautiful. Stunning. If you take that scowl off your face, you'd look even better."

"Oh, Beck, I'm so stressed."

Becky helped her relax with deep-breathing exercises.

"You don't want to use up all your adrenalin this early on. You'll be asleep by seven."

Cathy pulled her shoulders back, taking deep, cleansing breaths.

Becky stood in front of her, eyeing her chest. "Hold on, I just need to check something."

Cathy shot her hand up to cover the deep V at the front of the dress. I knew it, I'm too exposed.

"Stop, will you?" Becky swiped Cathy's hand out of the way. Do this." She shook her shoulders and torso, as if dancing to a 70's pop classic.

Cathy stepped back, watching her sister gyrate like a mad woman. "Why? Why should I do that?"

"Come on, Sis, just do it." Becky repeated the dance, this time bending forward and shaking her shoulders back and forth. Cathy copied her, shaking and shimmering, letting it all hang out. Everything went fine until she bent forward and her left boob popped out. She wasn't wearing a bra because of the V-neck design, and now she realised there wasn't enough support to keep everything in the right place.

"Oh, sweet Jesus," she gasped, stuffing her wayward boob in and pulling the fabric back into place.

Becky laughed out loud. "Better to have it happen here than when you're giving it loads on the dance floor."

Cathy groaned. "Great, I'll have to sit like a bleeding statue for the night, afraid to move in case I expose myself to someone."

Becky continued to laugh. "Not sure the men would mind so much. Here, I have something that'll help." She rooted in her handbag and produced a roll of double-sided sticky tape.

"Sticky tape?"

"Titty tape." Becky tore off a strip. "You put it on your boobs and use it to stick your dress in place. Rihanna uses it all the time. How else do you think she can dance around without her puppies flying all over the place?"

Becky worked her magic, securing both sides with the magic tape. "Now, do it again."

Cathy shimmied and shook as hard as she could, giving the tape its ultimate workout. To her relief, everything stayed in place. Now she could dance the night away without giving some poor creature a heart attack.

"That's brilliant. Where did you get it?" She picked up the package to see if there were any special instructions for removing the tape. She winced inside, hoping it wasn't like waxing, where you just had to grab and pull.

"In the chemist. I always keep a roll in my bag, just in case. You never know when you might have a nip-slip."

Cathy almost choked laughing. Only Becky could be so prepared. What other supplies did her sister keep in her handbag for *just-in-case* eventualities?

With the dress now decent, Becky lifted the hem. "Those shoes are still fabulous."

"I know." Cathy looked down at the Louboutin glitter, sling-back heels she'd worn on her wedding day, her pride and joy, and something she knew Becky would love to get her hands on. All the girls had chipped in and bought them as a wedding present, and she treasured them. They were her equivalent to a precious masterpiece of art or sculpture, and something she would never afford herself, so she was careful to look after the pair she had. She turned and lifted her leg to give Becky a good view.

"And that's as close as you'll ever get," she warned.

The doorbell rang and they hugged with giddy excitement.

"Here's your man," Becky said. "Make sure he looks after you tonight. And mind that dress. No ripping it off or you'll be minus a nipple or two."

Cathy went to answer the door while Becky rounded up the children to say goodbye.

"Wow!" Sam's jaw dropped. He repeated the exclamation when Cathy twirled and the skirt swung around her legs. "You look incredible." He leaned forward and kissed her full on the mouth.

She couldn't help but respond, even though she knew the children and Becky were watching. Sam looked so kissable in his sexy black tuxedo.

"Believe it or not, I'm ready to go whenever you are," she said, untangling herself from his arms before she dragged him upstairs and forgot all about the charity dinner. She pointed to her overnight bag by the end of the stairs.

"It's a miracle," Sam said to Becky and the children. "A woman actually ready to go when she said she would be."

Sam put her bag in the car while she said goodbye to the children and Becky.

"Behave yourselves," she warned, directing it as much at Becky as to the kids.

"You too," Becky said, winking, "but not too much. Ah, no, Sis, enjoy yourself. You deserve it." She shouted out to Sam, where he stood by the car. "You mind my sister tonight. And hands off that dress, it's one of a kind."

She winked again at Cathy, then hustled her out of the house to join her fabulous man, on her fabulous night.

*

They met up with Byron and Tom in a small cosy pub a short distance from the Conrad Hotel. Tom looked handsome but uncomfortable in his black-tie suit. He fidgeted with the collar, moaning about being choked, and wondering when he could lose the jacket.

"Keep it on, a least until after the dinner," Byron said, rolling her eyes. "When he went to hire the suit, he actually asked the man did they not have anything a bit more casual."

Cathy found it easy to imagine the burly fireman begging for something less restrictive.

Byron eyed Tom across the table. "God only knows what he'll want for a wedding suit. Bermuda shorts and sandals, and probably a big Hawaiian shirt to complete the outfit." She looked at Cathy, a knowing smirk on her face. "I know him, Cathy, he'll make a holy show of me."

As always, Byron looked stunning. Cathy had seen her dress before, but because of some clever accessories and different shoes, she'd transformed her outfit into something right-on trend and fabulous: black, silky, and oozing chic. With her unique ability to accessorize, Byron could do wonders with any dress.

Her long dark hair was pulled into a fishtail plait, circling around the nape of her neck, the tail-end resting seductively over her left shoulder. No doubt half a tin of hairspray held her tousled look in place and Cathy warned her against standing too close to any smokers for fear of going up in flames.

"Don't worry, I've got my own fireman here, more than willing to throw me down and roll about the floor." She winked at Tom, who confirmed he would do more than put out her fire if he got her on the floor in that dress.

Cathy loved the easy banter between them. A few more drinks and they could be up dancing on the table. "How's everything going with the wicked witch of the west?" she asked Byron, keeping her voice down so the men couldn't hear.

Bryon scowled. "I don't know. I haven't seen the old gasbag since the day she more or less flung me out of her house. I need more time to straighten my backbone before I can tackle an afternoon with that nasty bitch again."

Cathy linked her arm. "Try not to let it get in on you. You were having so much fun organising your wedding, don't let her ruin this special time for you."

"I know, I'm trying not to. I just need more time to feel sorry for myself, then I'll probably have to go and make peace with her, for Tom's sake. He's no good at being stuck in the middle. He did have it out with her, though, told her to cop on and stop treating me like someone off *Big Fat Gypsy Weddings*. But you know men, once they feel they've done their bit, they just want the problem to go away."

"Well, just ignore her, By, you're doing great. This wedding is yours and Tom's, no one else's. You do what you want and feck everyone else, especially that loony tune."

Just before eight, they made their way to the Conrad Hotel. Cathy had never been there before and gripped Sam's hand as they entered the lobby. The hotel, a mixture of modern, bright and airy chic, oozed expense with every one of its five stars.

As Byron went to look for Annabel, Cathy drank in the immense wealth that pulsated from people all around her. Diamonds flashed at the necks and wrists of expensively-dressed women. Men

265

wore hand-tailored, custom-made tuxedos, no doubt one of many that hung in their walk-in wardrobes. The heady odour of French perfumes and expensive aftershaves tickled her senses, mixing with the odd whiff of St Tropes fake tan and hairspray. Sam fitted right in with this crowd, dressed in his own impeccable custom-made tuxedo and Italian leather, dress shoes.

But it wasn't only his clothes that made him look so at home here. He had class and poise, along with the natural ability to converse with anybody he met. His manners were faultless, always introducing Cathy and Tom, before letting them continue with their conversation. He held Cathy's hand, reassuring her that she was just as good as any of the people present.

Byron returned, followed by Annabel and her date. Annabel air-kissed them all, paying particular attention to Sam, who she already knew but had never met in Cathy's company.

"Good to see you again, Annabel," he said, kissing her on the cheek.

"You too, Sam. Delighted you're all here." She beamed at their little group, and then introduced her date.

"Jean Luc, I'd love you to meet my friends." She gestured to each of them in turn, introducing all by name. Jean Luc's smile broadened as Annabel spoke, then to their surprise, he kissed Byron and Cathy twice on each cheek.

"En chante," he said, his words enveloped in a deep French accent. "It is a great pleasure to meet any friends of this beautiful woman." He shook hands with Tom and Sam, asking them what they did for a living.

Bryon and Cathy listened wide-eyed to Jean Luc make small talk with their boyfriends.

Annabel leaned between them and whispered, "Do you need a tissue, By? You're drooling."

"We need the toil... Ladies Room," Byron said, grabbing Cathy's arm and motioning for Annabel to follow them.

"Excuse us." Cathy felt like doing a little curtsy, as if she was in the presence of royalty. They tottered away on their high heels, leaving the men to get better acquainted.

"Oh, my God," Byron cried as she entered the bathroom. She turning to Annabel. "Where in the name of Jesus did you find that Adonis?"

"And why didn't you tell us he was French?" Cathy added, amazed. "The sexiest male species on the planet?"

"He's a doll, all right," Annabel said, a wicked grin dimpling her cheeks. "I didn't tell you because it's only a casual thing. We know each other through work and are only interested in sex." She checked her reflection in the mirror. As usual, she looked like a

Greek goddess, all tall and lean, not a hair out of place, and her dress was an up-to-the-minute Louise Kennedy creation.

"Well you could have warned us," Cathy said. "I won't have a clue what to say to him. I'll be too busy trying not to drool while listening to him roll that accent around his mouth."

"I bet that's not all he can roll around his mouth," Bryon said, quick as a flash.

"Hands off. You two have your own hunks to drool over, remember?"

"Yes," Byron said, "but I bet Sam can't roll his Rs like Jean Luc can?"

"Come on." Annabel squeezed them both. "What are we doing gas-bagging in here when there's an open bar waiting for us out there?"

"Yes, yes, let's go." Byron gave herself a quick once over in the mirror, then, nose in the air, led them out to join their men.

*

Dinner was delicious, and Cathy was impressed. No half-cooked, grizzle-ridden beef for this lot. The chef had outdone himself. For starters she had pan-fried scallops with angel-hair pasta and a champagne-cream sauce. With each one melting in her mouth, she enjoyed every bite of the well-cooked food. Sam encouraged her to try the venison for her main course. She didn't like the idea of eating deer. However, once she tasted the velvety-tender meat, she knew why people raved about the quality and texture of a venison lion.

The meat was pan-fried with a black pepper crust, served with creamy mash potato and thyme jus. Al-dente garden vegetables completed the course, leaving Cathy regretting having missing out for years by her refusal to try this delicious delicacy. Dessert was like a fairy-tale on her sweet tooth. Each mini selection complimented the previous courses, and by the time the individual cheese and biscuit board was placed in front of her, she knew she would burst if she ate another bite. Waiters were assigned to each table to ensure a glass was never more than half empty of red or white wine.

Thoroughly enjoying herself as the conversation flowed around their table, she found it easy to speak with people when Sam introduced her, but let him do most of the talking. Every now and then she'd look around, checking out the guests at other tables.

There were women of all ages, polished and coifed to within an inch of their lives. She'd never seen so much gold and jewels brought together in one place. Some women had faces so frozen by Botox, their startled expressions seemed permanent. She imagined them spending summers in the south of France, or on a yacht off the coast of Italy, and wondered what it would be like to lead such a life. However, she also noted some dodgy fake-tan lines, which got her thinking that even the rich can get it wrong. Seems like everyone needs a bit of help sometimes.

"This is like a wedding," Byron said, interrupting her thoughts. "When is the music starting? I need to get moving. Too much food and wine is making me sleepy."

"We have about an hour's worth of boring corporate speeches to get through first, I'm afraid," Annabel said, leaning back in her chair and stretching herself from head to toe.

As the speeches got underway, Cathy clapped and smiled with the rest of them as recipients received awards for a job well done. With copious amounts of wine flowing through her veins, and Sam's hand inching higher on her thigh, she found it difficult not to crawl under the table and give him a taste of his own medicine. He deserved to be teased back and made as sexually frustrated as he was making her.

She turned to him and smiled, pressing her shoulders forward to deepen her cleavage, making him follow her eyes down, then pushing her breasts out to enhance the effect. His eyes nearly popped out when she slipped a discrete hand under the tablecloth and brushed his groin. He stared straight ahead as she felt him grow beneath her fingers. Good boy, my Sam. She rubbed him and winked, and less than two seconds later he shot up, excused them both, and almost dragged her out of the ballroom. He led her to the *Disabled* bathroom tucked away in the corner of the main foyer.

"What are you doing?" she asked, her breath coming fast. "I was only teasing."

Sam groaned as he opened the door and pushed her inside. "I'm not."

He locked the door and pressed her back against the wall, grinding into her, taking her mouth in his, licking and sucking until she had to break off for air. Her head spun with a delicious desire as she groped and clawed at his trousers, releasing his rock-hard length. She wanted to please him until he cried out her name.

She dropped to her knees and took him into her mouth. He went to put his hands in her hair, but she shrieked at him, "Don't mess the hair!" She held his cock and looked up at him. "If you wreck Becky's masterpiece, she's not here to put it back together."

"Sorry." He guided her back to her business, urging her to continue what she'd started.

"You are the sexiest woman I've ever known, Cathy. God-damn beautiful."

Licking and teasing him, taking his heavy breathing as a sign that he was enjoying the experience, she took him deeper, sucking and kissing his member, working him into a frenzy.

"You're so gorgeous, so beautiful, so sexy," he growled, pushing himself into her.

His balls cupped in her free hand, Cathy pumped and sucked, faster and faster, catching his eye as he approached the point of no return.

"Holy fuck!" he roared, coming long and hard, gripping the radiator as he strained forward.

She kept his cock in her mouth, only releasing him when she was sure he was spent.

"Cathy, Cathy, Cathy, you are fucking amazing." He helped her up off her knees, then kissed her with a passion she didn't expect from a man who'd just come as hard as he'd done. He broke contact and kissed her face. "I love you so much."

"I love you, too," she said, trying to regain her composure. She spent time fixing her hair, tucking away curls that had come undone, then rubbed a finger under each eye to get rid of stray mascara flakes. Sam also looked to be getting himself respectable again. She pulled him closer by his jacket lapels. "I can't believe we just did that. You definitely bring out the bad girl in me."

"*Bad girl* suits you." He ran his hands over her bare back. "What else can you do?"

"I'm not doing anything else." She pushed him away, then added, "It's my turn next. I'll wait until later for you to pleasure me, unless you can find a shower here we can use?"

"Let me look into that."

"No, I'm only joking." She was looking forward to the shower in Sam's apartment later, not some half-baked affair in a hotel en-suite. No matter how swanky a hotel was, their bathrooms were no match for Sam's sex room.

"Come on, we'd better get back in there before we're missed." She unlocked the door and poked her head out, making sure they weren't spotted leaving together.

*

Back in the ballroom, Annabel grinned as they returned to their table. "And where did you two disappear to?" she asked, causing a number of heads to turn.

"Nothing. Nowhere," Cathy said, acting casual, but aware of her face burning as a deep blush betrayed her embarrassment.

"Ya boy ya!" Tom roared, going to high-five Sam, then pulling back when he caught Byron's warning look. He gave Sam a thumbs-up instead.

Annabel roared laughing. "You go, girl." She pointed at Sam. "You've been the making of her."

Cathy's face grew hotter. Why can't the ground just swallow me up now? "I don't know what you're all talking about. I wanted to get some fresh air after dinner and Sam very kindly took me outside."

"He took you, all right," Tom scoffed, earning himself a dig in the ribs from Byron.

Mortified by the attention, Cathy's relief was huge when a man interrupted Annabel, wanting to introduce her to someone. The table settled back down and they watched as the Jazz band began to play.

The evening continued in a relaxed and entertaining manor. Every now and then people would approach Sam, telling him how happy they were that he was back in Ireland, wanting to arrange a meeting in the future. Cathy marvelled at how casual he was with these people. It appeared he really had been one of the jet-setters back in the day. She looked at him as he stood chatting to an elderly couple who had money dripping out of their pores. Did he miss the high life?

He returned to his seat and rested an arm along the back of her chair, his fingers brushing her shoulder. Byron smiled over, raising a questioning eyebrow to ask if she was okay. Cathy nodded. She was already grinning like a Cheshire cat, so she reckoned Byron knew the rest.

"Come," Jean Luc said, standing and extending a hand to Annabel when she returned to the table, "let us dance."

Annabel hooked a hand through his proffered arm and followed him to the dance floor. Bryon and Cathy watched as they swayed to the sensual music, letting the rhythm set their pace.

"That's more than a casual fling," Cathy said. "She's totally captivated by him."

"I know." Byron nodded in agreement. "The way he said, *'Come, let us dance'*, and she followed him like a puppy dog,"

"I thought she'd would punch anyone who tried to order her around," Tom said, joining in the conversation.

"She normally would. That's why we're saying she must be more serious about him than she's letting on. Keep up, Tom," Byron snapped. "Seriously, why do men never understand these things?"

Cathy watched Annabel and Jean Luc. "I wonder will it last past the flirty-sexy stage and actually go long-term for her." Annabel didn't do long-term with anything, apart from her career. It was a real eye-opener for her friends to see her showing so much interest in one man, even hanging on his every word.

"As long as she's happy," Sam said, rubbing a thumb along Cathy's bare shoulder.

Tom stood and offered a hand to Byron, "Come, let us dance."

"Not quite the romantic French invitation that Annabel got, but, eh, who cares?" She smiled at Tom, his earlier stupidity forgiven.

"Let's go," Sam said, pulling Cathy to her feet and leading her to the dance floor.

"Oh, you old romantic." She nudged him with her shoulder, delighted he wasn't one of those men afraid to dance in public.

They spent the rest of the evening enjoying the music, dancing and drinking until Cathy's feet could take no more. At 2am, Sam rang for taxis to take them all home.

Cathy kissed Byron and Tom goodbye, then hobbled out to the front entrance. Annabel and Jean Luc were staying at the hotel and had already called it a night. Sam helped her into the taxi, then pulled her feet onto his lap and started rubbing her toes.

"That was a good night," he said, sliding a careful hand over her ankle, massaging the feeling back into her legs.

"If you think part one was good, wait 'til you see what I have planned for the second half." She ran her tongue over her parted lips, giving him an idea of what was to come. He raised an eyebrow and told the taxi man to step on it.

22nd September

Sunday

Becky had the children up, dressed, fed, and watered by the time Sam brought Cathy home.

"Thanks, Beck," Cathy said after she hugged the children hello. "I don't think I'm up for much today."

"A good night, so?" Becky winked at Sam.

Cathy nodded and groaned into her coffee cup. Her head pounded, her throat was like sandpaper, and all the muscles in her legs ached like she had run 10k. "I think I'm getting the flu."

"The flu? You feckin' chancer. How much wine did you have last night? Enough to float a small village, I'll bet."

Cathy refilled her mug with more strong coffee. "A bit."

Becky laughed. "Roughly translated, that means a bottle or two of wine and possibly a few shorts to mix it all up."

"Then there was the dancing," Sam said. "Don't forget the dancing. Maybe that's the reason for your legs being like blocks of cement today."

Cathy squinted at them both, willing them to go away and leave her alone.

Mark, Becky's boyfriend, came in from the garden where he was playing with the children. "It's a real cracker of a day out there. You should come out, make the most of it." He wiped the sweat from his face with some kitchen towel, then let his floppy fringe fall back into his eyes.

"We should have a BBQ," Becky said. "Better not to waste this fine weather. We might not get another day like this." She got a sheet of paper and started a shopping list, to which Sam offered to go and buy.

Cathy sipped her coffee. Burgers and sausages. Just what the doctor ordered.

*

Sam and Mark fought over who got to cook on the BBQ, while the girls stretched out on two sun loungers, letting the hot Indian-summer rays toast their skin. Mark lost the battle of the grill, so instead turned his attention to blowing up a paddling pool for the children to splash around in and keep cool.

Becky hitched her shorts higher, exposing as much skin as she could without being indecent. Cathy knew that only for Sam being here, she'd be stripped down to her bra and knickers, not giving a hoot what the neighbours or anyone else thought. She was grateful, for decency's sake, that her sister seemed to care what Sam thought of her.

Sam cooked burgers and steak on the grill, resting them just enough to let the juices flow and the marinade seasoning do its job. Several cold bottles of beer went down well, lifting Cathy's hangover to a level where she could enjoy the fine weather. She checked on the children and relaxed into the sun lounger.

"I love these Indian-summer days," Becky said, lashing on more factor-20. "It's even better when you can spend them outside in the fresh air, instead of stuck in a musty old lecture theatre or classroom."

"What are you studying?" Sam asked, finishing off a plateful of steak and salad.

Becky rolled her eyes. "Child psychology. I'm back in tomorrow, but I don't know if it's really me, to be honest. There are a lot of difficult emotions involved. Just reading about some of the stuff you might need to deal with is pretty rough. It brings me down sometimes."

"Understandable," he said. "Sounds like a lot of deep, meaningful study is involved."

"Yeah, it's tough sometimes. Anyway, I'm thinking of changing and doing something completely different. Something more suited to my personality and expertise."

"Like what?" Cathy asked, lifting her sunglasses onto her head. "What are you talking about? I thought you loved college? What will you do if you give it up?"

"I'm not sure. I didn't really give the last year my full attention. To be honest, I shouldn't have done the course, but they make you choose when you're only seventeen. How the hell was I supposed to know what child psychology was all about? They should put a warning on those CAO forms." She shook her head and sighed. "Anyway, I've been offered a job if I do decide to chuck the books."

"What's the job?" Sam asked. "Snake charmer? Tattooist?"

"Ha, ha, very funny, Sam. Well, if you really want to know, there's this band I know. They're doing really well around the Dublin pubs and clubs, and they're looking for, like, a tour manager."

Cathy's jaw dropped. "A tour manager? What the hell does that mean? What would you be doing? This'd better be a wind-up, Becky."

"It's just an idea. Something I'm rolling around in my head. Another path my life might take. And, anyway, nothing's finalised yet."

Cathy sat up in the lounger. "Who is this band? Are they any good?"

"They're good, really good," Mark said. "I've heard them play a few times."

"They're called the Screaming Dolphins," Becky announced. "They play in college every couple of months. That's where I met them."

"This all sounds a bit farfetched," Cathy said. "The Screaming Dolphins? Are you serious?"

Before Becky could answer, Sam said he'd heard of the band and that they were really good, and going places fast. Becky winked at him, her relief at his intervention obvious.

"Look, Cathy, nothing's decided yet. They have a string of gigs lined up for November, and they need someone to organise the travel and B&B, and stuff. It's no biggie."

"It's a biggie if you're thinking of dropping out of college for it. Mum will do her nut. Do you realise that?" Maybe playing the disappointed-mammy card might scare some sense into her.

"Mum knows all about it." Becky puffed her chest out. "She knows I'm not happy with the course. It was her told me to check it all out, and if it seemed kosher, then to go for it. She said it would be a great experience."

Cathy was stunned. Where were the strict pro-education parents she knew and loved? And where did her mother learn to use the word 'Kosher'? She was catholic, for God's sake. How had they not blown a gasket when Becky announced she was dropping out to run off to become a groupie? They'd almost needed a triple by-pass when she'd told them she was pregnant at nineteen, and another tankful of oxygen when she'd announced it was twins.

"I think we played a venue with them last year," Sam said, filling the deafening silence. "Did they get picked up by a label recently?"

"That's right," Becky answered, giving Sam another grateful smile, "a small indie company are giving them a shot. They lined up this mini-tour, all over the country. It's mostly pubs and clubs, but they've already got a pretty secure following, and it's only a matter of time before they go big. I'm sure of it."

"And what do you think about all this?" Cathy asked Mark, waving a hand around in frustration.

"It's the bomb, so it is," Mark said, bouncing up and down on his chair like he was sitting on a space hopper. "Becks is miserable doing that course. It's really bringing her down. This is an awesome chance to do something different with her life, to get in on something at ground level and work up to the top."

Cathy looked at the three of them. How come none of these guys can see where I'm coming from? "Beck, you'll be away all the time. Have you thought about that?"

"D'oh, what do you take me for? Of course I've thought about it. Stop trying to find something wrong with this, Cathy. It's a great opportunity. There isn't anywhere in Ireland more than a three-hour drive from Dublin. If something goes wrong, or I get stuck somewhere, it's not Outer Mongolia I'm going to. I can easily hop on a bus, or something, and get home. And Mark said he'll come and stay with me on his days off from work and college, and the guys in the band are really nice and down to earth. There's even a girl in the band. Mandy."

"Does no one else find this all a bit sudden?" Cathy rubbed her eyes, trying to focus on her point. "One minute you're living at home with Mum and Dad, going to college, living the high life, and the next you want to travel the country with some band in the back of a van, living out of a suitcase. I just don't see it, Beck, it's not you."

Becky sat up straight and gave Cathy her most serious, responsible look. "Cathy, I'm nineteen. I need some fun, some adventure, and some God-damn rock and roll in my life. Would you be so dead set against it if I told you I was going to Australia for a year?"

Cathy thought about that, suspecting she was beaten. "No, I suppose not, but Australia is different. I'm not sure how, but it just is."

"This gig is a four-week tour. It might turn into nothing, but then again, it could be the start of something big. Huge. We'll know by Christmas how things have worked out, and if there's any chance of a future for the band. It's not the end of the world, Cathy. If it doesn't work out, I can't say I didn't try, right?"

"Right," said Sam, high-fiving her.

Cathy got up, aware of how excited Sam seemed about the whole thing. Everyone was, except her. She knew that Becky's decision wouldn't be made by anyone but Becky. It couldn't be denied that her little sister had a good head on her shoulders, and it was seldom she landed herself in situations she couldn't handle. Becky was street smart.

She hugged her. "I hope it works out for you so, if you decide to go ahead with it. But you know I'm just a phone call away if anything goes wrong. If you need anything, just ring, okay?"

"Okay, Sis, thanks. I know you're concerned for me, but I'm well able to look after myself."

"Awesome," Mark said, holding up his bottle of beer. "Arsehole of nowhere, here we come." He clinked bottle necks with Sam and continued to bounce on his chair like an excited child.

Becky laughed, telling him to calm down or she'd ban him from coming to any of the gigs. Sam promised to keep an eye on the Dublin dates and would try to make it to one of the venues, even if he had to drag Cathy along.

They discussed the ins and outs of what Becky might have to do in her new job. Even though Cathy wasn't happy about Becky giving up college, inside she envied her the freedom to be able to do such a thing. Becky didn't have a care in the world, or responsibilities, except herself and not to make a holy show of her parents. She had no serious financial debt or worries, and if this job worked out and the band did well, she might get to travel the world, all expenses paid, doing and seeing the things Cathy could only dream about.

Cathy felt a little sad for the time she'd spent in her early twenties changing nappies and raising two babies. Who was she to tell Becky she was making a mistake by giving up college? Okay, so she'd got pregnant at nineteen, but she'd also tried to do the right thing by getting married, buying a house, and endeavouring to live happily-ever-after with her childhood sweetheart. That didn't work out too well.

She had to admit that she was jealous of her sister. Even though she couldn't imagine for even one second not having her children, she wondered what her life would have been like if she'd not got pregnant so young. Would she have travelled? Australia or Canada perhaps? Would college have been an option for her, spending her summers in America on a J1 visa, working in bars and motels? Would she have enjoyed all the summer festivals she'd missed out on? Oxygen and Electric Picnic were two she would love to go to. Maybe she would have taken long weekends away and travelled around Europe on a Usit Railcard, exploring beer festivals and cultural sites in a foreign language.

Would she have ended up with Gary had it not been for the children being born? She doubted it. That heartache was always going to happen, whether she'd had the children or not. Once a cheating rat, always a cheating rat. Having the children just made it that bit more difficult to deal with, sad as it was to think that.

She realised she was imagining a life she would never have, a life that was never to be. Her chosen road had taken her in another direction, and this was where she was now. Would she have been any happier had things been different? Hard to know. She could do without the crippling mortgage and the fact she would be divorced before the age of thirty, but as for the other stuff, who could tell. One thing she did know for certain was that she would not change a single second of the time she had with her children, nor would she regret for a moment ever having them. They were a blessing; her whole life, and now Sam was in her life too. It was all looking good. She was happy now, and that's all that mattered.

She glanced at her phone when it pinged, alerting her to a new message.

"Oh, for fuck's sake, this is all I need," she said, rubbing a hand across her face as she read a text from Gary.

Sorry won't be able to take kids tomorrow. Will try organise something next week. G

Sam raised an eyebrow, but Cathy shook her head, indicating that it was nothing and she would tell him later.

She sent off a 'don't mess with me' reply to her ex-husband: *Stop the crap Gary. It's your day tomorrow. Sort something out. No excuses.*

She drained the beer in her bottle, then lay back on the sun lounger feeling like she'd won at least one argument that day.

23ʳᵈ September

Monday

A beam of sunlight crept under a set of ill-fitting bedroom curtains. Sinead twitched as the light hit her face. The aroma of coffee tickled her senses and dragged her back into the land of the living. She sat up in the bed and looked around. The reason for her nakedness sat on the side of the bed.

Oh God, is this the guy I ended up with last night? Regret and disgust flew through her as she pulled the duvet over her chest.

"Wakey, wakey, sleeping beauty," he said, leaning over and whispering in her ear, "I've got coffee."

Sinead groaned, trying to formulate an escape plan. "What time is it?"

"Its half-eleven. I have to go out soon…to collect my kids from school. They're staying with me tonight."

She grimaced at the toast and the cheap instant coffee he handed her, then realised it was probably the best she would get until she escaped. The coffee was way too weak. She closed her eyes and tried to recall how she'd ended up in this man's bed.

At first her recollections were vague, but then she remembered going to Sam's pub yesterday to speak to him. He wasn't there, but she started chatting with the cute barman she'd met last week. Gary. She'd sat at the bar while he'd bought her drink after drink. He'd spouted an unbelievable amount of charm and tacky lines, but somehow she'd felt a huge turn on at the idea of bedding this pauper. It was like a living fantasy. Never before had she been with a working-class man. A bit of rough and tumble was just what she needed, until she could get Sam back onside, of course. It was surprising, she had to admit, that the sex was good.

Gary had lived up to the cheesy one-liners he'd used to get her attention. With more than half a bottle of free vodka flowing through her veins, Sinead was easy when he'd suggested she spend the night with him. He knew his way around a woman's body, that's for sure, demonstrating years of practice on her, making her orgasm multiple times by his touch alone. She didn't know if it was Gary, the vodka, or being in such a different environment that gave her the thrill, but one thing was for sure, it had been one good night of satisfying stress-releasing sex.

Last night had fulfilled her fantasy; the princess and the frog, but, somehow, she didn't think Gary was the type of frog who would turn into Prince Charming after a snog. She knew his type. He'd always be a slimy toad. Now she had to get herself out of here.

She dressed as fast as she could, annoyed that she'd have to make the walk of shame in her new Karen Millen dress. Where the hell was she, anyway? Bray? She couldn't quite recall where Gary had taken her.

He offered to drop her to the Dart station. She refused, scowling at him as she rang a pre-set number.

"Yes, a taxi asap." She looked around the room, almost afraid to breathe. Her disgust that Gary was not willing to drive her home was evident, but she didn't care. This guy actually had the gall to think she would ever step foot onto public transport. The cheek.

*

Gary needed to think about his next move. He knew he'd hit the jackpot with this one. She was a cracker. Maybe a bit of a snob, but still a cracker. They'd had a good laugh in the pub last night, and when he'd laid it on thick he'd gotten her into the sack without a problem.

This was a good move for him. Possible leverage with both Sam and Cathy if he played his cards right. Also, this chick was minted. She could be the answer to all his problems. All he needed to do was keep her onside and not fuck things up like he usually did.

He cleaned the kitchen while he thought of a way to make sure Sinead would see him again. Okay, he'd messed up by suggesting she get the train home. He should've seen that coming. Damn it, no way did a woman like that do the walk of shame on the Dart or bus. He'd offer to pay for her taxi. That would impress her.

She appeared in the kitchen doorway, holding the half-empty mug and plate of uneaten toast. Gary took a bite from the cold toast before throwing the rest in the bin. He stood by the sink, casual, not knowing if anything more intimate would be welcome.

"I'd like to see you again," he said, but knew straight away from the look of annoyance on her face that his lines weren't going to work on her now she was sober.

"Look," she said after a long silence, "I had fun, but I have to go." She laughed, more to herself than him. "I haven't heard so many cheap, cheesy lines coming from one person for a long time. I thought most of them had lived and died back in the 80s."

Gary grinned, mistaking her sarcasm for a compliment. Maybe there might still be a chance. "I'll see you around so, in the pub, maybe?"

She shrugged. "Maybe. I have to call back in to talk to Sam. I might see you there."

"Look, why don't you give me your number and we'll arrange something sometime?"

Her nose scrunched up. "Eh, no, I don't think so."

"Just your number, Sinead. Stop being such a stuck-up bitch. You had a good time last night. I know you did. No way were you faking anything that happened in my bed. Not a chance." He saw the blush creep into her face and his confidence soared. The body never lied.

She flicked her hair back and stood taller. Gary wondered if she was picturing them in the throes of the nasty business. She took a step towards him, but stopped short of actual contact, then reached behind his back to the kitchen counter and retrieved her handbag from the place she'd left it last night.

After rummaging through it, she produced a small black business card and handed it to him. "There's my number. But don't call me. I'll call you. Oh, and do you have Sam's number, by any chance?"

"Sure."

He saved her number into his phone, then sent her a business card with Sam's.

Her phone beeped. "There's my taxi."

Gary watched as she collected her coat and made her way to the door.

"So, I'll see you around sometime," she said, giving him a brief peck on the cheek.

"Yeah, give me a call when you want to hook up."

And then she was gone.

*

In the taxi, Sinead closed her eyes while she tried to sort out how to move things forward. She felt a bit sorry for Gary and his puppy-dog eyes searching her face for a hint she might be interested in him, but she wasn't sure if she'd ever go for the Princess and the Frog fantasy again. If she did, she vowed the rendezvous would take place in a hotel suite the next time. Never again would she set foot in his dingy little flat. She didn't care how broke he was. He didn't even have a *nespresso* machine, for God's sake.

Turning her mind to another issue, she smiled to herself, self-satisfied that at least one good thing had come out of her night with barman. She now had Sam's phone number.

Now that she had direct contact she could avoid the pub, avoid Gary, and work on Sam until he gave her what she wanted.

She wanted Sam back in her life more than she could admit. His connections were too good to be ignored. She needed a second crack at the whip, aware of the years ticking by and that time was running out for her to bag an eligible bachelor. Her looks would soon fade. To avoid being left on the shelf, God knows what sort of middle-aged wombat she would have to settle for.

Meeting Sam in Dundrum had really shaken her up. Seeing him with that other woman and her two little brats had left her seeing red. Sam belonged by her side, and come hell or high water that is where she would have him. After all, she thought, blood *is* thicker than water.

As the taxi sped towards Donnybrook, her mood lifted as she felt all the pieces of her plan falling into place.

24ᵗʰ September

Tuesday

Sam had just hung up from talking to Cathy when his phone rang again. He didn't usually answer withheld numbers, but this time he did without thinking. Cathy had him distracted with the things she'd done to him last night, and what she was going to do tomorrow when she saw him again. His growing erection disappeared the instant he heard the voice on his phone.

"Sam? Hi. It's Sinead."

"Sinead? Where did you get this number?" He gritted his teeth to stop him from shouting.

"Not important. Now, Sam, I just need to set a date with you to discuss something rather urgent. Does tomorrow night suit?"

"Sinead, whatever it is you need to say to me, say it now. For Christ's sake, I'm listening. I've no interest in meeting with you. Say what you have to say, then leave me alone."

She was pissing him off with all this crap. He regretted the day they'd bumped into her in Dundrum. He should've ignored her, not given her the time of day. Perhaps if he had, she wouldn't be harassing him like this.

"Sam. I need to meet with you in person. I have something to say. It's quite personal, and believe me, you will thank me for insisting on a meeting."

He thought for a moment. The only reason she could want to meet him was to try to get back with him. Did she think a fancy dinner, with all the good food and wine that entailed, was going to make him want to leave Cathy and declare undying love for her, his ex? She needs her head examined.

Although, if meeting in person and letting her have her say was the only way to get rid of her, maybe that's what he'd have to do. He'd need to have his wits about him, that's for sure. No way could he let that conniving cow get under his skin with her sob stories about regrets and all that was lost.

He agreed to meet her for dinner the following evening. The sooner he got her sorted out, the sooner she'd be gone from his life and he could concentrate on moving forward with Cathy.

"I'll book Shanahans for seven," she said. "I'll reserve a private table at the back so we can avoid any media attention."

"Make it eight. I'm working late tomorrow. I won't make it before then."

"Okay, eight it is. Will you come and collect me?"

Her voice had his teeth on edge. "Don't push your luck, Sinead. This is not a date. I'll meet you there at eight o'clock. Oh, and, Sinead, I'm only meeting you because of your insistence that there's something you need to say. Once it's said, that's it. No more. I won't want to see you or have anything to do with you again." He figured being so blunt was the only way to deal with her.

"We'll see," she said, her voice lighter than earlier. "See you tomorrow." Then she hung up.

Sam's mood had swung from horny and wanting, to annoyed and frustrated. How could one woman, Cathy, give him so much pleasure and make him want to run barefoot, like a happy sap, through a field of wild daisy's, while the other, Sinead, made him want to poke his eyes out with a fork to let the pressure inside his head escape?

Such different women. He'd had intimate relationships with both of them, and he knew who he wanted to continue it with. Cathy. It would always be Cathy. His mind drifted back to last night again. Then he realised he wouldn't be able to see her tomorrow night, as arranged. He growled through gritted teeth. Feck it, he'd just have to make it his business to finish work at a reasonable hour tonight and drive to Wicklow to see her.

He spied Gary skulking outside his office door. Whatever he wanted would have to wait. There was too much to do, and he didn't feel like dealing with that asshole today.

"I haven't time today," he shouted when Gary knocked at his door five minutes later.

"Well, it's about my extra shifts and paying back the money I owe," Gary said, a leering smirk turning one side of his mouth up. "If you're not interested…"

Sam watched him turn to leave. "Wait. Look, I'm up to my eyes today sorting out this messed-up delivery. I'll be leaving here in about an hour, so if it can wait until tomorrow, we'll talk then."

Sam had to give him a chance. Even though he didn't like the bollox, he was at least making an effort to sort himself out.

"I'm not in here tomorrow. I'm at the other pub doing an extra shift. I'll be back for the early on Thursday, though, so will I'll catch you then?"

"Okay, Thursday morning. Come and find me before it gets busy. Well sort things out then."

Sam sighed as Gary walked out of the office. He sent Cathy a text letting her know he'd be down to her tonight, and then got back to work, sorting out the mystery of the missing beer kegs.

25th September

Wednesday

Cathy rang Sam. She really wasn't happy about him meeting his ex-girlfriend for dinner in one of Dublin's poshest restaurants, even though he'd told her a million times it wasn't a date. As far as he could see it was the only way of getting Sinead to say whatever was so important, then leaving him alone.

"After tomorrow," he'd said, "she can crawl back into whatever sap's bed she's been warming for the past eight years."

Thinking about it, she could see where he was coming from. If he gave Sinead what she wanted then there'd be no excuse to contact him again. He'd let her know once and for all that he wasn't interested and she'd have to leave him alone.

Cathy was still nervous, though. What if Sinead turned on the charm and came at Sam with all guns blazing? Would he be able to resist? How could he compare her to the beautiful Sinead?

"Trust me," Sam had said, "nothing is ever going to happen with me and Sinead. This time tomorrow night she'll be well and truly out of our lives. I'll make sure of it."

Now the panic rose in her chest as she spoke on the phone to Sam in his car. "Are you there yet?"

"Just coming around the green," he answered. "Don't worry, babe, I'll get this mad yoke to go away, if it's the last thing I do."

"Okay. Good. Sorry, Sam, I'm just being stupid." She wished she didn't feel like a bunny boiler stalking her prey. "I'll let you go and get it over with."

"Here I go. Into the lion's den," he joked, though she knew he didn't like this any more than she did.

"I love you, Sam," she said, her voice quiet, hoping he would remember that, no matter what Sinead had to say.

"I love you, too. I'll ring you later, okay?"

"Okay, bye." She hung up.

*

Sam took a deep breath then climbed the three steps to the entrance of the exclusive eatery. "Here goes nothing," he whispered to himself as he opened the door, praying that this would be quick and painless.

The maître D showed him to the table where Sinead was already sitting, then took his drink order.

"Mineral water, please," Sam said, intent on staying on the dry. It was important that he keep his wits about him to fend off any sneaky advances Sinead might make. He wasn't being big-headed, but he knew what she was like. She was so insistent on them meeting alone together, he knew she had something up her sleeve.

Sinead looked stunning. Her dark, luscious hair was pulled high on her head in a messy bun, and her face was almost glowing. She made jeans, t-shirt, and a blazer look like something that had come off the catwalk. But it was more than that; she had a presence about her, like she belonged here. She looked comfortable with her surroundings, expecting nothing but the best.

But she was nervous. Sam could tell. She fidgeted with the silverware while she made small talk as they waited on their food, telling him about people and problems that were of no interest to him. He could do without all this. The last thing he needed was to hear the gossip-laden woes of people he once knew but now had no connection with.

They ate their starters in silence. The sautéed garlic shrimp was delicious, but he couldn't enjoy it waiting for Sinead to drop her bombshell. And why was she drinking so much? Glass after glass of wine disappeared until she seemed to have acquired enough Dutch-courage to allow her to speak frankly.

"Did you ever love me, Sam?"

Her left-field question startled him. He stared at her, put down his fork, giving her his full attention. "Yes, Sinead. I did. I loved you very much. But things changed. You. I did, too, but not enough, and so our lives went in different directions.

"Would it have worked out for us if…? Well, you know, if I hadn't got pregnant?"

"I don't think so," he answered, but seeing a flash of hurt on her face, he added, "It was good when it was good, Sinead, but it was never going to last." He paused a second, then continued, wanting to explain himself a bit better. "You were my first real, serious girlfriend. I don't know about you, but I was so naive. Way too young to be tied into that kind of relationship, the kind that is meant to be forever. When things got serious, and then the pregnancy, I panicked."

"But is that not what you're planning on doing now with your current squeeze?"

Her bitterness didn't surprise him, but he couldn't let her away with it. "Don't call her that. Her name is Cathy, and not that it's any of your damn business but, yes, that is where I hope we're is going."

He'd hit a nerve, but he could also see where she was coming from. What made Cathy so special? Why did he want to set up happy families with her and the twins? Why hadn't he wanted that with Sinead? For them to have a child of their own? His own. Cathy's face lingered in his mind, and he knew there was good reason for that. He didn't want to hurt Sinead by being blunt with his answers, but at this stage, she was grating on him.

Sinead coughed into her hand. "Cathy looks quite young. What makes you think she's ready to settle down into a committed relationship? Because it's what you desire doesn't mean she has to want it, too. You just admitted you weren't ready at that age. Why are you so sure it will work out with you and her now?"

Sam's eyes nearly popped at the neck of Sinead. How dare she ask him such personal questions about his life. He slowed his breathing, gritting his teeth to reign in his temper. "Watch it, Sinead. You're walking on thin ice. Nothing that happens between me and anyone else is any of your fucking business."

He ate faster to make this godforsaken dinner finish sooner, continuing to watch as Sinead drained another glass of wine. Time to put her straight once and for all, before she got too drunk to remember anything he said.

"Sinead, if the only reason you asked me here tonight is to quiz me about my long-term plans with Cathy, then you're wasting your time. I have no interest or intention of discussing that or any other issue with you. You need to forget my name. Forget my number. After tonight, I don't want to see you again. Not socially, not in the pub, nowhere. Do you understand?"

He forced the words out in a clear, strong voice, ensuring his point got across. "It's never going to happen between us. It's over. We are well and truly over."

Sinead looked at him, her face showing a cocktail of emotions all at once: hurt, anger, regret, all mixed with tears rolling down her cheeks.

What the fuck was she crying for? Sam's anger was barely contained. She must be deluded if she believed they had a future together.

"That's the thing, Sam. Our relationship may be over, but we will always have one thing in common."

Sam stared back at her. Is this the wine talking, or has she really lost the plot? "What, Sinead? What is it you think we will always have in common?" He wished this conversation was over and he could get the hell away from her.

Sinead's eyes were full of tears, with several sliding down her face before she wiped them away. "We will always have one thing," she said, her voice shaking with emotion.

"For fuck's sake, Sinead, just spit it out. What is it?"

"Our daughter."

Sam nearly choked as a numbing wave flushed through him. "What?"

"I thought you would like to know, Sam, that we have a daughter."

26th September

Thursday

Cathy checked her phone for the fiftieth time. Still nothing. No call, no text, no Facebook update. Where the hell was Sam, and why hadn't he contacted her? It was well after 3pm and she'd heard nothing since before he went to dinner the previous night. She was rattled, and by now she expected the worst. Why had he his mobile phone switched off? All she could do was leave a couple of voice messages asking him to ring her back. Nothing. The silence was deafening, and now her nerves were frayed. She rang Byron for advice.

"What's up, babe?" Byron said.

"I'm having a meltdown, By. Sam hasn't phoned all day and I can't get through to him and his phone is off, no text, no message, nothing, and I'm freaking out."

"He hasn't phoned you since last night? The bastard!" Byron chuckled, but the ensuing silence took all the mirth out of the moment. "I'm sorry, honey, what's going on?"

Tears brimmed in Cathy's eyes. "He met Sinead last night and now he's disappeared."

"Okay, okay, let's think about this rationally. So he went to meet the ex last night? Were you talking to him beforehand?"

"Yes, just before he met her."

"And how did he sound?"

"He was pissed at having to go and meet her in the first place. He didn't want to, but thought it might be the only way of getting her to leave him alone."

"Okay, so it looks like he was taking no interest or pleasure out of meeting this one. Right?"

"Yeah, I suppose," Cathy agreed, shaking her head and sighing.

"So, maybe, just maybe, his phone simply ran out of battery and he forgot to charge it when he got home. Perhaps he doesn't have a spare charger in work."

Cathy sobbed into the phone. "He's not in work today. I rang earlier and Gary said he didn't turn up, no phone call or anything."

"Well, perhaps he's sick then. Come on, Cathy, you're letting your imagination run amuck. Sam isn't Gary. Remember that."

"I know, By, but I'm still sick in my stomach that he hasn't contacted me."

"I understand, honey, but he's probably sick in bed with a migraine or something. That's it. He's forgotten to charge his phone and is out for the count on Migraleve and doesn't even know what day it is."

"You think?" Cathy's voice wobbled. Her nose was blocked and her vision blurred with welling tears. She took a deep breath. Maybe it could all be explained away like that. "He does suffer from migraines, all right. He said it drives him to bed sometimes. The stress of meeting that bitch probably brought one on."

Relief came, but she was annoyed for not thinking of it sooner. Of course he was sick, and his phone battery must be dead. True to form, she'd jumped right to the wrong conclusion, nearly giving herself a stroke in the process.

"Thanks, By," she said, wiping her eyes on her sleeve. "Thanks for talking me down. I was spinning out of control there."

"I know," Byron said, "and I know you, always assuming the worst. You need to calm down, girl, and trust your man. Sam is one of the good ones. Maybe a bit simple for forgetting to charge his phone, but who's perfect, eh?"

Byron's wit lightened the mood and after a few more minutes of reassurance, Cathy had calmed down and was feeling better. She said goodbye, promising to let her know what happened.

As soon as she ended her call, she checked her phone again: voicemail, text, email, and Facebook, still nothing. Having a grip on her emotions now, she felt foolish for freaking out. If he didn't contact her by tonight, she'd go and do something about it.

*

Byron had been right. Sam was sick. He'd been vomiting all night. Every time he relived what Sinead had told him, his stomach heaved and bile flushed into his mouth. Gone were the starters and main course. All that remained was green stomach acid that stung every time he retched into the toilet.

Bryon was also right about his phone. The battery was dead, but Sam didn't want to recharge it. A phone with battery life meant contact with the outside world. He couldn't face that yet. What he needed was time on his own, time to think, time to uncurl the gripping fingers that threatened to squeeze his heart so tight it would burst.

Poor Cathy. He wanted her there. Needed her, but he also needed to straighten this out at least a fraction before he could get her involved. It was torture not being able to ring her, or talk to her. He knew it wouldn't be fair to land this on her when he hadn't even figured it out himself. If she was here to hold him, tell him everything would be okay, things might be better, but he couldn't have that. He wanted her to sympathise with him about the years he'd lost out on with his own flesh and blood, but he couldn't. There was no doubt she'd be as furious at Sinead as he was for keeping something so huge from him all these years, but he couldn't let her. He couldn't do it to her, because none of this was her fault.

Cathy had her own problems to deal with and she didn't need this kind of twisted shit landed on her doorstep. How could he let her get involved in all this? There was too much wrong with the whole thing, it would take years to pick through. All the emotions and regrets, with so many what-ifs. It was going to have a huge impact on his life, and he couldn't let Cathy's life get bogged down with it.

He charged his phone and at 10pm switched it on to send a text to Cathy.

Cathy, we need to talk. Can we meet tomorrow? 9.30 in the café at Avoca Handweavers. Ok with you? I miss you, see you tomorrow. Sam.

He switched his phone off again, afraid Cathy would ring. If he spoke to her now he would make no sense. He could see himself begging her to stay with him and take on this life-changing torment. But that's not going to happen. This is my problem, I have to deal with it. This will not ruin Cathy's life. I fucked up. Sinead screwed me over, but it's up to me to stand up and be responsible now.

He cried for the first time all day as total exhaustion washed over him. Tears ran for the child he'd just gained, but mostly for the woman he was about to lose. He would never forgive Sinead for what she'd done, because losing Cathy would be the biggest regret of his life.

27th September

Friday

With the kids dropped off at school, Cathy drove north along the N11 towards the tiny, gateway village of Kilmacanouge. Tension had her temples pulled tight while her stomach flipped back and forth in a panicked shuffle. It reminded her of being summoned to the head-nun's office in school, not quite sure what she'd done wrong, but knowing it wouldn't turn out good.

She hadn't slept last night and no amount of make-up could conceal her swollen eyes or the underlying bags. Her hair was pulled back into a severe ponytail, giving her a gaunt look that she could do without. She wasn't at her best. However, if her suspicions about Sam having bad news for her were correct, then she couldn't care less what she looked like. Her saggy, grey track bottoms and sweater were comfortable and that's what she needed right now - comfort.

Sam was already waiting in the car park when she arrived. He approached while she parked her car, then grabbed her into a tight hug when she got out.

"Cathy," was all he said as their mouths connected.

She was caught off guard by the sheer emotion in his voice as he uttered that single word. He clung to her like he'd just emerged from the jungle, seeing sunlight for the first time in ages. His kiss was deep and needy, his body almost crushing her bones as he pressed her back against her car.

"Cathy," he said again, taking her face between his hands and studying it like a precious Fabergé egg. He shook his head, pain coursing through his eyes.

She guessed by the look of him that he hadn't slept the previous night, either, or the one before that. He was dressed in jeans and a shirt, but two days of stubble scratched at his face and his eyes were bloodshot. Like a hangover from hell. He looked rough, but the real damage was evident in his eyes. Her heart skipped when she saw so many emotions looking back at her, and she knew all this was the result of whatever had happened at dinner the other night.

She pulled back and straightened herself, took a deep breath, then looked Sam straight in the eyes. "Sam. Tell me the truth. What happened between you and Sinead?" Did you sleep with Sinead?"

His eyes closed and she thought she had her answer. She backed away, but he reached to stop her, his grip soft but firm as he held her arms by her sides.

"Do you trust me, Cathy?"

She pushed a sob back. "Yes."

"I didn't sleep with Sinead, I promise you." He looked so sad. "Please trust me."

"I'm sick to my stomach here, Sam. Obviously there's something going on. What else am I supposed to think? No contact yesterday, your phone switched off, you don't turn up for work, and then to top it all, the 'we need to talk' text last night.

I'm not a mind reader, Sam. Your signals are all over the shop. What else am I supposed to think?"

"I didn't sleep with her, Cathy," he almost roared, frustration getting the better of him. "I told you I wouldn't and you have to trust me." He took a deep breath. "Will you please, just for one moment, stop thinking that she's better than you in any way? I'm not interested in her, never will be. Jesus, you're as hard to convince as she is."

He shook his head, his anger and frustration evident in his tense posture and reddened face.

"Well, what is it then?" She held firm, her chin up, her body ready for the blow. "If you didn't sleep with her, what happened that had you out of contact yesterday and looking like shit today?"

Sam looked away, one hand covering his brow as he exhaled a long sigh through puffed cheeks. He didn't turn back to her. "Sinead told me something the other night. Something she should've told me a long time ago."

Cathy's heart pounded. "What?"

He turned to her, his dark eyes pained but unwavering. "She didn't have a miscarriage, nor did she have an abortion." He held both sides of his face, his eyes blazing anguish. "She had the baby, Cathy. I…have a daughter."

Cathy's hands flew to her mouth. My God. She searched his face. Could it be true? His whole body shook with the depth of his turmoil: confusion, heartache, anger.

"But how? When?" It was all she could say.

Sam groaned through another long exhalation and took her by the hand. "It's a long story. Come on." He led her towards the cafe, looking for a quiet place to continue.

They found an empty table in the corner of the outside terrace. Sam got two mugs of strong black coffee and two scones. Cathy didn't feel like eating, but needed something to keep her hands busy. She was shaking like a leaf and clung to her mug, letting the strong sweet black liquid ease some of her shock.

"I take it this is all Sinead's doing?" she said, her voice shaking.

Sam tried to speak, and Cathy watched him as the words caught in his throat. "I've been over and over this in my head a million times." Then his head went down and his shoulders shook.

She leaned across the table. "Sam?"

He shook his head and covered his face with both hands, his whole body shaking as huge sobs racked him.

Cathy stood, her heart breaking. "Oh, Sam." But he brushed her hands away and almost growled as he sat up, jaw clenched, eyes shut tight against escaping tears. He took the deepest breath she'd ever seen anyone take and let it out in a slow, steady, exhalation.

When he looked at her, she noticed how he gripped the edge of the table, as if keeping hold of his raging emotions. "Sinead didn't lose the baby, or have an abortion. The plane ticket I found was due to her going to London to find out about DNA testing. She stayed with her cousin while she was there. When she came back and realised I still didn't want anything to do with her, she faked the miscarriage, letting me think the baby was gone."

"Oh, sweet Jesus. How could anyone do that?" Cathy felt helpless at his distress, but urged him to go on.

"She hid the pregnancy for the next few months, then after I left, she returned to England and had the baby there. She told everyone she'd signed up to do a modelling course, or something, No one suspected a thing."

"So where's the child now? Does Sinead even know anything about her?" She paused, aware of how sceptical she sounded. "Are you sure the baby was even yours, Sam? You said yourself that she played around while she was with you? Maybe her trap didn't work all those years ago, and now she's coming back for a second crack at the whip?"

"The child." He took another deep breath. "Sorcha. She's in London. She lives with Sinead's cousin who couldn't have a child herself and offered to adopt the baby when it was born. Sinead was a bit sketchy on the details, but by the sound of it, the one thing she didn't mess with was the DNA test. She had one done and it confirmed that I'm Sorcha's father."

Those words seemed to hit him hard. He rubbed his eyes and ran his fingers through his hair, then leaned his elbows on the table and stared at his open hands. "After that, nothing was done by the book. It looks like Sinead just left the baby there, returned home and got on with the rest of her life. She didn't have any interest in being a mother to her little girl."

Cathy shook her head. "You didn't have any interest in being a father, either, so you can't really criticise her for that." She loved Sam, but he'd been willing to turn his back on a child all those years ago as well, and that bothered her.

He bowed his head. "I know. It's tearing me apart thinking of what a heartless bitch she was, but really, I'm no better. I turned my back on Sinead and that innocent child." He looked off to his left. "It's hard to explain, but when I thought the baby didn't exist, I felt like maybe I'd dodged a bullet or something. Yeah, I was sad and felt guilty for the way I'd acted, but then it was over. Done with. Of course, I thought about it at times, but I didn't have to live with it."

314

Cathy could hear the droplets of guilt fall off every word he spoke. Her heart went out to him. "How do you know she's telling the truth?"

"I saw the DNA certificate on Wednesday night. There's no doubt about it, Sorcha is my daughter." He racked his hands through his hair again, then sat back to let Cathy digest the fallout from the bomb he'd just dropped.

He cradled his cup in his hands, looking into the steaming brew. "Now there's a part of me out there somewhere that I know nothing about. A child who was unwanted by both her father and her mother." He looked at her, the torment obvious in his eyes. "We're not talking about something that could have been any more, Cathy. This is a real-life little girl. A person. My daughter."

He scrubbed his hands over his head and face, perhaps trying to shake some of the tension lodged behind his eyes, the darkness in his expression mirroring the heavy cloudbanks building to the east. Cathy remained silent, stirring her coffee, her scone untouched. She didn't know what to say, didn't know how to feel. Her heart was breaking in so many ways she never knew possible. All she knew was that she bore an incredible sadness for Sam and what he was going through, and for his family and parents for missing out on so many wonderful years with their granddaughter.

As for Sinead, Cathy didn't have an ounce of sorrow for her. She didn't deserve sympathy from the devil himself, being as rotten to the core as she was. How could she do that to an innocent baby?

Abandoning her like that and forgetting she ever existed. How did she justify what she'd done to Sam? Okay, so Sam had rejected her and her pregnancy at the time, but for understandable reasons. He'd doubted the baby was even his. Now, it seemed Sinead had proof by way of a DNA certificate of Sam's paternity.

And what about the cousin in London? Cathy hoped with all her strength that this woman had loved and cared for Sorcha like she was her own. It must be excruciating to know you can't have a baby, that your body has failed you in the most feminine way. Being offered the chance to love and raise a child after all her personal heartache must have been like a ray of light breaking through a thunder cloud. Maybe this was fate's way of letting her be the mother she always wanted to be, even if the pages in her book were skewed and someone else's selfishness was the answer to her prayers.

There was one person Cathy couldn't think about just yet. Sorcha. It was too sad. She would need peace and quiet, with some time on her own, before she could even start to imagine her as a real life little girl. The child deserved the benefit of her full attention when she thought about her. The little mite was due that much at the very least.

There was no doubt Sam's head was like a volcano ready to erupt. But with all the complicated emotions, had he considered Sorcha and the consequences his actions had on her? Cathy didn't think so. Men seldom thought like that. They did the anger and hurt bit first, but it was only when that was squared away that they got down to the nitty-gritty. She supposed it could take a few days before he was ready to think about his daughter as a person.

As they sat there, nursing two cups of cold coffee, Cathy sensed a tormented anger pulsating from Sam. He was still caught up in the shocking deceit that had been inflicted on him nine years ago. Nothing else could be considered until he came to terms with that.

"What are you feeling, Sam? What can I do to help?"

He didn't answer, but it was obvious that he was struggling inside with something that had pain and despair rippling through every line on his face. He took her hand across the table and held on, as if for dear life, a lone tear leaving a trail down his cheek.

An awful fear rose into Cathy's throat and she had to swallow it back in order to speak. "Please, Sam, talk to me. Tell me what I can do for you."

He cleared his throat, wiping his face with the back of his hand. "I can't let you help me, Cathy."

She stared at him, unsure she'd heard him right. Why wouldn't he want her to help him? She tried to say it, but her throat was too choked up.

"I can't drag you into all of this. It's not your life, Cathy. It's mine. This is the result of decisions I made and things I did years ago, before I ever met you."

"Are you mad, Sam? I can't walk away, if that is what you're suggesting?"

"You have to, Cathy. I'm sorry, but you don't need this shit in your life. Look at the state of me." He gestured with both hands at himself. "Imagine what I'll be like from here on in. I've made it crystal clear to Sinead that this changes nothing between me and her. I need to find my daughter, but it's not because I want to play happy families with her mother. Sinead won't even tell me where in London her cousin, and my daughter are living. She thinks that by revealing this to me, it's going to make me run back to her and play happy families. She is never going to get what she's after. My ring on her finger. I'm only interested in the child, Cathy. She is my priority now. I have to make up for lost time."

Cathy couldn't stop the tears. Her heart felt like it was squeezing every drop of hope out of her. Why was he rejecting her? She'd done nothing but love him. Why didn't he want her? Why could he not let her help him?

She grabbed his hands, forcing him to look at her, to see her anguish. "Sam, please. I'm here to help you. You can't push me away. I won't let you. You need help and support."

Her sobs built as her heart threatened to explode, but she held them back, keeping them below the surface. "I'm not afraid of this, Sam. I love you, I love you so much. I need you to believe that. It's killing me to see you so messed up. Let me help you with this. We'll work it out together. Please, Sam, don't push me away."

318

She saw what she thought was a flicker of hope on his face, like he was trying to figure out if having her in the mix would work. Then the shutters came down and steely determination took over. He released her hold on his hands and leaned away, his lips thinned, teeth showing, his eyes squinting at her, as if convincing himself that she was really there.

"I can't do this with you in my life, Cathy. Don't you see? When I'm with you, you're the centre of my world. You and the children. I'm so utterly consumed by you, wanting to be with you all the time, every hour of every day. But now, things have changed. I have a daughter, and I need to find her." He leaned forward, steel in his eyes. "I need to find her."

"I understand that, Sam, but you'll also need support, and who better to provide it than the woman who loves you? Me!"

"No, Cathy, you have to understand how tough and emotional this is going to be for me. If you're in my life, I want you 100%, no distractions, no interference. It's what you deserve. But I can't do both. I can't give you that now. It's not fair on you, I know, but I need to concentrate on Sorcha now. I need to do the right thing for once in my life. No more running away."

Gulls circled overhead, waiting for an opportunity to attack the abandoned scones. Cathy sobbed into her hands. This couldn't be it. We can't end like this. She rose from her chair just as the heavens opened and fat raindrops landed on their heads. Other customers ran for cover, grabbing pots of tea and soggy breakfasts in their rush, but

319

Cathy and Sam just stood there. Within a minute they were soaked through, but neither seemed to notice. She stood there, numb, unable to comprehend what was happening to them.

28ᵗʰ September

Saturday

Gary was anxious to use his newfound power sooner rather than later, but he couldn't find Sam. The guy hadn't been in work for two days. Gary knew there must be something going down for Sam to miss work like that. He'd tried ringing Cathy last night to snoop around a bit, but her phone went straight to voicemail. What the hell was going on? He'd worked his ass off all week, pulling double and extra shifts, trying to earn enough to pay back his debt. There was no way he could keep going like this. He was exhausted and needed to bribe a break out of Sam.

His chance came after lunch. Sam arrived and headed straight for the office. Gary finished serving a customer and followed him in. Sam looked rough, like he hadn't slept for a week. His hair was all over the place and he carried at least three days stubble. But the most shocking change was in his eyes. Gary saw pure pain. What was going on? Could it be finished between him and Cathy? It would certainly explain the state he was in, and why Cathy's phone was turned off. Today probably wasn't the best time to tell Sam about his dance with no pants involving Sinead, but he knew it had to be now or never. It looked like Sam was packing up to go somewhere, so he probably wouldn't get another chance to spill the dirt.

"What's going on, Sam? Is everything okay?" He didn't really care how the other man was. The important thing was to get him talking.

Sam looked sideways at Gary, a sneer on his lips. "Like you give a fuck about me."

Gary tried a different approach. "Are you going somewhere? On holidays?" He knew it sounded lame, but he needed to get this done. Sam was packing up all his personal belongings. He was obviously leaving for longer than a couple of days. What was going on? Surely a break up with Cathy wouldn't cause Sam to quit his job and run for the hills. No, there was something else going on here and he'd make it his business to find out what. But first he needed to negotiate a little deal with Sammo before he left and his chance was gone.

"Sam, you're obviously going through some personal stuff..."

Sam held a hand up. "What do you want, Gary?" His words came out as if their weight was too much to handle. "Spit it out. You're not here to lend a shoulder to cry on, so tell me. What are you after?"

Gary hesitated, unsure if he should go through with his spoof. Fuck it, why the hell not? "I think you should know something. Sinead and I hooked up the other night. We got it on, if you know what I mean?"

Sam's face drained of what little colour was there. He stared hard at Gary.

Gary shrugged. "It was just one night, but we, like, you know, really connected. Anyway, I thought I'd let you know, we'll probably be seeing a lot more of each other in the future."

He watched Sam, then continued, "I suppose I wanted to give you the heads-up before things went any further."

Sam's face was hard to read. It was blank, void of any expression or emotion. Then his cheeks flushed and a spark lit in his eyes. Gary didn't see the fist coming. He only realised he'd been punched when pain erupted through his jaw. He crashed back against the desk, sending files and papers scattering to the floor. Sam rushed him, grabbed him by the front of the shirt, pulled him up, and punched him again and again.

"You fucking nutcase!" Gary roared, breaking away and ducking to the ground. "I'll fucking have you for this." He tried to stem the blood gushing from his nose, the warm fluid flowing over his throbbing split lip. His left eye was swelled shut. "Fuck!"

Sam said nothing, just stood over Gary, watching him try to catch his breath and right himself. Gary sensed the furious tension in Sam's rigid stance. The guy looked like he could do real damage.

"Stupid fuck," Sam said. "You screwed the wrong woman."

Gary was trying to stand up, roaring and shouting about assault charges and getting the Gardai in to deal with this unprovoked attack.

Sam sprang into action again, yanking open a drawer in his desk and grabbing out a large chequebook. He scribbled for a few seconds, ripped a cheque out, and thrust it into Gary's shaking hand.

"Take this and lodge it to your account. Pay back what you owe to my family, then get the fuck out of my life. You're done here, Gary. I should have done this weeks ago. Your face in here every day is the stuff nightmares are made of."

Gary looked at Sam, then at the cheque in his hand. €10,000. Enough to clear the best part of his debt, but he was also getting the can. Not a bad deal, even though he felt like he'd been through a tumble dryer. He could pick up another job handy enough. It wouldn't be that hard. He had friends that could sort him out. The money would clear his debt, letting him start again.

"This is between you and me," Sam said. "You ring Tony and hand in your notice today, pack your stuff, then get the hell out of my pub. Stay away from me, my family, and anything to do with me if you know what's good for you. That little rough and tumble is only the start of it if find you breathing near anything of mine again."

Gary eyed Sam one last time before nodding and pocketing the cheque.

"He's lost it," he mumbled between swollen lips as he walked away. "He's lost the fucking plot." Poor Cathy, I hope for her sake she's well shot of the psycho.

He walked out the door with money in his pocket, ready to start fresh, or as fresh as his miserable little life would allow.

29th September

Sunday

Cathy's breath stank. Her hair stuck to her head like an oil slick. Barely able to keep her stinging eyes open, she rolled over in the bed to check the time: 9.30am. She would have to get up soon to bring the children to Gary's. Byron had stayed on Friday and Saturday to mind them while she locked herself in her bedroom and went to pieces.

How had she ended up here again? Fresh tears stung her raw eyes as she remembered Sam's parting words. Almost a year since she'd had her life shattered by Gary, it had been repeated by Sam. Only this heartache was different, stronger and unimaginably more painful than anything Gary had done to her.

The intensity of everything they had experienced as a couple far outweighed any feelings she'd had for her husband during their marriage. Cathy and Sam had stepped onto a mile-long rollercoaster after that first meeting, starting off a slow climb up the first hill, inch by inch, then taken a dive into the unknown at the next hurdle. They'd whistled their way through twists and turns, almost veering off-track at some points, screaming and whooping around the course, holding on for dear life.

The whole experience had given her highs and lows she could only have dreamt about before, but the final crash had knocked her so off balance she'd tumbled into a terrifying spiral, hurtling through the darkness towards an unknown, heart-breaking destination.

Sam rang twice the previous day, but Byron had intercepted his calls. All Cathy's fighting to save their relationship had been done on Friday. Nothing had changed since, not as far as she could see. Sam had a daughter he needed to find, and he didn't want any help from her.

*

Byron and Cathy had sat long into Saturday night, empting a few bottles of wine, and taking apart the whole sorry saga, piece by piece.

"I know he's hurt you, Cathy," Byron said, her voice soft, "but I have to admire him at the same time."

"Oh yes, he's a real knight in shining armour." Cathy's words dripped with sarcasm. She knocked back the dregs of warm wine in her glass. "One click from Sinead's fingers and he's back on side with her. A real gent, if you ask me."

Byron refilled her glass half-way. "No, I didn't mean that, Cathy." She pulled her legs under her on the couch and sat back. "Look at it from his point of view. He's mad about you, and yes, he probably wanted to spend the rest of his life with you, too, but now this has happened. He needs to take a different path to the one originally intended."

"Why can't he take me with him down that path, though, Byron? Why is he leaving me to find my own way?"

"Because he loves you. He loves you so much he doesn't want to drag you into this whole sorry mess."

"But I offered. I want to help him with this, be there for him. I can handle it, By. I'm a big girl. I've been through a marriage and separation to the biggest love rat in Ireland. I think I can handle a round of the forgotten child and any other shit Sinead has locked in her murky closet."

"You're right," Byron said, "you can handle all of this, no doubt about it. You're the strongest woman I know, bar none. Look at all you've been through and you only twenty-six. Most people don't have to deal with that much crap in a whole lifetime."

She shifted on the couch and leaned forward. "The thing is, Cathy, you shouldn't have to deal with this. Sam knows that. He loves you too much to let this affect your life too. He knows what you've been through. It's enough. He's giving you a way out, a chance to lead a normal, happy life with your children, without getting dragged into another drama."

Cathy shot up from her chair. "I can't believe you're on his side, Byron Kelly. You are supposed to be my best friend. No, don't say another word." She held a hand out to Byron, whose mouth had dropped open. "Gary treated me like dirt. Like I didn't exist. Even though Sam made me feel like the most wonderful woman in the world, he shot me down, just like Gary." She stopped and took a deep breath. "Sam O'Keefe decided I wasn't good enough to be in his life. He doesn't want my support. He doesn't want me."

"Hold on--"

"No!" She paced the room, Sam's words tumbling through her mind. "For God's sake, Byron, he's going to a huge city and he hasn't the slightest clue where the child is. He's racing off on the wildest goose chase I've ever seen. Not one ounce of thought has gone into this, but still he's dumping me because he doesn't think I deserve less than his full attention? Well, fuck that, I deserve more."

She stopped pacing and stared at Byron. "Do you know what? He's right. Why am I wasting my life on someone like him? Someone who's obviously able to compartmentalise his feelings way better than I can."

"Dammit!" She raised her wine glass in the air, spilling some on the carpet. "Au revoir, Sam. Have a safe journey and a nice life. If you want to call the shots on this, well, who am I to argue with you?"

She flopped down onto the couch beside Byron, exhausted beyond belief. As she lay her head back against the cushions, she whispered, "Never again will I let a man make me feel this way. Good riddance, Sam O'Keeffe. I wish you luck."

*

She dragged herself out of bed and showered. At least the children were dressed and packed for the next few days at Gary's, thanks to Byron acting like a sergeant major rounding up the troops.

"How come Gary is taking them today?" Byron whispered as she ate burnt toast with marmalade.

Cathy sighed. "Something to do with him having an extra few days off. I don't really know. He wasn't forthcoming with information on the phone last night, just saying he'd be able to take the kids today and tomorrow, and drop them back down on Tuesday after school."

"I thought he was working double shifts and overtime?"

"I don't know what's going on, By, I'm just glad he's able to take them for a couple of days. I need to get my head sorted and you can't stay forever, can you?"

Byron shook her head.

"I didn't think so. I need to cop on before I end up stuck on this downward spiral. Damn it, I'm not the only person in the world who's been dumped." She produced a weak smile, then went to pack the kids into the car with all their bags and baggage.

Byron promised to stay for the rest of the day. Tom was working the weekend shift so she was at a loose end, anyway. Cathy was glad. As much as she needed to get her head sorted, she also needed adult contact; someone who would listen to her 'poor me' whining; someone who would slap her face and shout at her to calm down when she spun out of control. Most importantly, someone who would hold her, rubbing her back while she sobbed her heart out.

"I'll be back in about an hour," she called through the open car window. "My phone's on the kitchen table. If Sam calls, don't answer. It's killing me, but he had his chance and now I have to consider myself and the twins."

"Oh, Cathy, I really do wish I had your strength, but don't cut him off. If you at least talk to him, there might be a chance of something being sorted."

Cathy pulled out of the driveway and took off up the road, wishing she was as strong as Byron thought she was.

*

"Cathy, I'm sorry," was all Sam could manage when she bit the bullet and returned his calls later that evening.

"I'm sorry too, Sam," she said, choking back a lump in her throat. She'd sworn she wouldn't cry during this call, but her resolve broke the second she heard his voice.

"What do you think you're sorry for? I was expecting a curse-ridden rant."

"I'm sorry that all this has happened to you. To us, when everything was going so well." She bit back a sob, her voice dropping to a whisper. "We could have been great."

"We are great," he said.

She took a deep breath to steady her nerve. Though she was mad at Sam, she still needed him to know what she was thinking. "Sinead is being a total bitch here, landing this on you now, after all these years. She's after something, Sam, and it's not the welfare of your daughter that she's concerned about."

"I have to give her the benefit of the doubt, Cathy. At least she finally owned up to what happened."

Cathy was shocked by his response. "Are you going soft or what? Why the sudden change in attitude towards her? Last Friday you wanted nothing to do with her."

"I've had time to think about this, Cathy."

"So have I, Sam. Every waking hour since last Friday morning, and most other hours when I should have been asleep."

"I'm going to need Sinead on-side for this. If I don't, she could make things very difficult for me."

"Like she already hasn't?"

"Cathy, stop," he said, his voice sharp. "Do you think I don't know this? I've been over and over this in my mind until my head is swimming so bad it hurts. I've already said how terrible I feel for putting you through this much already. It's driving me insane."

A silence hung between them while they both regained some composure.

"You hurt me, Sam."

"I know, but--"

"No, Sam, let me speak. I'm barely hanging on here. I need to get this off my chest." She paced the kitchen floor as she clung to the phone. "I've cursed you from here to hell and back, Sam O'Keeffe. You've stomped all over my life, and my heart."

"I know. I'm sorry." He let the words dissolve between them before continuing. "This is something I need to do. For my own sanity."

"Yes," she said, "your sanity. But what about mine?"

There was no answer from Sam. What did she expect him to say? She didn't know. "How can you just walk away from us, cast our relationship, our intimacy aside, so casual like? Is this what it's about, discarding your baggage and tying up loose ends, before starting out on a brave and noble quest?"

"Cathy, it's best this way." His voice was low. "You know that." She could hear his pain, but let him continue. "I have no idea where this is going to go. I have wrecked my brain trying to see another way of dealing with this that means we can still be together. But I can't, it won't work. I can't focus on you and your needs, as well as trying to find my daughter."

Cathy saw red. "Do not make this about me and my needs. This is all about you, Sam. I've never asked you to choose between me and your daughter. How dare you."

"Cathy, that's not what I meant--"

"Maybe I can't drop everything and run off with you on your noble quest. I have responsibilities. Maybe I'm not the one you want to comfort you when the going get rough." She took a breath. "Is that it, Sam? Is it Sinead you want to run to, to hold your hand and pat your back? I can't compete with her, Sam, and she knows that. She's using this as a stepping stone back into your life, and damn you, but you're letting her do it."

Before he'd a chance to utter a word, she hung up. She'd said enough.

30th September

Monday

Sam made his way through Terminal 2 at Dublin Airport. With yet another sleepless night behind him, he was relieved to be finally making this important journey.

Hundreds of people mulled around him, like soldiering ants going about their business. People who had places to go, people to see. Just like him.

Sinead had given him the email address of her cousin, Aoife Bennett, and told him to contact her for more information. He had, and Aoife replied with a short, terse response, threatening legal action if he showed up anywhere near her or her daughter, warning him in no uncertain terms to stay away.

Well that's not going to happen. He ordered a strong black coffee from the barista. Tony, his brother, had come up trumps by searching the London electoral register and emailed Sam her address. At least he now had a beginning for his journey. Where it would end, God only knew.

In saying that, he'd no intention of barging into a stranger's house demanding parental rights to his long-lost daughter, but he needed at least some contact. He needed to see her, in person. His imagination ran wild, wondering what this little girl was like. Was she dark like him and Sinead, or had she picked up the skipped-generation gene and inherited his mother's red curly hair? What did she like, dislike? Could she sing? Sinead was a good singer, he remembered. Was Sorcha good at school, at art or music perhaps? Did she sometimes pick up a guitar and strum the strings wondering where she got that talent from? So many questions buzzed around his head, but the most important one he needed to answer for himself: Was she happy?

He settled at a small table and sipped the strong dark liquid, allowing the coffee take its desired effect. His head ached as he waited for his flight to be called. Then, for no reason he could discern, a calmness came over him, and for the first time in days he felt like things would be okay.

Something, maybe a celestial force, had lifted most of the weight from his shoulders, leaving him with a burden he could manage. His thoughts turned to Cathy. She was rarely out of his head, but right now she was bursting through and becoming crystal clear in his mind's eye.

Things were going to be okay. He could sense it. Despite the fact he'd hurt her beyond anything he thought he was capable of, he now felt that all was not lost.

*

In Wicklow, Cathy was having a panic attack. "Breath. In, out, in, out," urged Annabel while Byron unfolded a paper bag.

336

"I can't," Cathy stuttered, trying to force the words through the choking sensation. Tears streamed down her face as Byron pushed the bag over her mouth, holding it while rubbing her back.

"Deep, even breaths, Cathy. Come on. In, out." Byron puffed with her, trying to slow Cathy's panicked gasps.

Becky looked on from her perch on the kitchen counter. "Pretend you're in labour, Sis. Imagine you're just about to push your two lads out again."

"Shut up, you," Annabel shouted. "You're not helping."

"Oh, calm down, for Christ sake." Becky rolled her eyes as she went to kneel in front of her sister. "Look deep into my eyes." Resting a hand on the centre of Cathy's forehead, she pushed forward, throwing her own head back with dramatic flair while chanting a mantra. "Release and breath, release and breath."

Cathy burst out laughing, her tears of panic turning to tears of hysteria. "Jesus, Becky! I swear, you should be on stage."

Becky released her hand and patted her sister's cheek. "You're welcome." She performed a little curtsey.

"Bleeding nutcase," Byron said, shaking her head.

The girls settled back around the table, crisis averted. They had to figure out what Cathy should do.

Before her panic attack, she'd cleared her head and listened to her friends. The realisation that she could not let Sam leave like this hit her like a lightning bolt. Anger and pride had prevented her from begging him to change his mind last night, but this morning, the penny had finally dropped.

"Yes, I'm mad and angry as hell at the stupid fecker, but, do you know what? He's my stupid fecker. I can't let him go."

She looked around, wide-eyed and shaking. "No matter what he says, I won't let it happen. He needs me. I'm not letting him call the shots on this one." Her words came out in a rush of realisation.

Byron and Annabel looked at other in obvious relief that their girl had finally battled through the fog and pulled herself together.

"He may be going away, but I can't let it be the end." Cathy sobbed, her breath shallow as she gasped. "I cut him off on the phone last night. Just like that. I was hurting so bad, I wanted to hurt him back." She hung her head, wringing her hands on her lap, trying to rub the numbness away.

Knocking over the chair as she leapt to her feet, she grabbed Byron by both arms. "I need to fix this, right? I can't let him go like this. I need to see him."

The room spun as she forced air into her lungs. A huge weight bore down on her chest with the realisation that she'd messed this right up. She needed get it straightened out before Sam was lost to her forever.

"Help me. Help me fix this, Oh, sweet Jesus, I can't breathe. I can't breathe!"

Fifteen minutes later they were speeding their way towards Dublin Airport in Annabel's Mercedes.

"What time is the flight again?" Annabel asked.

"11.11am. Terminal 2, I think. Will we make it?"

"By Jesus, if I have to sprout wings and fly you there myself, we'll make it."

Flight BA740, London Heathrow, boarding now at Gate 16, the announcement squawked out of the overhead speaker system.

Sam looked over to where a queue had started to form and decided to stay put for the moment. He preferred to be one of the last to board a plane. Less time cooped up in an aeroplane seat while passengers banged into you going up and down the aisle.

He looked at his phone and noticed a few missed calls from Cathy. Sadness swam through his heart as he thought about her. Wishing again that things could have been different, he returned the phone to his pocket. There was nothing more to be done. He didn't have the strength to return her calls right now, fearing his fragile thread of resolve would snap and leave him in the depths of distress in the departure lounge. Going to pieces was something he preferred to do in private.

"What now?" Cathy asked, her frantic words coming as they screeched to a halt outside the airport terminal.

"We really didn't think this through, did we?" Annabel said. "He's hardly going to be waiting for you at the front door. Not after what you said to him last night, and there's no way security is going to let you through without a ticket."

"Ring him again," Byron screeched, bouncing up and down in the front passenger seat.

"I've tried, he's not answering." Cathy sobbed again, hysteria clamping her lungs around her heart.

"Here we go again." Becky cursed as she tried to open the back door to get out. "Lemme out! Oh, for fuck's sake, why have you got the child locks on, Annabel? You don't even have children."

Annabel leapt out. "I don't know," she answered. "For safety, I suppose. I've never even been in the back of this car before, so how should I know."

Becky shook her head as she jumped out, dragging Cathy with her. "God help us if there's ever a nuclear disaster. You lot are brutal."

"Shut up, Becky," Annabel shouted.

"Shut up, both of you," Byron snapped. "Now, what's the plan?"

"If you will let me speak," Becky said, throwing a look at Annabel, "it seems I might have the solution. I just happen to know someone, a friend of a friend, let's say, who might be able to get our Cathy here through the airport and close enough to see Sam."

Each of them looked at Becky, mouths wide open. "Is this one for real?" Annabel said to Cathy. "Does she think she's in a bloody cartoon?"

"Come on, come on," Becky urged. "We haven't time for this. Let's get this princess to her frog and shut this thing down."

Three girls raced towards the departure hall, while Annabel parked the car. As they ran, Becky pulled out her phone and spoke in hushed tones. "Yes. Yes, now if possible. Can it happen? Is it possible? Yes. Good. I'll deliver her now." She grabbed Cathy and they headed towards an emergency exit door close to the security line.

As they reached it, a burly, balding man in a high-vis jacket walked through, setting off the alarm, but continuing on without batting an eyelid.

"Is this her?" he asked Becky.

"Yes, she needs to get to gate 16, ASAP."

Mr High-Vis glanced about, then looked at Cathy who was barely able to contain herself. What if this didn't work? What if she couldn't reach Sam on time? She was teetering on the edge of her last nerve when he nodded and beckoned her to follow.

Becky squeezed her hand. "We have to leave you here, Sis."

"Good luck, honey," Bryon gushed.

"Go get him," they yelled, as Cathy rushed after her personal escort.

"Here, put this on." High-Vis handed her a lanyard with a security tag attached. "You need to look like a VIP coming through." He removed a pair of sunglasses from his shirt pocket and handed them to her.

He led the way to the security door, speaking into his radio as they moved. Cathy was astonished when they more or less strolled right through, having gained clearance from the fuzzy radio voice replying to High-Vis's request for admission.

Adrenalin surged through her as they rushed towards the boarding gates. She was shaking. Half in fear about being arrested by airport police, half worrying about Sam's reaction if she did reach him on time. She sent out a silent prayer to the universe that the right words would come when she saw him. If she saw him.

She checked her watch as they ran. Don't let us be too late. "Please let him still be here," she whispered. "I need to see him. I need to touch him. Please, God, let my luck hold out for a few more minutes."

Gate 16 loomed ahead. She broke into a sprint as she approached, looking around at the empty seats. "He's gone," she sobbed, her body turning cold as all hope drained from her heart. "I missed him."

Mr High-Vis touched her arm. "Who's that over there?"

She spun around and caught a glimpse of Sam's back disappearing through a door that closed softly behind him.

Cathy sank into the nearest chair. "He's gone." She looked up at her escort, blood pumping through her ears. "My man is gone." She stared down at her open hands. "My man is gone."

"Ah, fuck this," High-Vis said, grabbing Cathy's hand. "Coming down." The radio squawked to life as he led her through yet another secure area. They rushed down steps and out onto the apron of Gate 16.

Cathy saw Sam about to take the first step up the stairs onto the plane. The plane that would carry him out of her life, for good. Her heart almost stopped.

"Sam!" she yelled over the noise of the roaring engines. "Sam, please, I'm here."

Sam kept going and she was sure the engine noise had shattered her chance of talking to him. Then a tanned man in a white shirt appeared in the plane's doorway. He smiled and gestured to Sam, who turned around.

Her heart leapt when he dropped his bag and raced back to where she stood.

"Cathy." He lifted her straight off her feet into a sweeping embrace. She met his mouth with hers and drank him in, like he was the last water on earth.

Sam twirled her around, holding her tight to his chest, his strong arms forming steel bands around her. She clung to him, their faces together, her tears mixing with his.

"I love you, Sam O'Keeffe."

"I love you, too, Cathy."

"I tried calling. I tried to get through to you. I couldn't let you go. Not without sorting this out between us."

"Cathy--" he began, but she cut him off, putting a finger to his lips.

"Sam." Her breath came back off his mouth. "I wanted to tell you how proud I am of you. Of course going to look for your daughter is the right thing to do. It always was, I never disputed that. I just wish you would let me come along on this part of your life journey. For support, if nothing else." Tears threatened to drown her words. She had to make him accept that she was a firm part of his future. No argument.

"You need to know that when things get so unbearably rough, that I will always be there for you. You need a focus in your life, Sam, to look back at and regain normality. The future is going to be a roundabout of madness. Things that never touch the likes of you or me in normal situations. You'll need a constant positive in your life, allowing you to cling onto reality when the going gets tough."

The look of adoration in his eyes told her she was getting through. She'd made him listen, and he was letting her in.

"How are you such an incredible woman, Cathy? Look at what you're getting yourself into here. It's a mess. I don't want you to be left playing second fiddle to the drama I have to deal with."

She smiled, relief flooding through her when she realised that Sam too had turned a corner. "Let me be your anchor, Sam." Her voice broke, but she forced the words out. "I will always be your anchor. Here, patiently waiting, whenever you need me." She drove that point home.

Sam's eyes closed as he pulled her close to him, not letting a whisker of air separate them. Shouting in her ear above the plane's engines, he made her a promise. "Cathy, let me do this first, on my own. I promise I'll come back and fix us. I know it's a lot to ask of you, but I promise, it will always be you I will be striving to return to."

"You won't need to fix us, Sam," she said, tears streaming down her cheeks. "We will never be broken." She kissed his mouth, hungry for his taste, willing this moment to last forever.

"I'll be here, whenever you need me, whenever you're ready. That is *my* promise."

With strength she didn't know she possessed, she let him go. She forced a smile, masking her aching heart, as he turned and walked back to the plane.

"Thank you," he called back to her as he picked up his discarded bag. A kiss blown from his hand as he ascended the steps caught and held close to her heart.

She stood for a long time, watching as the plane doors closed and it taxied away. Her heart had been shattered into a million pieces, but now she could feel it start to pull itself back together. She knew, as each splinter repaired itself, that Sam was hers, and she was his. Forever.

"I love you, Sam O'Keeffe," she whispered as his plane thundered down the runway, taking him away from her.

*

"I love you, too," Sam whispered as the plane tilted back, climbing into a soft arc towards his destination. Sorcha.

The End

Book 2 in the Calendar Days Series

Out Now

April...

Three best friends, three very different relationships.

Watch out Wicklow, the girls are back.

High-powered businesswoman, Annabel, is suddenly finding life very tough. Can she rely on her friends for support, or will she try to weather the storm alone?

Single mum, Cathy, knows just how tough long distance relationships can be, but supporting Sam on his quest for answers was something she promised to do.

Obsessed with wedding preparations, Byron's perfectly made plans are thrown swiftly out the window, when someone else's life gets rudely in her way.

Land yourself straight into spring and see if these best friends can survive any of the April showers.

42450708R00194

Made in the USA
Middletown, DE
12 April 2017